10 THINGS
I HATE
ABOUT
PROM

10 THINGS

I HATE

ABOUT

Elle Gonzalez Rose

joy revolution

Text copyright © 2024 by Assemble Media, LLC

ASSEMBLE
MEDIA

Cover art copyright © 2024 by Rebeca Alvarez,
bouquet icon by Muhammad/stock.adobe.com,
hands showing heart shape icon by Pixel-Shot/stock.adobe.com,
smile emoji by Vadymstock/stock.adobe.com,
bee drawing by nenilkime/stock.adobe.com

All rights reserved. Published in the United States by Joy Revolution, an imprint of Random House Children's Books, a division of Penguin Random House LLC, New York.

Joy Revolution is a registered trademark and the colophon is a trademark of Penguin Random House LLC.

GetUnderlined.com

Educators and librarians, for a variety of teaching tools, visit us at RHTeachersLibrarians.com

Library of Congress Cataloging-in-Publication Data is available upon request.
ISBN 978-0-593-70517-9 (hardcover) — ISBN 978-0-593-70518-6 (lib. bdg.)
ISBN 978-0-593-70520-9 (tr. pbk.) — ISBN 978-0-593-70519-3 (ebook)

The text of this book is set in 11-point Warnock Pro Light.
Interior design by Cathy Bobak

Printed in the United States of America
10 9 8 7 6 5 4 3 2 1
First Edition

For the real Nurse Oatmeal: Doctor Porridge

CHAPTER ONE

THERE'S NOTHING WORSE THAN working a double shift on the last day of spring break.

Except turning around to find a guy you barely know holding up a sign that says *PROM?*

My jaw locked the second the bell over the door chimed. Most weekends I don't get a moment to breathe. The rush at Casa Y Cocina is constant from brunch all the way through dinner, the hours passing by in a mad flurry of fritura samplers, piña colada mimosas, and crumpled dollar bills. But today was unusually slow. Like, keep-an-eye-out-for-tumbleweeds slow. Tío Tony even gave me the green light to head home at two if no one else came in after I finished wiping down my tables. The last time he let me dip early was when I chipped my tooth nose-diving to save a plate before it hit the ground. *Nepotism* isn't a word in the Santos family dictionary.

I can feel Tío Tony's glare on the back of my head as my

gentleman caller, Chris Pavlenko, sets the box under his arm on a table so he can get down on one knee.

Chris's brow quirks, his hot-pink duct tape sign halfway into the air when he pauses. "You're Ivelisse, right?"

Wow. A promposal from a guy who isn't even sure who I am. Shakespeare could never.

The temptation to say no is strong. Chris is usually stoned on days that end in *y*, and last month he almost drank a beaker of liquid iron because he thought it was green-apple Gatorade. But even if he doesn't immediately smell the lie, roll call in chem tomorrow will be a pretty big giveaway.

I take my time replying. Opening my mouth too soon could lead to (a) projectile vomiting, (b) saying something I'll regret, or (c) saying something I regret while projectile vomiting. So I take a deep breath, decide to use the rational part of my brain, and nod instead.

Chris grins, his eyes half open and tinged pink. "Sweet."

The smell of weed and stale tortilla chips comes with him as he shifts closer to me, overpowering the usual smell of sautéed onions and cilantro wafting from the kitchen.

"So, you down?" Chris asks as he holds the sign up over his head.

"To go to prom?"

"Yeah," he says in the same tone one might say, "Duh" or "No shit, I'm holding a sign that says *PROM?*"

My cheeks flush as I choke out a laugh, scratching the back of my neck just to give my hands something to do. It's not like he walked in here to ask Tío Tony or one of the fry cooks to prom but asking me makes just as little sense. In the four years we've known each other, Chris has said maybe ten words to me. Five of which were *Did you do the homework?* You can't blame me for being shocked that *prom?* is the eleventh.

"Ivelisse," Tío Tony barks, wiping down his knife as he slowly approaches us. "You good?"

"Yep, fine," I reply to keep the peace. Tío Tony's heart may be made of marshmallow fluff, but he definitely gets a kick out of leaning into his "bulging muscles and intimidating tattoos" exterior. I wouldn't put it past him to lift Chris up by the scruff of his neck and toss him onto the street like a rag doll.

"Oh!" Chris exclaims with a grin, as if there isn't a six-foot-five man with a meat cleaver glaring at him. "I brought these."

He gets up off his knees to grab the box he set aside. My nose wrinkles as he pulls up the lid with a lazy wave of his hand, the hairs along my arms rocketing to attention as a familiar scent wafts over me.

The peanut butter cookies make me recoil like a vampire would at garlic. Any hope I had of getting through this interaction without throwing up is long gone. I'm not afraid to admit that a box of cookies can strike the fear of God into me—not when one wrong move could land me in the emergency room with anaphylactic shock.

I jump back as Chris takes a tentative step toward me, nearly tripping over a broom. He frowns, glancing from me to the box. "I guess you don't like peanut butter?"

At this point, expecting him to remember my nut allergy would've been too much to ask.

"I'm allergic." I take another step back for good measure. "Really allergic."

"My bad," he replies as he closes the box. "Anna likes these, so I figured you might like them too."

All the nerves that calmed within me when Chris put the cookies away come again. "Anna?"

He nods, picking his PROM sign back up and wiping some dirt off the *R*. "I asked her yesterday." He wrinkles his nose, picking at a dust clump that's now stuck to the tape. "But she said no."

Finally, this bizarro situation starts to make some sense. Chris spends more time sighing over Anna Adebayo's perfume than he does taking notes. If he spent that time actually listening to her or paying attention to the pins on her backpack instead of trolling "How to Get Girls" subreddits, he'd know she's a lesbian.

"So . . . you decided to ask me instead?"

Anna and I don't have many other friends at Cordero High besides each other, which *is* how we prefer it, but that doesn't make us interchangeable. I guess proximity makes me his runner-up.

He shrugs, giving up on the dust clump and flipping the sign around to face me once more. In the new light, I spot the patches where tape has been pulled off. Sticky residue spells out *Anna*.

"You seem chill."

At least I have that going for me.

The silence goes from awkward to strained to painful as excuses sit on the tip of my tongue and die when I open my mouth. If Chris wasn't actively stoned, he might call out my hesitance. Instead, he grabs a cookie for himself, not noticing

4

when I put a safe distance between us. Even a crumb could send me down a dangerous spiral. Though breaking out into hives *would* be a very effective way of getting myself out of this situation.

Maybe I can sneak off and camp out in the kitchen. Hiding from my problems isn't the solution I need, but I do my best thinking after a long, cathartic scream into a bag of frozen corn. There's a reason freezer screams are the backbone of the service industry. Plus, it'll give me time to think of an excuse or, better yet, an escape plan.

"I actually—"

"Chris!" another voice cuts in before I can finish.

My heart leaps from the pit of my stomach as my best friend and saving grace, Joaquin, sweeps Chris into the bro-iest of bro hugs.

"I thought you lived up in Anchor Heights?" Joaquin asks without missing a beat.

"Y-yeah, I do." Chris gives Joaquin a bleary once-over before glancing at the front door, as if to confirm he didn't materialize out of thin air. "I was just—"

"Oh, I meant to ask you," Joaquin interrupts, wrapping an arm around Chris's shoulders and guiding him toward the door. "I had this issue with my bike last week, and one of the guys mentioned you might know what the deal is."

Their voices trail off as Joaquin leads them to where his bike is locked up out front, letting the door shut behind him. I collapse onto the chair beside me, heaving a sigh with every bit of breath I have left in me.

"Ivelisse," Tío Tony calls out yet again, hovering by the entrance to the kitchen. "No more boys allowed unless they pay for food." As if I had any choice in the matter. His thick gray mustache bristles as he peeks through the front window, jutting his chin toward Joaquin. "Except for El Conejito."

Over a decade of friendship and Joaquin still can't shake off the nickname my abuela gave him when we were six. My family watched in awe as Joaquin happily nibbled on his carrot sticks instead of begging for more cake like the other sugar-high six-year-olds at my birthday party.

In our defense, he *does* have rabbit teeth.

I give Tío Tony a nod and sink back into my chair, massaging my temples in hopes of fighting off the steadily building headache. The smart thing to do would be to haul ass and slip out the rear exit while Chris is distracted, but I never make smart decisions when I'm under extreme duress.

Thankfully, Joaquin was smart enough for the both of us in that moment. My heart has stopped pounding and my headache has subsided to a dull throb by the time he returns, sans Chris Pavlenko, wearing a cocky smirk that tells me I'm never going to live this down.

"So," he singsongs as he drops into the chair across from me. "Seems like you had fun while I was gone."

I'm still too mortified to do anything other than groan and let my head fall onto the table with a thump.

"Gotta say, I didn't see this relationship coming but it makes sense. Y'know, since you two have"—he pauses to do a drum roll on the table—"chemistry."

His corniness is enough to bring me back from the dead. "Shut *up*," I snap as I lean across the table to smack his shoulder.

He tries to appear wounded, holding a hand over his heart, but he can't hold in his giggles. "Don't fight your feelings anymore, Ive. This could be the beginning of a very beautiful romance."

I roll my eyes as I slump back into my seat. "I'm sure my grandkids would love to hear about how their grandpa only asked me to prom because the girl he asked first said no."

Joaquin lets out a hiss. "Oof. Okay, never mind, that's harsh."

That's an understatement, and I didn't even tell him about the peanut butter cookies. As sad as it is, having a close brush with death the first time a guy asked me out since freshman year is a very appropriate metaphor for my love life: dead on arrival.

Using a dishrag to protect myself from any stray crumbs, I take the box Chris left behind to the kitchen and write out a note for the line cooks to help themselves.

"He did say I was chill, though," I add. Joaquin snorts, immediately trying to cover it up when I turn to glare at him. "What? You don't think I'm chill?"

He scrunches up his nose in thought, waving his hand from side to side. "On a scale of one to ten, I'd say you're like a . . . four?"

Great, so I *don't* have that going for me.

I go to whack him with the dishrag—a very chill response—except he catches the tail end of it before it can hit him. "Jesus, you're fast," I mumble as he lets go of the towel with a shit-eating grin. "Did you get any radioactive spider bites over break?

Because you can't get a tan *and* superpowers in the same week. That's just not fair."

"I wish." He leans back in his chair, one hand coming up behind his head while the other gestures down the front of his shirt. "But I did get this."

His new shirt is . . . loud. Somewhere between a Hawaiian shirt and a bowling jersey, complete with orange, blue, and white palm fronds. Paired with black jeans, it's definitely a switch from his usual wardrobe of hoodies with gray sweatpants or basketball shorts and slides.

"Interesting choice," I reply delicately as I slide back into my seat across from him.

He quirks an eyebrow. "The good kind of interesting?"

I take my time replying, rubbing my chin as I take in the full ensemble. "You look like my abuelo."

His smirk falls into a frown. "Well, then, I'll just have to give your souvenir to someone who appreciates my fashion sense." With a *humph*, he stands up from the table and heads for the door.

Roasting Joaquin Romero is by far my favorite hobby, but I'm a material girl at heart. I bolt from my seat, racing to cut him off before he can get to the exit. "Souvenir?" I ask with a raised brow.

A smirk plays at the corner of his lips for a brief moment before he slips back into his role, lifting his nose high in the air and crossing his arms as he turns his back to me. "I have nothing more to say to you."

The man plays a dirty game. Then again, he learned it from

8

the best: me. And the hours of telenovelas we watched in middle school. But mostly me.

I give it a few seconds before finally admitting defeat. "You're a fashion genius. An icon. Your invite to the Met Gala will arrive any day now."

He tries and fails to hold in his amusement. "You're forgiven." He holds up a warning finger as he faces me. "Just know you're on thin ice."

If that was true, the ice would've cracked five years ago when I told him his new haircut made him look like an egg. But I give him an overly gracious smile and hold out my hands like the greedy gremlin he knows and adores. "The souvenir . . . ?"

"Is at my place," he finishes, nudging past me to open the door. "Come over after your shift's done?"

"Actually, I get to cut out early today."

Joaquin gasps dramatically, bracing himself against the door-frame. "Did hell freeze over?"

I untie my apron and let my hair down from its oppressively tight bun. "No, but I did see some pigs flying around this afternoon."

After I promise to be ready in five, I head to the storage closet and grab my stuff. I rush through pulling on my sneakers and storing my apron in my designated cubby. With my luck, a party of fifteen will come strolling in any minute now and keep me here past closing.

"Bye, Tío!" I call out as I hurry across the dining room, back-pack in hand, and close the door behind me before he can change his mind.

Joaquin's waiting for me on the curb, his bike propped against a fire hydrant. Before we do our usual dance to squeeze onto the seat together, I pause on the sidewalk to breathe in a deep lungful of the cool spring air. "Sweet, sweet freedom."

Joaquin takes a sniff of his own, his face crumpling into a grimace. "Freedom smells like car exhaust."

It does, but that doesn't make it any less sweet.

CHAPTER TWO

EITHER JOAQUIN'S RIGHT AND I'm a four on the chill scale, or his cycling skills have seriously tanked.

It's a miracle that we manage to get home with our limbs intact. Maybe that's thanks to the prayer I said under my breath when he almost sideswiped a soccer mom's minivan. It's only a ten-minute journey and yet Joaquin managed to make my life flash before my eyes twice.

"Are you trying to kill us?!" I shouted into his ear when he plowed through a stop sign.

"Calm down. Car rules don't apply to bikes."

"They do if you want to survive."

My protests went ignored, so I chose to squeeze my eyes shut and bury my face in the crook of his neck instead. If we were going to die at the hands of a Suburban, I didn't want to see it coming.

As soon as he stops in my driveway, I launch off the vehicle and collapse to my knees, leaning down to press my forehead against the asphalt. I'm grateful to be alive, but not grateful enough to put my lips where car tires and motor oil have been.

"Never again," I whisper against the pavement, just loud enough for Joaquin to hear.

"You lived, didn't you?" he calls back.

I stick my tongue out at him as he wheels his bike into his garage. His shoulders are engraved with dozens of crescent-shaped moons my nails left behind. I'd apologize if he wasn't the exact reason I had to cling for dear life.

"This is why I need a car," I proclaim to the universe. "To save myself, and innocent bystanders, from reckless cyclists like you."

"You're such a saint," he replies dryly, even though we both know a car would make our lives here in Jersey substantially easier. Herbert, the car his mom passed down to him before she moved back to Puerto Rico last summer, was ancient when she bought it. Now it can barely handle the twenty-minute drive to school every morning.

Joaquin nods his head toward his place. "You coming?"

Thanks to the fear and adrenaline coursing through my veins during the ride home, I started sweating in places where *no one* should sweat.

"I desperately need a shower. Meet at mine in ten?"

He gives me a thumbs-up before disappearing into his house, and I lug up the driveway to my own.

Opening the door, I'm met with a round of earsplitting barks.

My twenty-pound terror of a dog, Nurse Oatmeal, comes tearing through the living room, growling and snarling beside me as I step into the entryway to take off my shoes.

"¡Cállate!" Joaquin's grandma, Doña Carmen, bellows from the kitchen, even though there's no point telling her to be quiet. Nurse Oatmeal is the only terrier on this planet that can't smell her humans coming a mile away. In the four years since Joaquin and I found her, she's never once let anyone come through the door without giving them a symphony of high-pitched barks for at least thirty seconds.

Sure enough, she settles down once she realizes "Oh yeah, this person fills my bowl every day" and returns to the very important task of chewing on a throw blanket in the living room. It'd be one thing if she just barked at everyone who comes through the door, but no, she's a chewing menace too. Her massive pile of destroyed stuffed animals, shoes, and old T-shirts is practically part of the living room décor.

"Thank you again for walking her," I say to Doña Carmen after our usual cheek-kiss greeting.

"Claro, claro," she replies, waving off my thanks. Doña Carmen had jumped at the chance to watch the dog when I'd mentioned it in passing over dinner at their place last week, insisting that we didn't need to pay a sitter when she knew how to tame the beast herself.

Both she and Joaquin have been over at our place more often lately. Probably since theirs is unusually lonely now that Mrs. Romero is back in Puerto Rico taking care of her mother, who has rapidly progressing Alzheimer's, and Joaquin's older sister, Isabella, left for her freshman year at American University in DC. Without the cacophony of Isabella yelling at Joaquin to let her use the TV, or Mrs. Romero singing along to the radio in the kitchen, the house feels deserted.

Doña Carmen hoists herself up and starts gathering her things. "Hiciste mucho chavo?" she asks with a raised brow, waiting for me to show off the spoils of my labor.

I frown, pulling the few crumpled dollar bills out of my pocket. Barely thirty bucks. "Nah, slow day."

Doña Carmen gives me a consoling pat on the shoulder. "You'll get there," she whispers before shuffling over to the living room to give Nurse Oatmeal a parting scratch behind the ears. "I made arroz con gandules, if you want any."

I cross the kitchen to the pot on the stove, lifting the lid and taking in a deep whiff of her signature rice. The intoxicating scent of her top-secret sofrito blend makes my mouth water. Watching our goblin of a dog while Mami and I are at work *and* making us food? Forget me, she's the real saint around here.

Pulling my tongue off the floor, I head to my room to store my tips, then go to the bathroom to scrub away the smell of a hard day's work. By the time I make it back to the living room, hair in a clumsy braid and dressed in my finest semi-clean sweatpants and concert T-shirt, Joaquin has made himself at home.

He and Nurse Oatmeal are sprawled out on the couch, her body flopped on his chest while he rubs her belly and talks to her in his signature For-Nurse-Oatmeal-Only baby voice.

"Who's the best girl?" Her ears perk up. "You are!" Her tongue rolls out of her mouth in delight.

It's a cruel twist of fate that Nurse Oatmeal lives at my house instead of Joaquin's. She's always preferred him over me, even though my belly-rubbing technique is *far* superior. Even the day we found her freshman year, eating oatmeal next to the dumpster behind the nurse's office, she ran up to Joaquin the second she saw him and completely ignored me and the hot dog I offered her to lure her in. The only reason we wound up taking her in was because Isabella is allergic to dogs. Now Joaquin has an empty house, and I'm in an unrequited relationship with our dog.

"Can you please tell the best girl to stop chewing on all of my stuff?" Last week the little shit destroyed my favorite pair of sneakers.

Joaquin leans in close to Nurse Oatmeal, his brow furrowing as if the two are having a heated discussion. "She says no." He ducks his head close to hers again. "And that you should give her more treats."

"Shocking how she always says the same thing whenever I ask you to translate," I reply as I stand between him and the TV with crossed arms and a raised brow. "So." I pause for dramatic effect. "My souvenir?"

"Yeesh." Joaquin groans as he sets Nurse Oatmeal aside and stands up. "It's like you're only friends with me for the gifts."

"Duh, wasn't that obvious?"

He ignores my reply in favor of covering my eyes and guiding me carefully into the next room. "Keep 'em closed," he whispers before letting go of me and walking off. I hear what I think is the fridge door, then his footsteps approaching before he rests his hands back on my shoulders. "Okay, open."

My eyes fly open and my jaw almost hits the ground as I take in the surprise. "You did not."

With a flourish, he waves his arms toward the dozen slushies spread across the dining room table. "I did."

Backing out of our spring break plans had hurt my soul, but nothing pained me as much as having to cancel our slushie-taste-test road trip.

Slushies have been our ultimate guilty pleasure for as long as we can remember. Probably because our abuelas told us about savoring the piraguas they'd save their allowances for as kids growing up. Sadly, shaved ice desserts haven't made their big break in Elmwood yet—though Tío Tony is strongly considering adding them to the Casa Y Cocina menu—so we've had to settle for the next best thing.

The mini road trip was the perfect addition to our shoestring-budget spring break adventure. Better known as *Spring Broke*. On our way down to Wildwood, we'd stop at seven different restaurants to sample their slushies, collect our ratings, and crown the Ultimate Slushie Champion. Spending my spring break at home sucked, but missing out on the slushies just made the FOMO that much worse.

But thanks to Joaquin, I'm not missing out after all.

"How did you even get these here?" I ask, peeking into a white paper bag beside the slushies and finding an assortment of French fries and chicken nuggets, our slushie accompaniments of choice. "Shouldn't they have all melted by now?"

"Borrowed a cooler from one of the guys," he explains, carefully removing the slushies from their Styrofoam holders. Two cups per establishment. "They're not perfect but should still be good enough for us to give impartial rankings. And I had to skip the place in Harrison. They're closed on Sundays, so we'll need to hit them another time."

Eagerly, I sit down at the table and pull up the Notes app list I'd created weeks ago to keep track of our rankings. Once Joaquin is seated across from me, I reach for the closest option—from Iggy's Ices—smiling when I notice my name written in Joaquin's handwriting on the side of the cup.

On the count of three, we each take our first sips, savoring the sugar racing through our veins. My eyes widen as the sweet but not overpowering taste of piña colada washes over me—the taste so rich that if I closed my eyes I could easily picture myself sipping this straight out of a coconut on a beach in San Juan.

"You good?" Joaquin says around a laugh as my body trembles while I come down from the high of that mind-blowing first sip.

"So good," I mumble, doing a little dance as I take a second sip. "Amazing. Life changing. I could die right now, and I wouldn't even be mad."

Once he's sure I'm not going to collapse from delight, he reaches for my cup and takes a sip for himself. His eyes go wide, his cheeks flush, and his shoulders shimmy in the same mini-dance I performed seconds earlier as he goes through the same life-altering experience I did.

"That shouldn't be legal," he says as he helps himself to another sip. "I would do *very* dangerous things for that."

I nod in agreement and join him in one last shoulder shimmy. I'd gladly give up my firstborn if it meant getting to have these for the rest of my life and not risk my health. As Nurse Oatmeal paws at my leg, I wonder if they'd take her instead.

Joaquin's cherry slushie isn't as exciting as mine, but still pretty solid. Definitely not dance break worthy, though. After two sips each of both, we pop open the lids and go through our practiced routine of carefully mixing the two together to create our own masterpiece. The combo definitely bumps the cherry up a few points but doesn't top the OG piña colada.

"All right, ranking," I announce after we've sampled our swirl flavor. "I give Iggy's a nine and a half. Would be a ten if their fries were crispier, but a very impressive start."

Joaquin nods, chewing a chicken nugget and rubbing his chin thoughtfully before giving his own ranking. "Seven. Cherry could've been better, and I'm docking points for them not having a drive-through."

"You can't factor that into your ranking," I protest. "This is supposed to be objective!"

"My ranking, my rules," he insists.

Well, I can't argue with the person who made this possible in the first place.

"So, did I miss anything exciting while I was gone?" Joaquin asks. "Besides you rendezvousing with Chris Pavlenko."

"Oh, plenty," I reply. "I went to work. Binged three seasons of *Gilmore Girls,* and watched Nurse Oatmeal try to take a skunk in a fight. Thrilling stuff."

Joaquin snorts, swirling the straw in his cup. "Did she win?"

We look down at where she's given up on trying to snag a French fry and has flopped onto the floor and presented her belly for pets instead.

"She got a few intimidating barks in," I reply, leaning down to give her the attention she so desperately needs. "But then the skunk just sprayed her and bounced."

I'll never forget that smell. Like the love child of a rotten egg and a McDonald's dumpster.

"Dirty game," he says with a snort, waiting until his laughter has subsided to peer up at me with a more ominous expression. "Hear anything from Sarah Lawrence yet?"

"No," I reply with an attempt at a nonchalant shrug.

Not that I've been counting the days since I found out I was waitlisted at my dream school—but if I had, it'd be seventeen. Hope started fading over break, when I realized I only have three weeks left to either put down a deposit at one of the schools I actually got into or risk my entire future on a school that may not want me.

No pressure.

"It'll come," Joaquin is quick to reassure, knocking his knee against mine. "And if not, you've still got Rutgers."

My smile is as stiff and awkward as the thought of Rutgers makes me feel. The day I got my acceptance email was the happiest I'd seen Mami in months. She may have dropped out her junior year after she discovered she was pregnant with me, but that hasn't stopped her from singing Rutgers' praises. And there are plenty of pros, more than any of the other schools I got into.

But I can't shake the nagging feeling that the only reason I can see myself there is because it'd make her proud.

Mami wasn't over the moon about Sarah Lawrence, at least not the way I was. The campus, the theater program, the city. The chance to live somewhere new and reinvent myself was so intoxicating I'd filled out an application the second we got home from our visit. All Mami saw was the distance between here and

New York, making it seem like I'd be flying across the country instead of just hopping to the next state over. But no other place has given me that all-consuming, have-to-be-there feeling like Sarah Lawrence did.

There's nothing wrong with Rutgers, really. They even have a solid theater program. The biggest problem is that more than half our class will be there next year. College is supposed to be about discovering yourself, finding new friends, yadda yadda. How am I supposed to do that when I'm only twenty minutes from home and surrounded by the same people I've known my entire life?

"Right," I reply, brushing off the post-grad-plan cloud that's been hanging over me for seventeen days, twelve hours, and forty-five minutes, and focus on the more important task at hand: trying slushies from restaurant number two. Limeade and watermelon from Talk Frosty to Me.

While Joaquin combines our—unfortunately mediocre—slushies, I pause, struck by how . . . *different* he looks. Besides the bold fashion choices, everything else about him is a stock-photo-worthy image of your classic high school spring breaker. An unfairly even tan, freckles dotting the bridge of his nose, and the smell of salt water and suntan lotion rolling off him in waves.

Something tugs at my heart, a weird, empty type of sadness as I dwell on the fact that I should've been on the beach with him, sampling slushies by the ocean instead of at my dining room table.

"Five. Nothing special," Joaquin says after a lukewarm final sip. I jot down his ranking. "So, how was your mom's Vegas extravaganza?"

As if on cue, the front door bursts open and Nurse Oatmeal springs into action, barking at top volume as she races to greet whoever just walked in.

Mami comes barreling into the kitchen with an armful of shopping bags, wearing the most god-awful cheetah-print jumpsuit I've ever seen.

"Hello, party people!" She greets both of us with a kiss on the cheek before setting her bags on the ground.

"Did you hit big?" I ask, eyeing the Chanel shopping bag on her arm.

She scoffs, rolling her eyes as she grabs a seltzer water from the fridge. "Lost three hundred bucks. Don't gamble when you're older, kids," she warns before taking a long sip. "It's a scam."

While Mami quenches her thirst and Nurse Oatmeal inspects the bags on the floor, I scan the entryway for any sign of her travel companion. "Where's Doug?"

The whole reason Mami was even in Vegas was to celebrate her latest fling's divorce anniversary. Who the hell celebrates getting divorced?

"*Dave* is at his place," Mami replies, emphasizing his name. In my defense, he looked like a Doug. "We, uh . . . didn't work out."

Joaquin gives her a sympathetic frown, while I hold back an eye roll. I saw that coming from a mile away. When Mami asked me earlier this year if I'd be okay with her slowly dipping her toes into romance again, I'd insisted on helping her take a new set of photos for her dating profile. It's been over a decade since she and Papi split, and almost as long since either of us have seen him. No one deserves to be swept off their feet more than she does.

But when I was helping her apply winged eyeliner for the first time, I didn't think the next six months would pass in a blur of dozens of different nondescript men hanging out in our living room every other week. We already rarely see each other thanks to her new job as an overnight ER nurse. Most days we're on opposite timelines—her fast asleep when I get up for school in the morning and vice versa. With her days off now reserved for dates, I'm lucky if Mami and I can get a single night alone together every week, if I even see her at all. For years it was just the two of us, holding on to each other like lifelines, and now I'm off at sea alone.

I'd been talking about my own spring break plans for months when Doug—sorry, *Dave*—sprang the weeklong trip to Vegas on Mami. A weeklong trip that happened to be at the exact same time as *my* spring break. With my abuela down in Virginia and Doña Carmen off at a church retreat for a few days, Mami begged me to stay home and watch Nurse Oatmeal. Or at the very least bring the dog with me. Because, of course, their hotel and travel weren't refundable.

But mine were.

Every potential dog sitter already had spring break plans of their own, the local pet hotel banned Nurse Oatmeal last year after she bit someone, and the Airbnb Joaquin and I booked had a strict no pets or late cancellation policy, so the decision was made for me.

Spring Broke was supposed to be perfect. Every year, Cordero High seniors flock to Wildwood—a resort town in South Jersey far away enough from Elmwood that parental supervision is minimal, but close enough that Herbert's engine wouldn't crap out on us halfway there.

Spring break in Wildwood is as essential to the senior year experience as existential dread about your future. After nearly four years, it was our turn to feel like the protagonists in a Disney Channel movie. Beach volleyball and bike rides on the boardwalk and finally using the fake IDs we spent all of our birthday money on last year.

But just because my mom decided to wreck my plans didn't mean Joaquin should suffer. He'd insisted that he was fine with canceling his trip too—since we are co-dog parents—but he couldn't hide his disappointment. Spending a week at a beach house alone isn't ideal, but it's not like he'd have to search hard for company. Most of our class was staying in the same budget-friendly block of rentals as us, and, unlike me, Joaquin never had trouble making friends. Within ten minutes of me officially backing out, he was making plans to go boogie boarding with his friends from the baseball team.

Mami sits down beside me, not clocking the pissed look on my face as she helps herself to a sip of my third slushie. "Did you have fun while I was gone?" she aims the question at me, even though we both know my disrupted plans were the exact opposite of fun.

"Just worked," I mumble, the annoyance from her wrecking my spring break making the limeade slushie taste bitter.

Mami stiffens, clearly sensing my irritation, but doesn't call me out on it. Instead, she grabs her bags and heads for the stairs. "I'm going upstairs to unpack and shower. Let me know if you two need anything, all right?"

I give her a noncommittal nod, waiting until she's gone before slumping in my seat. "Looks like it went as well as I thought it would," I say, answering Joaquin's earlier question from before she arrived. "So, was Spring Broke everything we dreamed it would be?" I ask him, eager to switch to a less frustrating topic.

"Not exactly," he replies with a coy smile. "Kinda hard to live up to the dream when half of it isn't there." Beneath the table, he nudges his foot against mine.

"Please tell me you and the guys didn't spend your entire break playing video games." Joaquin and his teammates have a one-track mind when it comes to video games. They see a TV, they sit, they play. For hours, unless someone comes along and offers them food. Then they learn to multitask.

"Not exactly," he repeats. His smirk is even wider this time, like a mischievous imp.

"Stop being cryptic." My leg hoists up to nail a kick against his shin, but he catches my ankle before I can make contact. Seriously, what is up with his reflexes today?

The mood shifts after he releases my foot, his teasing smile falling away. The color starts to build in his cheeks, as rosy as our cherry-stained tongues.

I've seen this expression before. It's the same one from when he told me he had a crush on our ninth-grade homeroom teacher, Ms. Woodsen.

"Oh my God." I lunge out of my seat. "You met someone!"

24

He doesn't say a word, keeping his eyes on his remaining nuggets, but the silence speaks volumes.

For the shortest blink-and-you'll-miss-it-moment, his lips tug into a smile. And that's all I need to know that I'm absolutely right: Joaquin has a crush.

"I knew it!" I shout, slamming a triumphant fist on the table.

My response soothes whatever nervous energy has built up in him, his smile blossoming into a full-on grin as I shove his shoulder.

"Why didn't you tell me?!" He bats my hands away, but it doesn't wipe that dopey smile off his face. The boy has it bad. "Is it someone from school? That girl from the track team who's always asking you if you like documentaries?"

"No, not her. It is someone from school, though," he answers after a beat, going back to avoiding my eyes again.

"That could be a lot of people." One person comes to mind, someone he might hesitate to tell me about. "You're not getting back together with Chelsea, are you?"

Despite being a hopeless sap with a penchant for cheesy love songs, thanks to his intense baseball schedule, Joaquin's only relationship was a month-long fling with Chelsea Sanchez sophomore year. A fling that came to a crashing halt when Chelsea dumped him in front of half the school because he was "too focused on sports to deserve her." Which is bullshit if you ask me.

"God no, no, definitely not," he reassures with a grimace, waving his arms to clear the air of that accusation. That doesn't do much to settle my nerves. Other than Chelsea, who else could it be?

"It's Tessa . . . Hernandez."

Oh hell to the mother fucking no.

"Oooh." My smile might be convincing, but the crack in my voice ruins the façade. Everything comes together—the shyness, the lack of eye contact. This doesn't *not* make sense. Tessa and Joaquin would be a match made in cliché heaven. With Joaquin going to the local technical school after graduation to follow his late electrician father's footsteps and Tessa going to Rutgers, they wouldn't even have to deal with some dramatic over-the-summer breakup due to long distance.

The only problem is Tessa is the worst.

Tessa Hernandez has been at the top of the social pyramid since elementary school. Maybe even since birth. Popular, pretty, and loaded as hell, she's had people scrambling to be in her orbit for as long as I can remember. Being in Tessa Hernandez's inner circle means summers at her abuelo's villa in Punta Cana and winters skiing at their Colorado chalet. Dinners with private chefs and shopping sprees charged to an Amex with a sky-high limit. And she's not small-town beautiful, either. She's the real thing—thick, silky dark brown hair, legs for days, and glowing, blemish-free brown skin. The type of girl you wouldn't be surprised to see on the cover of a magazine years after you last saw her.

While she has enough admirers to start up a fan club, thanks to her overly strict dad, she's never truly been on the market. Sure, she's had her down-low hookups here and there, but until her crabby older sister, Julia, starts dating, Tessa's strictly off-limits.

Or, she was, until Julia went social-media official with her boyfriend last week—the one time anyone at Cordero cared about a college student's dating life. And thus, the floodgates have officially opened. The race for Tessa Hernandez's heart is on.

Watching Joaquin compete in the Tessa Hernandez Hunger Games would be bad enough. What makes it worse is our—well, *my*—history with her. My first, and only, relationship lasted a whopping fifteen days freshman year. In retrospect, Danny and I were never meant to be. It was awkward enough that he was Joaquin's teammate, but besides being in the same bio class, Danny and I basically had nothing in common. Still, that didn't make finding out that he hooked up with Tessa Hernandez at a party barely two weeks into our relationship hurt any less.

And now Joaquin has a crush on her.

"I know what you're thinking, and I swear, I have a shot," he says, holding his hands up in defense of my judgment. "We ran into each other and got to talking and she seemed . . . I dunno . . . sweet. She made me dinner one night, and we went roller skating on the boardwalk, and talked for hours, and on the last day we watched the sunrise together, and it was . . . really, really nice."

By the time he finishes and gulps for breath, the blush on his cheeks has traveled down to his collarbone. The spark never leaves his eyes, not for a second.

"That's uh . . ." I take my time, knowing I should choose my words carefully.

It's not that I mind that he met someone. Boys like Joaquin

are hard to come by. Sweet. Thoughtful. Doesn't smell like a wet sock. Watching him and Chelsea make out every lunch period the month they were together was stomach turning, but after that mess he deserves something good. A cookie-cutter romance that doesn't end with him getting his heart broken in front of the entire school.

But couldn't he have picked *anyone* else?

"Ive, I promise, she really is different. She's not . . . y'know . . ."

"Still an asshole?"

I bite my tongue the second the words slip free. Tessa is a . . . *delicate* subject. Something we skirt around or avoid because the wound still feels fresh four years later. Obviously, I was way more pissed at Danny than I was at her, but I'm sure she knew that we were together. It was front-page news that someone on the illustrious baseball team—one of the better players at that—had decided to grace a nobody like me with his presence. According to Danny, the hookup had been Tessa's suggestion. Granted, he's a piece of hot garbage and I take his word with a grain of salt, but now just the thought of Tessa makes me feel uncomfortable. Like one wrong step could make me snap.

And I'm very close to snapping.

"Ive . . ." That's the only thing Joaquin can think to say. My name. But he says it with those stupid expressive eyes and his stupid pouty face and even though I'm pissed, I can feel the ice around my heart begin to thaw.

"Sorry." Uncrossing my arms is the first step. Followed by unclenching my jaw. The final piece, making it seem like I'm not about to explode, is too much to tackle yet. "So . . . you said"—*you fell for the Wicked Witch of the West*—"you guys ran into each other?"

The question is tense, my voice unsteady, but Joaquin lowers his guard. There's a strange boyishness to him as he tugs at a loose thread on the hem of his shirt, the color in his cheeks fading from Flamin' Hot Cheeto to bubblegum pink.

"Umm, yeah. On the first day. I was at the boardwalk and saw her just standing there. At first, I didn't think it was her, since . . . well. She's never by herself."

It's true. Tessa's flanked by a minimum of two of her adoring fans around the clock. Her henchwomen probably take shifts guarding her while she sleeps.

"I thought she was lost, so I went over to ask if she needed help, and it was . . . freaky. She had makeup streaming down her face, and a bunch of tissues in her hands. At first I thought maybe someone had like . . . just died or something, so I started backing up before things could get awkward. But then she told me to stay . . . so I did."

"And now you two are gonna run off to elope in Vegas like my mom and Dave?"

"Ha ha," he replies with an eyeroll. "We're saving that for the second date."

"How chaste," I grumble. "If you two are a thing now, does that mean she has to ride with us to school in the morning? Because she might break up with you as soon as she sees your back seat."

"We're not a *thing*." He waves his hand dismissively. "Yet, I mean."

"Did you kiss her?" I ask, even though I'm not sure I want to know the answer.

He shrugs sheepishly. "No."

"Did you *try* to kiss her?"

"No!" he replies while throwing his hands in the air. "I was respecting boundaries!"

Further proof that he's an anomaly among our peers. A teen boy who thinks with his heart and not with his dick.

"I want to ask her to prom," he says, sitting up straighter, his voice more confident. Like a general prepared to address his troops.

Except he's asking for the impossible.

"You want to ask Tessa Hernandez to prom?"

It's hard not to scoff. Prom season at Cordero High is sacred. The month after spring break is like a cotton candy sugar rush. Promposals in every hallway and empty classroom and rumors about who's wearing what dress and how much they spent on it. Not to mention the school pep rally, which is less of an assembly and more of a school-wide rave, and senior skip day, then senior lock-in, two opportunities for us to get discreetly wasted on school grounds. But prom is the main event. Needless to say, it's exhausting.

And with Tessa now officially on the market, she's sure to be at the center of it.

"It can be romantic!" Joaquin says with genuine enthusiasm.

"Promposals? Romantic?" I reply skeptically. Promposals at Cordero High are lots of things. Over-the-top. Cringe-worthy. Capitalism in its purest form, as Anna would argue. But definitely not romantic.

"I know things usually get out of hand, but I have an idea!" Joaquin pauses to pull out his phone, opening the Notes app and scrolling through a list of items ranging from *Write her name in the sky* to *Hire a flash mob*. "Well, lots of ideas."

Being a good friend means being supportive. And sometimes being supportive is saving your best friend from going bankrupt at eighteen over something that has a 90 percent failure rate.

"Are you sure you want to do this?" I ask warily. Promposal season is cutthroat, high stakes. Stepping into the ring for Tessa's hand in promtrimony means making enemies and an ass out of yourself.

"I do." His voice is sincere, honest, and that's even more terrifying. "When we were together at the beach, it was *electric*, Ive. Sparks, chemistry, all that stuff they talk about in those telenovelas you always made me watch."

He made *me* watch them, but I don't protest.

"But I can't do this alone," he continues. "Or, I could, but it would probably suck. But if I had help from the master of making magic happen behind the scenes . . ."

Oh no.

"N—"

"Please, Ive," he begs before I can respond. He even takes it one step further, sliding onto his knees, hands clasped together in prayer to his almighty God: Ivelisse Santos. "I promise, promise, *promise* I'll never ask you for anything else again. And I'll buy you lunch for a week—two weeks!"

His sales pitch stalls long enough for him to inch closer to me, resting his chin on my knee, gazing up at me with those sweet bunny eyes. "Pretty please," he says again, this time barely louder than a whisper.

For the second time in an hour, I feel an overwhelming urge to say no. But turning down your best friend is way harder than turning down someone from chem that you barely know. I've already disappointed Joaquin once this month by bailing on our trip. And every year after spring break, we hardly see each other. Baseball season goes into full swing—especially now that they're moving on to the championships—and I'm usually tied up with running tech for the spring play—a fact he'd reminded me of by praising me as the "master of making magic happen behind the scenes." Which is correct, but still a dirty move. With Joaquin and Isabella planning to spend this summer in Puerto Rico with their mom, these last few weeks of the year are starting to feel more like a ticking time bomb to goodbye than the most "care-free time of my life."

Spring break was supposed to be our last hurrah. Neither of us said it, but it was always there in the fine print of the high school rulebook. Everything about us—where we are, *who* we are—is going to change in a few months.

This may not be the prom season I imagined, but Joaquin is still a part of it, and at the end of the day that's the only thing that matters. Weathering the last couple of months of senior year with the person who's been in my life since the beginning. Even if it means having to help him win over someone I can't stand.

"Okay."

Joaquin looks up from his prayer hands, lips parted in shock. "Wait, seriously?"

"Your lack of confidence in me is very insulting."

Instead of replying, he leaps to his feet, pulling me into a hug tight enough to make me lose my breath.

"You're the best friend ever, you know that, right?"

"I do," I reply quietly, patting him on the back and hoping my kindness doesn't backfire.

CHAPTER THREE

A LEGION OF PROM elves snuck in over break. They've sprinkled glitter glue and confetti over every surface they could find. The halls are covered in crepe paper and neon posters advertising nominations for prom court and pre-prom limos that still need one more person to make the down payment. One very artful flyer outside the gym asks if anyone has access to a horse-drawn carriage. Somehow every room looks like the aftermath of a tsunami, though the real theatrics haven't even begun.

By eight a.m. sharp, there's a crowd forming in the hall outside the cafeteria seconds after the homeroom bell rings, everyone clamoring to get closer to the front.

"Did someone get caught with weed again?" I ask Joaquin as we linger in the back of the crowd. Fortunately, he's tall enough for the both of us. He can get a bird's-eye view of the action without even going on his tiptoes. Meanwhile, I have a fantastic view of the dandruff in the hair of the guy in front of me. Since I can't see what's going on anyway, I dig out my phone to refresh my email for the third time today, but my inbox is as empty as ever. No emails from Sarah Lawrence.

Joaquin's fresh tan pales. "Shit . . ."

Before I can ask him what's going on, the opening notes of a song I've only ever heard in laundry detergent commercials begins to blare over the intercom.

"I believe in miracles . . ."

Oh no.

I'm able to watch the horror unfold thanks to my dandruff-y friend holding up his phone to record the spectacle.

A boy I vaguely recognize from the basketball team is decked out in a lime-green tracksuit, holding a rose between his teeth and slowly making his way to the real center of attention: Tessa Hernandez.

"Where you from, you sexy thing," he mouths along with the lyrics unironically, pulling the rose from between his teeth to give to Tessa. Gross.

There's a smattering of giggles as Tessa accepts the rose with a tight smile before handing it off to one of her minions when he turns his back. The volume of the song dips as he spins back around with a poster board in hand, as glaringly neon green as his outfit. He two-steps his way back to Tessa before sinking down onto one knee, holding up the sign for the eager crowd to see.

I'LL BELIEVE IN MIRACLES
IF YOU GO TO PROM WITH ME

The crowd eats it up, gasping and hooting as if we don't already know how this is going to play out.

To his credit, he does get Tessa to laugh. Whether it's from amusement or condescension is unclear, though, and in this case, ignorance is his bliss. The crowd leans in as she pushes her freshly highlighted, dark brown hair over her shoulder. Joaquin starts chewing on his thumbnail—a nasty habit I thought he shook off years ago. Even I can't help holding my breath as Tessa takes a step toward her first suitor of the season. The hall goes completely silent, except for the closing notes of the song and the click of Tessa's designer ankle boots tapping on the tiled floor. Even through a cracked phone screen I can tell that he's started to shake as she peers down at him with her signature sly smirk.

"Keep dreaming."

An outsider might think we'd just found out classes were canceled for the rest of the year with the way everyone loses their minds. Gossip moves faster than the speed of light here—anyone who didn't see this stunt will know in approximately six seconds.

"This is a freakin' nightmare," Joaquin mutters around his chewed-up thumb. "I knew people were going to move fast, but I didn't think they'd be *this* fast."

"It should be illegal to stage a promposal at eight a.m.," I reply, pulling him out of the path of a gang of hollering boys.

Joaquin doesn't pay me any mind, so focused I wouldn't be surprised if steam started coming out of his ears. "I need to think of something. ASAP."

"Chill, Quin." I give him a reassuring shoulder punch as we start heading toward our lockers. No one's in a hurry to get to class even though the final bell just rang. There's no such thing as time during prom season. "Tessa's gonna get a million promposals. Just—"

"Hey, Joaquin," the woman of the hour herself says as she glides through the crowd to stand between me and my best friend.

"H-hey!" Sweat beads on Joaquin's forehead as he whips around to face Tessa, subtly readjusting his jacket to cover the protein powder stain on his T-shirt. "How was the rest of your break?"

"Not bad." She smirks like she's holding back a secret, her voice as smooth as silk. "See you in third period?"

I can hear him audibly gulp. "Y-yeah. Totally. Wouldn't miss it."

Tessa gives him one last parting smile before brushing past me and into a nearby classroom. I hate to say it, but she smells incredible. If luxury had a scent, it'd be her.

Around us, a new round of commotion breaks out over this latest development. Tessa turning down a promposal *and* gracing Cordero's baseball golden boy with a conversation he didn't initiate? Stop the presses.

Joaquin is in a Tessa-induced trance, practically floating as he gazes longingly at the classroom Tessa went into, not noticing me even after I nudge my arm against his.

"See, you don't have anything to worry about. She's totally—"

He takes off before I can finish, calling, "Gotta go think of ideas. I'll talk to you later!" over his shoulder.

"O-okay, bye," I reply weakly, even though I know he won't hear me.

So much for weathering these last few weeks together.

"This prom shit is going to kill me," Anna announces as she storms onto the auditorium stage, almost knocking over a bucket of paint sitting beside Emily R., one of our sophomore tech crew members.

"My bad." Anna gives Emily R. a thumbs-up before carefully navigating through the sea of brushes and cans.

Anna's covered in a fine layer of hot-pink glitter. It nicely complements her purple overalls and rose-gold septum ring. Like Joaquin, vacation seems to have rejuvenated her. Her dark brown skin is glowing—even without the glitter—thanks to the facial she got with her mom at the day spa they visited over break.

And I can't say I disagree with her about prom. We've only been back for a day, and the chaos is already at a hundred. At some point last night, we were both added to a group chat with over three hundred of our classmates to post photos of our prom dresses to ensure no one wore the same one. By fourth period, all-out war had broken out over whether Yesenia Gordon's midnight-purple dress was too similar to Casey Zosnowski's deep-violet dress. Jury's still out.

I hand Anna a paintbrush once she's stored her stuff backstage and knelt down beside me. We only have a couple more minutes before the drama club finish their warm-ups and come wreak their usual havoc. Getting anything done set-design-wise is basically impossible when you have high school divas demanding you adjust their spotlight at the same time.

"Did Chris ask you out again?" I ask, not glancing up from the bush I'm working on solo. We still have to finish painting our Italian countryside, build multiple doors and windows, and construct an entire balcony before *The Taming of the Shrew*'s opening night. We may have more tech crew members now than we had freshman year—for a grand total of six, including me and Anna—but we're still way behind schedule.

"No, thank God. Some guy in my English class dedicated the sonnet we were supposed to write over break to Tessa Hernandez's 'cerulean eyes.' Except he (a) didn't even write a sonnet; it was just a list of ten things he likes about her, and (b) her eyes aren't even cerulean! They're brown!"

I wave my paintbrush at the clump of glitter stuck to the bridge of her glasses. "And the glitter?"

She dabs her glasses, rolling her eyes when her fingers come back hot pink. "That was from lunch. Guy gave his girlfriend a box that was supposed to 'lightly shower her with confetti' but it wound up going off like a pressure cooker. Glitter everywhere. Landed him detention for the rest of the week."

Anna pauses, stiffening halfway through pulling her locs out of her face with a banana-shaped clip. "Wait. How did you know about Chris?"

"Because he showed up at Casa Y Cocina on Sunday and asked me too."

Her jaw drops as she lets go of her hair to lean in closer to me. "He didn't."

"He did." I finally tear my eyes away from my half-finished shrub to wipe my hands on my painting jeans. "Even used the same sign. He took your name off and everything."

That gets a deep belly laugh out of her. "Men are trash. Absolute trash."

"Agreed," Emily R. says with a groan.

"You should keep your options open, though," Anna says once her laughter has died down. "Chris is obviously a no, but you can have my brother if you want," she teases.

Cool, my options are Chris Pavlenko and Anna's fourteen-year-old brother.

"Thanks, but no thanks. I'm staying away from all things prom."

For now, at least. I'll need to figure something out eventually, since Joaquin is dead set on going with Tessa. Joaquin and I have been a package deal for every dance of our high school careers, but Tessa's prom limo is as exclusive as a bougie sushi restaurant in Manhattan. There's no way in hell she's letting me take up one of those seats. Having Tío Tony drop me off at prom sounds mortifying, and Anna hates capitalism so deeply she probably won't be going. I can't say the thought of skipping doesn't sound appealing. If promposal season alone is this mind-numbing, I can only imagine the event itself.

"I'm just saying, you have options," Anna continues, delicately removing her star charm bracelet and tucking it safely into her pocket before getting to work on her own shrub. Her confidence in me is flattering, but we both know I don't have a line of suitors knocking at my door. "I know you're going with Joaquin, but you deserve a date that makes you feel special."

Except Joaquin does make me feel special. He's the only one who laughs at my jokes and entertains me when I'm panicking. He sits through horror movies with his head buried in a pillow because he knows they're my favorite, even though he can't sleep for a week afterward. He claims he hates reading, yet he's devoured every single book I've ever recommended. When we realized Herbert didn't have an AUX outlet, he burned dozens of CDs with my favorite songs just so I'd always have something to listen to.

He's my favorite person on the planet. And he's falling for a girl I can't stand.

And even if he wasn't, going with anyone else isn't exactly a possibility for me. I'm less of a wallflower and more like a fly on the wall—unnoticed and swatted at by those who do. And it's for the best. I've seen the way my classmates chew people up and spit them out. I have no interest in making nice with the same people who judged my appearance the second a popular guy expressed interest in me. Shit like that wrecks a fourteen-year-old's confidence.

After the Danny fiasco, I decided romance had to be off the table until college—that is, if I wind up at Sarah Lawrence. Which, according to my empty-as-of-ten-minutes-ago-inbox, remains up in the air. Rutgers' campus may be huge, but with my luck the only people I'll be meeting my entire freshman year will be the same people who I've spent the past four years avoiding. In which case, I can put off dating until my mid-twenties.

Plus, most teenage boys stink. Why would I want to go out of my way to spend more time with them?

"We're, um . . . not going together, actually," I mumble, half hoping she won't hear me and move on.

But of course she does. Anna has bat-level hearing when it comes to gossip. "What?!"

"We should hurry up. The drama kids wi—"

"No, hold up. You don't get to change the subject." She waves her brush dangerously close to my nose. "Since when are you not going to prom with each other? You two do *everything* together."

This implication may not be off base, but it gets under my skin nonetheless. It's in her tone, the way she makes it sound like it's a bad thing to have a person you hang out with all the time. Joaquin and I are not codependent. Seriously. He has his baseball friends, and basically everyone at this school is under his spell, and I have Anna, Mami (when she's actually around), Nurse Oatmeal, the tech crew . . . well, sometimes, and . . .

I guess that's kind of it.

I shrug, trying to play nonchalant. "He's not obligated to bring me. He's gonna ask someone else."

"Who?" She's fully abandoned productivity at this point, crossing her arms and gesturing for me to hurry up and spill.

If Joaquin is as set on speeding up this plan as he seems, it won't be a secret for long anyway. But Tessa and Anna have an . . . interesting past. The two of them were capital B best friends—matching jewelry sets, joint birthday parties, finishing each other's sentences. Our entire class knew about Anna even though she went to a different middle school. Anna and Tessa were as much of a two-for-one deal as Joaquin and I are.

On our first day at Cordero, everyone waited for Anna and Tessa to roll up, pinkies linked, and take ownership of the halls. But Anna never took her place as Tessa's right hand. They wouldn't even so much as acknowledge each other in the cafeteria. Rumors came and went—Tessa tried to hook up with Anna's older brother, Anna blew off Tessa's birthday sleepover for someone else's, gossip ad infinitum—but nothing really stuck. Being friends with Anna then meant taking sides in a feud no one understood. And in those first few days of freshman year, social currency was all that mattered. So, we found each other and formed our own little Reject Club.

The urge to ask what went down between them has sat on the tip of my tongue since Anna waltzed into the auditorium during our freshman year production of *Seussical* and asked if I needed help with my Truffula Trees. But just the mention of Tessa's name makes her scoff.

Needless to say, she wouldn't react well to Joaquin's crush.

"It's kind of a long—"

The door to the auditorium bursts open and I breathe a sigh of relief. For once, the drama club is coming to my rescue. Except it's not the overcaffeinated thespians I'm used to. They typically break into show tunes immediately. I can't quite make out who it is, their face completely hidden by enough bouquets of roses that the local florist could retire.

"Ive!" the walking centerpiece shouts from across the room.

Dear Lord.

"Hey," I call back weakly, setting my brush aside to help Joaquin before he drops one of the bouquets. "You've been busy."

The four other members of tech crew—all, strangely

enough, named Emily—flock to the edge of the stage to greet the reason our membership has gone up.

"Hey, Joaquin," Emily R. and Emily S. say in almost perfect synchronicity.

"Do you need help?" Emily W. offers.

"Those are so pretty!" Emily Z. adds.

Joaquin has been an unofficial member of the tech crew since I joined freshman year. From stopping by to paint whenever he doesn't have baseball practice, to helping us on trips to Home Depot for plywood, if he can lend a hand, he will. His reserved seat in the front row of every show is both a thank-you and a time-honored tradition. One that his many admirers must have caught on to this year.

He gives the Emilys a "'sup" nod before turning his attention back to the roses.

"Went after last period to grab these before practice," he pants, so out of breath he might as well have run a marathon. His forehead is dripping sweat, the roses pressed to his chest now damp and crumpled. "Tessa's already turned down five promposals." His phone pings, and he pauses to scan the text that just came in. "Shit, six."

The devil works hard but Tessa Hernandez's simps work harder.

"I figured something out," he continues as he hands half of the bouquets to me. They're piled so high I can barely see over the top of them. "But it'll have to wait until before class tomorrow."

I gesture for the Emilys to focus on painting the cobblestone wall while I help Joaquin with setting the roses down on the lip of the stage, the perfect excuse for me to avoid the confused looks Anna keeps sending my way. So much for keeping Joaquin's plan under wraps.

"Think you could do me a favor?" he asks once the roses are out of harm's way.

I'm starting to dread this question. "Y-yeah, sure."

"I need to run to practice. Coach'll kill me if I'm late, but would you mind holding on to these? Abuela's allergies are a bitch this time of year, so I don't want to upset her."

"You didn't think of that before buying all of these?" Anna snaps, wearing a frown that could pierce stone.

Joaquin is either immune or too good-natured to be fazed. "Gotta go big if you want a shot with Tessa Hernandez," he says with a shrug.

There's a collective sharp inhale from the Emilys as Joaquin wipes his face with the edge of his T-shirt, giving all of us a glimpse of his well-defined stomach muscles. My nose wrinkles—not at Joaquin, but the uneasy feeling in my gut. It's not the first time someone has gawked at Joaquin in my presence, but knowing your best friend is one of the hottest guys in school hasn't gotten any less weird over the past four years.

Now less sweaty, Joaquin taps his fist against my shoulder. "Thanks again, Ive. You're the best."

Before I can process how I'm going to get these back home in one piece, Joaquin's taking off the way he came. As soon as the door closes behind him, Anna pounces.

"Are you seriously going to help him ask out Tessa?"

She makes it sound like I'm helping him rob a bank.

Behind her, the Emilys deflate—their Joaquin Romero dreams crushed.

"He's not asking her out; he's asking her *to prom*," I correct, avoiding her gaze by moving the roses off the stage and into the wings where they'll be safe from the drama club.

"Right, because people only want to ask Tessa to prom because she's such delightful company." Every word drips with sarcasm.

"She could be, I don't know," I reply, not taking her bait.

Anna hops off the stage and stands right in my path. The face she gives me is so intense it shakes me to my core.

"Fine, yes, he wants to ask her out. Whatever."

"Did something happen between them?" she asks, her voice quieter. Likely to avoid spreading any gossip to the Emilys. "Like . . . did they hook up or something?"

"Not really." I shrug. "They hung out over break and Joaquin thinks there's something there. Nothing concrete."

That seems to soothe Anna's concerns. "You know he's asking for public humiliation, right? And you're helping him do it, Miss I Don't Want Anything to Do with Prom." She punctuates the statement by pointing her finger against my shoulder.

Sometimes I regret befriending someone as brilliant as Anna. At least Joaquin is too much of a himbo to ever call me out on my bullshit.

"This is different," I insist, pushing her finger away and walking around her.

"Uh, no, it is *not* different."

Groaning, I take a deep breath. "It's like being in tech crew," I say while gesturing to our still-in-progress set. "I stand in the back, make it look like the trees are swaying in the breeze, and let someone else be in the spotlight for two hours. Just because I helped make it happen doesn't mean I want to be an actor."

Building sets isn't a meaningless extracurricular for either of us. Unlike me, Anna has a set-in-stone future and a one-way ticket to study drama at NYU. We both know there's a distinct difference between the people behind the stage and the ones on it.

Even so, Anna doesn't seem convinced.

Before either of us can say anything else, the drama kids come barreling into the auditorium in a flurry of iced coffees and show tunes. Neither of us moves at first, eyes locked on one another until the drama supervisor starts barking out orders.

"Don't say I didn't warn you," Anna mumbles, leaving me to pick up the pieces of Joaquin's mess.

CHAPTER FOUR

THERE AREN'T MANY ITEMS on my senior year bucket list, and getting up at 6:00 a.m. to set up roses in the senior parking lot definitely isn't one of them.

At least Joaquin comes bearing breakfast.

"Caramel iced coffee with skim milk," he says in lieu of a greeting when I make it to his driveway, rubbing sleep crust out of my eyes. "Upgraded to a large as a special thank-you."

"You're too kind," I reply, though the statement lacks enthusiasm. It's too early to be anything other than exhausted.

"And *this*"—he pauses to hold up a foil-wrapped breakfast sandwich—"is because I like you."

I lunge for the sandwich like I haven't eaten in weeks, inhaling the intoxicating aroma of grease, melted cheese, and bacon. "From Marco's?"

Marco's may be the greasiest place within fifty miles, but their food is a religious experience. They're not afraid to smother their fries in every type of cheese known to man, and a single sip of their coffee could make you bulletproof. And, most importantly, their cherry and piña colada slushies currently have an iron grip on the top slot of our ranking list. It's a hot spot for truckers like Papi, who first brought us there when we were six, just a few months before he and Mami split and he disappeared to Florida.

"What am I, a monster?" he replies with a roll of his eyes. "Of course it's from Marco's."

Any annoyance over his inhumane call time melts away when I take my first bite, all gooey, cheesy goodness and perfect crispy bacon. It's impossible to stay angry when you're eating a Marco's sandwich. All that's missing is a piña colada slushie, but I can understand his reluctance to give me a cup full of sugar at six in the morning. I'd crash by fourth period AP Lit.

The sandwich is gone in record time, nothing left but a crumpled foil wrapper when we pull up to Cordero twenty minutes later. I was able to stash the roses in the drama club's prop closet instead of lugging them home on the bus. With everything we need already at school, and my keys to the auditorium in my bag, I was able to buy us an extra half hour of sleep.

"This is spooky," I say as we make our way back from the auditorium. I've never seen the lot so empty before.

Having your own parking spot is a mark of pride that most Cordero seniors take *very* seriously. Some graffiti their names onto their assigned spots on the first day of class while others spend months creating intricate murals dedicated to their senior year. Anna designed a galaxy on hers, complete with glow-in-the-dark paint. Joaquin, on the other hand, just wrote his name in plain, boring white.

Tessa's parking space is impossible to miss, though. Her name is written in hot-pink bubble letters, messages from her various admirers scrawled in every color of the rainbow with chalk paint.

"You're sure you want to do this?" I ask Joaquin as we struggle to hold the bouquets of roses we've just grabbed from the auditorium's cramped storage closet. They're still in surprisingly good condition.

"Totally," Joaquin replies a little too quickly.

Sweat dots his brow and the collar of his shirt.

"You just look a little . . . nervous."

And that's what's so concerning—he's *never* nervous. It's part of what makes him such a fantastic baseball player. He never lets the unexpected throw him off his game.

Joaquin is the cool cucumber, the level head to my chaos. The one who always reminds me that the things I'm worried about are valid but stuck in my mind. If he wasn't so set on becoming an electrician, he'd make an excellent therapist. I guess therapists have their days, too, because he seems to be moments away from popping like a balloon.

"No, nope, all good here," he rushes out, and starts working on laying his bundle of roses across Tessa's parking spot. He flits back and forth between the *P* he's constructing to the mostly finished *M* at lightning speed.

I set down my stack of roses and block Joaquin's path. He's too preoccupied with counting the roses to notice, walking right into me and nearly toppling both of us over. It does the trick of getting him to meet my eye long enough to hold him steady.

"Hey," I say, gripping his arms once I've caught my balance. "Talk to me. Because right now you're in Energizer Bunny mode, and it's kind of freaking me out."

He exhales slowly, taking the time to push his damp curls out of his eyes. "Right, sorry," he mumbles, and shakes his head. "This *has* to be perfect, and it feels like I'm already running out of time, and what if she hates it and—"

"If she doesn't love it, then she doesn't deserve you," I interrupt before he can finish, squeezing his shoulders. "You're amazing, Quin. And anyone who can't see that is an absolute dumbass."

He snorts, and such a gross sound has never sounded so charming. "You're pretty amazing too."

"Oh, I know." I let go of his shoulders to squat down and start rearranging his hot mess of an *R*. "Only a truly wonderful friend would wake up this early for someone as annoying as you."

He squats beside me, picking up one of the roses and poking the end of its stem against my arm. "Dick."

I swipe the rose from between his fingers, careful to avoid the thorns as I tap the petals against his nose. "I'm taking that as a compliment."

Instead of replying, he bites his lip but can't hold back his smile. Something in me wants to stay there, holding on to this image of him backlit by the glow of the sunrise. But I pull the flower and my attention away and get back to the task at hand.

Everyone knows you can't stare too long at the sun unless you want to get burned.

Considering our very sweaty start to this whole fiasco, the finished product is actually pretty swoony, if I do say so myself. The hit to Joaquin's meager summer job savings was well worth it for the sheer size of the spectacle alone, the question *PROM?* stretched out past Tessa's parking space and toward her neighbors, who hopefully won't mind. It's usually a free-for-all in the name of romance this time of year.

"Are roses too cliché?" Joaquin asks, as if he has time to return to the florist and buy a fresh truckload of daisies.

"I mean, I'm more of a peony gal, personally, but roses are classic. Can't go wrong."

"I should've gotten another two bouquets," Joaquin mumbles as he goes to fidget with the question mark for the hundredth time.

"And force yourself to declare bankruptcy?" I snap before smacking his hand away. "It's more than enough. Now, go get changed unless you want to prompose to Tessa in sweatpants."

I had the foresight to tell Joaquin to pack a change of clothes last night. Coming up with this plan on his own was impressive, but I had a feeling he'd forget that presentation isn't everything. Tessa would sooner drop dead than accept a prom invite from someone who looked like they just rolled out of bed.

While Joaquin heads off to change, I handle the finishing touches to the display. Weaving battery-operated fairy lights through the roses was a pretty good idea. *Good job, Joaquin.* The gently flickering lights pull his vision together. Spelling something out with roses isn't as easy as it sounds.

People start trickling into the lot. A group of stoners camped out on a nearby picnic table see me and giggle to themselves. For a second, I'm worried they'll start asking about the display, but they quickly become distracted by a more important debate: who's next in their blunt rotation.

A car comes barreling toward me at way too high a speed for a parking lot. I only have a split second to jump out of the way of the SUV, narrowly avoiding ruining our hard work. Whoever my oh-so-kind classmate is has the courtesy to blare their horn at me. The car finally slows down to a crawl in front of the roses, and I read the GUD VIBES vanity plate.

Nothing about this car or its driver says *good vibes* to me.

The bass of an EDM song keeps the car vibrating even when the motor turns off and the window rolls down, the music so loud it pushes me back like a tidal wave. A head pokes out, a boy in a letterman jacket who pulls off his sunglasses slowly, like he's some kind of action hero. Hank "The Tank" Azario. The meatiest meathead on the football team.

Hank runs a hand along his stubbled jaw, humming as he takes in the display in front of Tessa's parking space.

"I'm not the one asking her," I blurt out. It's common knowledge that Hank's been in love with Tessa for years. So much so that he even tried paying someone to ask out Julia just so he could stealthily make his move on Tessa. Long story short, it didn't go the way he'd hoped.

I'm surprised he didn't shoot his shot on day one like

everybody else, so he must be biding his time. Or scoping out the competition.

Hank's not going to tackle me because I might be asking out the girl he likes, but the intensity of his glare makes me weak in the knees. And not in a hot way.

"Then who is?" he asks, shouting over the radio instead of just turning it down.

I clam up, my lips pressing into a line to keep from babbling anything that might get my friend in trouble. Hank might have enough of a conscience not to pick a fight with me, but I can't say the same about Joaquin. The football and baseball teams are bigger rivals than our *actual* rival, Elmwood Prep. In a town dictated by high school clichés, the baseball team being more popular than the football team is considered a crime. Especially to the football bros. But I guess they should suck less?

After almost a minute of silence, Hank sucks his teeth and waves me off with a scoff, rolling up his window and screeching away so fast he almost bowls over a group of girls gossiping on the grass. I'm sure having to watch the entire school battle over your longtime crush is doing a number on Hank's ego, but luckily he didn't smash any of the roses. Though, he was close enough to leave a very un-sexy puddle of motor oil in front of the display. It's not as pristine as what we'd originally put together, but it's better than having to start over with five minutes to the bell.

Speaking of the time, if Joaquin doesn't hurry up, I may wind up promposing to Tessa for him.

I quickly scan the lot, double-checking for any signs of Tessa or any of her other exes who might want to derail this plan. With the coast clear, I dash toward the front entrance.

The sound of lazy, too-loud laughter stops me in my tracks. I turn slowly, afraid of what I'll find. The stoners break out into *oooohs* as one of them snatches the blunt out of the rotation and takes an unearned puff.

It happens in slow motion. An elbow against a shoulder, an arm pushed into a rib cage, the blunt flying through the air and rolling toward the roses, then catching on the puddle of oil. The burning smell. Smoke.

My body doesn't operate on rational thought, just instinct. I put my blind faith in the stoners to keep things from getting out of hand as I dart as fast as I can toward the bathroom, smacking right into Joaquin as we both turn a corner.

"Geez, watch—" Joaquin stalls when he realizes it's me, all the nerves he scrubbed clean returning in full force. "What happened?"

"Okay, don't panic." I rest my hands on his shoulders, marveling at the soft fabric of the royal-blue blazer he picked out for the occasion. While he was gone for what felt like forever, he's cleaned up spectacularly, his curls falling in front of his eyes, framing his long, thick eyelashes. The beach tan makes his brown skin glow and brings out the warmth of his eyes, glittering with what I'm now realizing is panic.

"She said no already, didn't she? I didn't even get to ask and—"

"No, no, she's not here yet," I reassure him, letting go of him and shaking myself off. Now is not the time to get distracted by the pull of a well-cut suit and a little hair product. "We just need to head outside. Now."

"Is everything okay?"

"Everything's fine." The high pitch of my voice betrays me. "Totally fine. It's just . . ." I inhale sharply, preparing myself to deliver the news. "The flowers may or may not be on fire."

CHAPTER FIVE

THE FLOWERS ARE ON FIRE.

I should've known better than to trust the stoners not to let a spark turn into a flame. By the time we make it outside, the *O* and *M* have disintegrated, and the flames are on their way to devouring the *R*. Most of our classmates stand around and film while we pour Joaquin's Hydro Flask and the rest of my iced coffee onto the fire in vain. I dash back into the building, grabbing an extinguisher and doing my best to put out the flame despite having no idea how it works. A smattering of applause breaks out along with a couple of cheers as the white fog begins to clear. Joaquin's head hangs low as he stares at his failed vision, likely contemplating how much money has gone down the drain.

Meanwhile, I take in two terrifying sights. Tessa Hernandez, window rolled down, eyeing the roses like they're charred roadkill.

And Principal Contreras, arms crossed and mad as hell.

"You're blocking my parking space," Tessa says in her usual

dry, bored tone before taking a slow sip of her iced coffee, making my stomach ache from the loss of my own. I bet it's delicious. "Hey," she says when Joaquin turns around, her tone softening. "This from you?" She gestures to the burned roses with a raised brow.

Joaquin buckles under the weight of her gaze, tripping and stumbling over his words while my attention is focused on the much bigger issue at hand—expulsion, or better yet, jail time for arson.

"Nope! Just being good citizens!" I shout, giving Joaquin an out with Tessa and hopefully one for both of us with Contreras.

"Romero. Santos. In my office. Now!" Contreras barks out, snapping Joaquin's attention away from Tessa.

Well, there goes that plan.

Joaquin follows him like a kicked puppy while I hazard a peek over my shoulder. With us out of the way, Tessa backs into her parking space with ease, what's left of the burned roses crushed to dust beneath her car. It stings, watching our hard work join the mud, dirt, and grass caked into the grooves of Tessa's tires. I breathe a sigh of relief at the sight of Joaquin's back, still trudging along behind Contreras. At least he didn't have to see it too.

"Care to explain how this happened?" Contreras gestures to a singed rose sitting on his desk, coated in flecks of white from the fire extinguisher.

Contreras isn't known for putting the *pal* in principal. He made us sit in the hall outside his office until he finished a five-minute guided meditation. We knew it was going to be a bloodbath before we even sat down.

"I was j—" Joaquin begins.

"It was me," I interrupt, drowning him out with an uncharacteristic strength to my voice.

Joaquin's eyes bug out like a cartoon character as he whips around to stare at me. Contreras doesn't appear convinced, narrowing his eyes as he leans across his desk.

"You're saying you organized this whole thing on your own, Ms. Santos?"

"No, she—"

I slam my foot down on Joaquin's, replying, "I did," while he yowls in pain. "Joaquin asked me to help plan something and put it together for him since he had practice early this morning. He'd just come from the field when the fire started. He was only trying to help me put it out."

Joaquin is glaring daggers at me, but I know he'll get over it eventually. If Contreras is going to come down as hard as I think he will, Joaquin will have more to lose. School policy says any student athlete with more than five detentions is barred from playing on the team. Getting kicked off the baseball team a month before their championship game in his final year would make Joaquin more than just a social pariah—he might as well be banished to his own deserted island.

No one cares if the drama club's tech crew manager is out of commission for a few detentions, but they will absolutely care if their star shortstop is.

Suspending Joaquin from the baseball team means all-out war with the student body. The whole point of our upcoming pep rally is to hand out the senior MVP award, and Joaquin has had that on lock since sophomore year. One wrong move could mean chaos in the halls. Anarchy in the cafeteria. Bags of hot, flaming dog poop on Contreras's doorstep.

Contreras knows it too.

He hums as he runs a hand along his jaw, considering me and Joaquin.

"Three weeks of detention, Ms. Santos. And, Mr. Romero, I highly suggest you find a less flammable way to ask someone to prom."

Before Joaquin can protest my sentencing, I'm out of my seat and dragging him toward the door. "He will—thank you! Sorry again!" I call out, slamming the door behind us before he can decide to tack on another week of detention just for the hell of it.

"You didn't need to do that, Ive," Joaquin says, crossing his arms and blocking my path.

"And let you get kicked off the baseball team before the championship?" My attempt to walk around him is swiftly blocked. His arms are long enough to trap me no matter which way I go, and I'm nowhere near coordinated enough to trick him. "If you get me another week of detention because I'm late to first period, I *will* bite you."

The threat doesn't make him budge either.

"It's not a big deal, I swear." I shrug. "Go win the World Cup, or whatever it is they give you for winning a baseball tournament."

"You have to let me make it up to you." His tone is as stern as a parent doling out groundings, even as he holds his pinky out in front of me.

"Well, since you twisted my arm . . ." I loop my pinky through his, and finally, he cracks a smile.

When the bell rings, I'm swept up by the flurry of motion. People spilling into halls, elbows shoving into me, and, suddenly, Joaquin pulling me to his chest. His arms are a warm, safe haven from the chaos around us, the steady thrum of his heartbeat and the comforting smell of his bodywash keeping me grounded.

"Stay out of trouble," he whispers into my ear, like we're in our own little bubble in the middle of the hallway.

"No promises."

I expect his arms to fall away immediately, but we stay there, wrapped up in one another as our classmates pass by like there's no one in the world but us. For a moment, it feels like our first day of freshman year all over again. The two of us with skinned knees and an unfortunate amount of acne clutching each other for dear life, too afraid to let go.

But he does let go, dropping his arms back to his sides when his teammate, DeShawn, comes rushing up to him.

"Bro, were you seriously trying to ask out Tessa Hernandez this morning?"

Whatever Joaquin says next, I can't make it out. He lets DeShawn whisk him away, not even giving me a wave or a "bye" before disappearing around the corner.

Watching him walk away shouldn't hurt when he's done it dozens of times before. The same way watching him pour his heart out for someone like Tessa Hernandez shouldn't bother me either.

But that doesn't stop the feeling.

CHAPTER SIX

NOTHING LIKE THE SMELL of burnt ground beef to welcome you home after a long day.

"Ive?!" Mami calls after I close the front door.

I pull out my headphones, so unused to her actually being home these days that I'm not sure I didn't imagine hearing her. "Yeah?"

"Can I get some help?"

I follow her voice to the kitchen, jumping back in surprise when I open the door to find the room shrouded in smoke and an overwhelming sense of déjà vu. Mami is bent over the kitchen sink, struggling to empty the charred contents of a pot into the sink while Nurse Oatmeal laps the ground for scraps. Smoke swirls around them, getting dangerously close to the flickering fire alarm on the ceiling. I don't wait for Mami to give me marching orders, immediately throwing open the back door and as many windows as I can. I cover my mouth with the collar of my flannel, fanning as much of the smoke out of the room as I can.

Miraculously, we're spared the rage of the fire alarm, and the room clears within a few seconds.

"I think I burned the meat," Mami says, breaking the silence.

And, just as quickly as the smoke dissipated, we're doubled over with laughter.

Walking into two almost-catastrophes in one day should be traumatizing, but as Mami leans against me for support as she struggles to keep herself up from laughing so hard, all I can feel is relief. Because our house didn't burn down, sure, but mainly because she's *here.*

"All right, all right, let's get this handled before the fire department shows up," Mami says as she stands upright, wiping tears from the corners of her eyes.

"Again," I add as I set down Nurse Oatmeal.

She scoffs, waving me off. "That was one time."

Two times, but I won't argue.

We work together to clear out the last of the smoke and scrub the charred contents of the pan. Whatever Mami was attempting to make for dinner is too crispy to be edible; the crumbles sitting in the sink are hard as coals.

"What was this even supposed to be?" I ask, nose wrinkling.

"Tacos," she replies with a sigh, holding up a pack of unopened tortillas. "Want pizza instead? Mushrooms, olives, and onions with extra cheese?"

I nod eagerly as she recites my go-to order, excitement dashing any lingering disgust over the smell. Who would've thought

I'd actually be happy about spending a night on the couch eating takeout with my mom? Most of our meals are enjoyed from the comfort of the living room while we binge whatever reality TV show has piqued our interest that month. A tradition we haven't honored in weeks.

Mami pulls out her phone, typing away while I scoop food into the trash. "Joaquin tried promposing to someone today."

In the madness of helping Joaquin with his plan and Mami heading back to work after her Vegas extravaganza, I haven't had a chance to catch her up on his lovesick quest.

"Uh-huh," she mumbles absent-mindedly, distracted by something on her phone.

My smile drops, familiar disappointment coursing through me. I'd gotten my hopes up too quickly. "We almost set the parking lot on fire."

She just keeps typing. "That's great."

"Arson is great?"

Finally, she breaks out of her trance and blinks up at me like a deer in headlights. "Wait—what?"

An obnoxiously loud car horn cuts me off before I can explain.

Mami rolls her eyes. "Carajo," she mutters, shoving her phone into her pocket and storming off to her room.

I carefully peek through the living room window, and my stomach drops. Leaning against the driver's side door of a double-parked black Tesla is a middle-aged man I've never seen before but who's exactly Mami's type. Salt-and-pepper hair with a thick mustache to match, wearing a perfectly tailored suit. When he catches sight of me, he leans through the open car window and presses the horn again. Classy.

Suddenly, the pieces fit together. Mami never said *we* were having dinner together. All she asked was if I was in the mood for pizza. She even neglected to mention our *real* order: half mushrooms, olives, onions, and extra cheese for me, half pepperoni and sausage for her. Not for the first time, I let my hopes get the better of me. At least this time she attempted to leave a homecooked meal behind.

"I told him I wouldn't be ready until seven-thirty," Mami says through gritted teeth, reemerging from her bedroom in a black wrap dress and heels, her hair up in a slicked back bun. "Pizza should be here in twenty. It's already paid for—just give them a tip from the jar in my room."

I'm grateful she's distracted as she darts around the room, grabbing her purse and coat while applying her go-to ruby-red lipstick. Tears cloud my vision, anger splitting through me like a pulsing headache.

Finally, she stops in front of me, cradling my cheeks like she used to whenever I came home with scrapes and bruises. "You okay, mama?"

I wish all I felt was anger. That I could push her away and send her off with Mr. Car Horn and not care that I'm eating dinner alone again. But, more than anything, I want her to stay. I want her to run her fingers through my hair and ask about my day.

"M'fine," I mumble, pulling my face out of her hold before she can see the tears. Maybe she wouldn't even notice. "Just a headache."

She coos, running a hand down my back that should feel comforting but just makes me angrier. "There's some Advil in the bathroom. Take two and call me if you're still not feeling good, okay?"

I nod, biting back a barbed reply. That stings too, knowing that even pretending to be sick didn't get her to cancel her date. Outside, said date slams the horn yet again, earning him a "Cállate!" from Doña Carmen next door.

"He seems great. . . ."

She sighs, shaking her head and pinching the bridge of her nose. "He's a decent guy, I swear."

She also thought Tim, the lawyer who stood her up three times in a row, was a decent guy. And let's not forget about the other decent guy—Luis—who stole our air fryer.

Not trying to upset Mr. Car Horn more than we already have, she presses a wet kiss to my cheek and heads for the door. "I'll be home by ten, and I want to hear about this whole arson thing. Love you!"

Before I can say I love her back, the door slams shut.

By the time I've finished cleaning the kitchen, my pizza's gone cold. Groaning, I turn on the oven and stick a few slices in the broiler. Microwaving pizza is basically a sin.

The ache in my body begs me to crawl into bed and forget this nightmare of a day. I've dealt with two different near-death experiences, my email inbox continues to be painfully devoid of any updates from Sarah Lawrence, and I landed myself three weeks of detention. Rushing out after my first detention to get two hours of set building finished in forty-five minutes has done a number on my joints. Anna was pissed to the high heavens about my sacrifice, but I promised her I wouldn't leave our already small crew down a person. Even if it means wrecking my body in the process.

Between getting up at the ass crack of dawn, bending over backwards for the drama club, and the emotional whiplash of my run-in with Mami, I could sleep for a week. But I still have a grueling amount of pre-calc homework left, and I don't trust myself not to pass out if I go anywhere near my bed.

So, I grab my pizza from the oven and head out to my safe haven.

The treehouse in our backyard has seen better days, but it's not any less comforting than when we constructed it over a decade ago. It was Joaquin's idea, a space for us to get away from our parents without giving them a heart attack. We spent the summer between first and second grade building it with our moms. A whirlwind summer of splinters and firecracker Popsicles. Since we were, y'know, seven, Mami and Mrs. Romero did most of the work, nailing and sawing while we handed them the tools they needed. When the hideaway was finished, Mami called it our greatest creation. And it absolutely was—*is*. She's a better carpenter than cook.

Ignoring my muscles' protests, I climb up the ladder to the treehouse's entrance. Over the years, Joaquin has sprouted enough that he barely bothers with the ladder. Meanwhile, puberty wasn't as kind to me. On a good day, I can pass as five one.

One flick of a switch and the treehouse comes alive—our

homemade paper lanterns casting shadows along the walls. It's been a while since I last came up here. The place could use a good wipe-down. Just the sight of dust on the windowsill sends me into a brief sneezing fit. As soon as my nose is under control, I sprawl along one of the blankets piled in the corner, yawning like a lazy cat. One of the perks of remaining tiny is that I can continue to stretch out across the floor and have room to spare while Joaquin has to scrunch up.

I nibble on my pizza while staring at the decorations we tacked to the ceiling. Finger paintings of our favorite things—dragons, cartoons, each other (but mostly dragons), and Polaroid photos tacked on every free patch of wall in between. We'd put the camera Mami gave us for my eighth birthday to good use, taking photos of everything we could possibly think of. Joaquin riding his bike. Me eating a peach. Mami on the couch with her hair wrapped up in a towel. Mrs. Romero giving Joaquin a piggyback ride. Isabella doing a cartwheel. A piece of toast that we found aesthetically pleasing. At the center of the collage is the last photo we took before the camera completely crapped out for good. Me and Joaquin on my eighteenth birthday four months ago, hugging Otis the Otter, the stuffed animal he'd given me to commemorate our day at the aquarium.

Hidden behind the playbill for my first show at Cordero is a photo of Mami and Papi at their sophomore year homecoming dance. The only thing bigger than Mami's hair is their smiles, their arms wrapped tightly around one another like they're worried they'll float away. A light pink peony corsage sparkles on Mami's wrist, a perfect color match for her floor-length dress and dangly earrings. For years, Mami kept dried peony petals in a glass jar beside the picture and that dress in her closet. Now the jar is empty, and the dress is being eaten by moths in the attic. If she knew I'd kept this photo, it'd go straight into the trash, but I can't help it. I don't remember much about what life with Papi was like, but when I think of him, I want to think of this moment. Of him and Mami, so blissfully happy they didn't notice the camera.

The treehouse feels unusually dark. Outside, the sun has only barely started to set. I sit up on my elbows, scanning our canopy of paper lanterns. Sure enough, some of the fairy lights we'd strung through the lanterns to give them a little extra shine are missing.

And look an awful lot like the ones Joaquin used in his roses stunt . . .

As if on cue, my phone buzzes.

look up

I finish the last of my crust in one ill-advised bite before crawling over to the treehouse's window. Joaquin is stationed at his bedroom window one yard over, pointing to his hand and mouthing something I can't make out.

"*Slow down*," I mouth back with some added hand gestures to convey the message.

He rolls his eyes before sticking his hand out the window, waving whatever he's holding at me until I finally piece together what it is. A walkie-talkie.

I take two steps to the opposite side of the treehouse to the dustiest surface of all: our toy chest. The walkie-talkie sits on top of a pile of headless Barbies and melted-down action figures. Somehow it has enough juice left to turn on. Joaquin's voice comes through a few seconds later.

"Red alert, I repeat, red alert. If you don't respond in five minutes, I'll assume you're either dead or these walkies finally crapped out on us."

"The walkie lives," I reply, though my mouth is so full of crust it comes out too garbled to be intelligible.

"Use your words, Ive."

"Shut up," I snap once I've chewed and swallowed. On the other end of the line, I can hear him groan as his spine cracks unsettlingly. "Rough practice?"

Usually, baseball practice keeps Joaquin busy until well past sundown, but with the championship game in a month, he's lucky if he gets home with enough time to heat up dinner and have a five-minute FaceTime with his mom before crashing.

"Coach actually went easy on us today since we have the pep rally on Friday. Not a great look if half the team is about to pass out onstage."

Fair point. Then again, half the student population looks like they're about to fall asleep on any given day.

"And speaking of which, I kinda need your help . . . again."

I make my way back over to the window, where I spot Joaquin sitting at his desk, his profile backlit by the colored light strips he installed over the summer. The lights flicker menacingly before shifting from purple to green.

"If it's with home décor, then my advice is to stop buying shitty sponsored products from influencers you think are cute."

His chair swivels around so he can turn to glare at me. "These lights were a steal," he retorts before disappearing from view, doing something to said lights that make them switch back to purple.

"More like a scam, but whatever you need to tell yourself."

He doesn't grace me with a reply. "You and Anna are running tech for the pep rally, right?"

My brow arches even though I know he can't really see me. "We are. Why?"

"Because I have another idea."

His excitement is palpable, even from a yard away. My stomach twists uncomfortably, as if it senses what he's going to ask before he can say it. He sits up straighter in his seat, his free hand gesticulating wildly as his words come through after a brief delay. "I know the roses majorly backfired, but this one doesn't involve anything flammable!"

"That you know of."

"Hush," he snaps, waving his hand out the window toward my direction. "I was thinking . . . I've been so panicked about this whole speech thing for the rally. What if I just kept it short and sweet and asked Tessa to prom at the end of it? The crowd would go *nuts.*"

Public spectacle aside, the thought of Joaquin pouring his heart out to Tessa in front of the entire school versus the entire senior parking lot makes my skin clammy. The seniors would've teased him mercilessly, but getting turned down by Tessa is practically a rite of passage by now. A rejection in front of the entire student body is totally different, though . . .

"You'd just have to play this song once I'm done." My phone pings with another new message from him. A link to a playlist titled "tessa hernandez pls say yes."

Gross.

I scoff as the opening notes of "Can't Take My Eyes Off You" begin to play. "Seriously? You couldn't have picked a song from this century?"

"When was the last time you heard a good, life-changing romantic song on the radio?"

He's got me there. If there's one thing Joaquin inherited from his mom, it's her taste in music. Before Herbert was ours, we'd get rides from Mrs. Romero in exchange for letting her have total control of the radio. We probably know more old-school ballads by heart than anything from the past decade. Now Joaquin passes as a cool, aloof music snob.

I rest my cheek on the windowsill, willing him to turn his chair around and face me too. "Are you sure you want to declare your love for Tessa Hernandez in front of hundreds of people?"

"It's not *love,* it's *prom.*"

"Same thing."

He sighs, leaning so far back in his chair I wonder if he'll topple over. "Yes. I'm sure. Again. I just have a good feeling about this one, okay?"

Even with his back to me, I can picture the hopeful smile blossoming on his lips. My best friend's smile is one of my favorite things about this too-small town. Right below Marco's, but above Nurse Oatmeal and the really good taco place down the block from school.

And I hate that this smile lodges a pit in my stomach.

"Yeah, I've got you," I say, settling down on my pile of blankets when it's clear that Joaquin isn't going to turn around. "Just don't say I didn't warn you when everyone roasts you for your song choice."

He snorts before letting out an exaggerated, "Fine." Then, "You're the best, Ive."

"I know," I say with a smirk. "Oh, also, my mom just—"

Before I can finish, our connection sputters. Leaning up, I watch Joaquin toss the walkie into a desk drawer and flip his bedroom lights off, gone before I could say goodbye, let alone finish what I was saying. Again.

Why is everyone in my life determined to blow me off today?

Slumping against my pillow, I try to calm the uneasy feeling in my stomach. Maybe I just ate my pizza too fast. Or the questionable food in the cafeteria is finally wreaking havoc on my body. Or I'm just still pissed about Mami leaving me high and dry. I'm considering taking her advice about that Advil when the sound of a crack makes me spring back up.

I'm on my knees in the nick of time, one of the ceiling planks snapping in half and crashing down right where my head was seconds ago. Almost got killed by the one place I can go to be alone. Cool cool cool. If there was ever an excuse that could get Mami to come home from a date, it'd be this. *Hey, what's up, almost got decapitated, you coming home yet?*

My heart races as I carefully peek at the hole in the roof.

The wood holding the top half of the treehouse together has become so warped I'm surprised it didn't cave in as soon as I entered. I can't find it in me to move, though, my attention drifting to the scattered decorations that came down along with the plank. One of the photos of me and Joaquin, holding hands on the beach, is torn down the middle. Our tiny, clasped fingers keep us together, but just barely. I cradle the photo carefully, making sure not to pull too hard or cause a bigger rip, and tuck it into my wallet. It's safe for now, but I can't shake off the fear it sends surging through me.

One wrong move could tear us apart.

CHAPTER SEVEN

PEP RALLIES BRING OUT the worst in the student body.

The senior parking lot is overflowing with tailgate parties, our peers decked out in Cordero's signature red and gold in various forms—mainly body paint, beaded necklaces, and backward caps. No one's bold enough to drink beers out in the open. Instead, everyone sits on the hoods of their cars passing sips of cold brew and neon-colored energy drinks. The real drinks have been stored away for the post-rally after-parties.

"Thank me later." Anna appears practically out of thin air as the final bell before the rally rings, shoving a can into my hand.

My nose wrinkles as I examine the nutrition label. There's about half a dozen different chemicals I've never heard of using every combination of letters in the alphabet. "Raspberry Unicorn?"

"Tastes like shit," Anna explains after gulping down the last of her own drink. "But it has enough sugar to send a sloth into hyperdrive, and you're gonna need it."

She makes it sound like we're headed into a battlefield and not a high school gymnasium.

And she's exactly right.

The gym is a madhouse even thirty minutes before the start of the rally. Someone took it upon themselves to bring a speaker, music blaring loud enough to make the ground vibrate. While the cheerleading team preps for their upcoming performance from the comfort of the front lawn, the rest of the student body takes advantage of the unsupervised gym, turning the lights down as best they can and transforming this school-sanctioned event into a rave.

Anna clutches my hand for dear life as we dive headfirst into the crowd to try to make it to the AV booth at the opposite end of the gym. She nearly loses me to the magnetic pull of a mosh pit, and we spend an uncomfortable amount of time shoved into our classmates' armpits, but we manage to make it through with our limbs, and some dignity, intact.

The AV booth is a breath of fresh air. Literally. I can finally inhale deeply without being assaulted by the smell of sweat. We chug water to catch our breath. If it wasn't for the Raspberry Unicorn, I might not have had the strength to dig myself out of that den of teenage sin.

"I thought you said I'd handle the music?" Anna asks while watching me unravel the AUX cord. She holds up her phone, open to her "music for meatheads" playlist.

"You will. I just need to do a tiny favor for Joaquin," I say so quickly I hope she either won't hear me or won't care enough to pry.

But, of course, I'm wrong. She has the hearing of an elephant.

Anna slides between me and the light board, brow arched high above her round glasses. "He asked you to do *what*, exactly?"

"Play a song."

"What song?"

"You wouldn't know it."

She snatches my phone out of my hand, immediately pulling up my Spotify. "Fine, I don't know this song, but it sure as hell sounds like it's for a promposal."

I plead the Fifth, ignoring her in favor of snatching my phone from her and keeping busy with untangling the wires beneath the light board.

"Is Joaquin trying to ask Tessa to prom *today*? Is he nuts?" Her voice is loud enough to echo in the cramped space of the room.

"I tried to talk him out of it, but he's going to do it with or without me, so we might as well help make it memorable."

Anna remains unconvinced, collapsing into the seat beside me with a huff. We sit in silence while she takes in the crowd beyond the window, our classmates bumping and grinding while our hands shake from too much Raspberry Unicorn.

"If she doesn't say yes, he's never going to be able to live that down," she says, as if that same line of thought hasn't haunted me since Joaquin first proposed this plan.

"I know," I mumble, tossing aside the now untangled wires. "And I told him that, but he thinks it—*she's*—worth the risk. And after they win the game, everyone will probably forget," I add with a shrug. "They'll be kissing his ass for centuries and dedicating monuments to him outside of the locker room." Their win isn't a guarantee, but a little optimism for once wouldn't kill me.

"Sure. But are *you* okay with this?"

The question makes me stutter to a halt. "Yeah. I'm not the one asking her. I don't have anything to lose."

"I *mean* all of this. Joaquin and Tessa. You bending over backwards to make a thing between them happen."

"I'm not bending over backwards," I reply, brushing her off with a wave of my hand.

"Hello, you literally took three weeks of detention for him. Right before tech week. Taking a bullet would've been less stressful."

"Don't be dramat—"

"We're in the drama club, we're supposed to be dramatic."

Technically we're in the tech crew, but something tells me making that distinction isn't going to change her opinion.

Yes, having to deal with detention on top of tech week and my shifts at Casa Y Cocina is already a nightmare. Yes, Tessa is very far from my first choice in a romantic partner for Joaquin. Yes, this whole situation feels Not Great.

But does it matter what I think? Being Joaquin's best friend doesn't mean I get a say in who he can and can't date.

"This year has been weird. With getting waitlisted, and everything with my mom, and . . . just, really weird. And I don't even want to think about how weird they'll be next year when we're not in the same place for the first time. But Joaquin has always been there for me, through all the weird. Even when things weren't easy for him either."

Anna's expression is impossible to read, her lips set into a straight line while her fingers toy with one of the gold cuffs clasped to the ends of her locs. She avoids my eyes, looking somewhere over my shoulder before turning to face the light board. "Being there for your friend doesn't mean throwing yourself under the bus."

Before I can reply, she switches off the gym's overhead lights.

The mosh pit breaks out into cheers, intensifying for half a second before Anna aggressively flicks the overhead lights on and off in warning. "Back to your seats and hands to yourselves, sheep. Before you get our prom canceled," she says into the mic, her words blaring through the gym's overhead speaker.

Whoever was in control of the music shuts it down to a wave of groans, but the sea of bodies listens to their disembodied overlord and trudges up to the bleachers. With everyone safely in their assigned places again, the real show can begin.

It's impossible to ignore the lump lodged in my throat throughout the cheer team's routine. The caffeine boost that got me through the crowd makes my heart pound so loud I'm worried Anna can hear it. My stomach lurches when the baseball team comes rushing into the auditorium to deafening applause.

I spot Joaquin, clad in his letterman jacket and cheeks painted red and gold. His goofy grin stands out in the crowd, bright enough to spot even from the tech booth. My fingernails dig into my palms as I watch him scan the room, immediately finding Tessa seated with the rest of the cheerleaders a few feet away. He waves at her, and when she waves back and gives him a wink, his cheeks flush and his teammates clap him on the shoulder in excitement.

"Settle down," Principal Contreras says as he steps up to the mic onstage in a dry, flat monotone. Instant vibe killer. "Thank you to the cheer squad for that wonderful performance." He's greeted with a polite smattering of applause, grimacing when someone takes the opportunity to shout, "Tessa, I love you" over the quiet cheers.

Contreras's tone is as dry as sandpaper, yet I cling to the edge of my seat as he goes through his pep rally spiel, congratulating the seniors on making it to the end of the year, telling the freshmen to aspire to great heights, and, finally, announcing this year's theme for senior prom—Under the Sea (how original) as well as the nominees for prom court.

"Your nominees for prom queen are . . . Amal Khan, Yesenia Gordon, Tessa Hernandez, and—" The final nominee's name is completely lost under the roar of applause for Tessa. Poor girl never stood a chance.

"And your nominees for prom king," Contreras continues once the excitement has died down to an anticipatory hush. "Hank Azario, DeShawn Harris, Joaquin Romero, and Danny Garcia."

I'm so caught up in my nerves that I don't remember to clap for Joaquin's nomination until Anna shoves my shoulder. Not that his nomination comes as a surprise. He's not a lock for the crown like Tessa, but there's no way Cordero's athletic golden boy wasn't going to nab a nomination. He's in good company with his teammate and (second) closest friend DeShawn, who's also president of the student council. Hank isn't much of a surprise either. The guy's a dick, but when clichés reign supreme, the quarterback always gets a nom. Obviously, I'm not thrilled about Danny either. But there's no way the resident class clown wins over the golden boy or the StuCo president. Or at least, I hope not.

By the time Contreras unveils the glimmering silver senior MVP trophy, I'm practically vibrating, resisting the urge to chew on my nails as he finally gets to the moment I've been waiting for.

"We're very pleased to present this year's MVP Award to a talented senior who's demonstrated his incredible athletic ability since he first joined Cordero's baseball team his freshman year."

A low hum breaks out among the crowd, the enthusiasm making its way to the tech booth. The boys on either side of Joaquin pat him on the back, jostling him by the shoulders as Contreras gestures for him to come onstage.

The music from earlier is no match for the volume of the cheers as Joaquin heads for the stage. A chant of his name starts up, breaking it into two syllables, with a stomp on the bleachers for "Quin." The chant picks up speed, rumbling the room so intensely it topples over Anna's last (thankfully, closed) can of Raspberry Unicorn.

By the time he gets up to the mic, Joaquin has to wait a full thirty seconds before he can speak, the applause and cheers drowning out his sheepish "Thank you so much." I join in on the cheers even though the tech room is insulated, clapping until my palms go numb. I don't even realize I'm standing up until the applause starts to die down and reality sinks in. As I slump back into my seat with pinkened cheeks, Anna keeps her eyes straight ahead and that anxious feeling comes crawling back.

"Thank you so much to my abuela for everything she's done for me this past year, and for giving me my first bat once I was old enough to hold it on my own. Obviously she's not here right now, but I know she'd be pissed if I didn't thank her anyway." A pause for *aww*s and quiet laughter. I kick myself for not thinking to record this for her.

"Thank you to my teammates, for always pushing me and covering for me that time I bailed on practice to go buy Jordans from some sketchy dude on Craigslist. Sorry, Coach." His teammates break out into their own set of laughter and applause, DeShawn standing up on his chair and starting a cheer so rowdy Contreras has to hiss at him to sit back down.

Joaquin doesn't continue, though, when his baseball bros have finally calmed down. He has everyone clinging to his every word, me included, as he rubs the back of his neck, his eyes suddenly shifting to his shoes. It's odd, watching someone with all the confidence in the world shrink under a spotlight.

His eyes scan the crowd again. Assuming he's searching for Tessa, I brace myself for the signal we agreed on. As soon as he says the code word, I'll dim the lights and crank up Frankie Valli, but his gaze goes right past Tessa. Instead, he finds me. A hundred feet and soundproof glass can't stop the chill that runs through me when he flashes his ultra-white smile, light brown eyes locked with mine.

"And Ivelisse Santos. I wouldn't remember to get up in the morning if it wasn't for you. You're the best person I know, and the world would be a much brighter place if there were more people like you in it. Thank you for being my best friend."

All the air has been sucked out of the room. No one says a word, not even another round of polite clapping, and maybe that would bother me if I didn't suddenly feel like my entire body is made of jelly. My lungs can't keep up with my heart, and I might be crying, who the hell knows. I just sense Joaquin's eyes on me, and this indescribable warmth that feels like coming home.

The silence doesn't faze Joaquin, and the spell he has on me breaks the second he turns back to the crowd. "Well, I won't hold you guys up anymore, but it's prom season and I . . ."

Shit, this is it. Prom—the code word. His eyes flicker back to me, but this time feels different. He nods, as if to give me the go-ahead in case I forgot my cue. My thumb hovers over the play button on my phone, less than an inch away. I only have to close the distance.

I turn the lights off instead.

"What're you—"

Before Anna can finish, I'm reaching across her lap, plugging the AUX cord into her phone, and cranking up her playlist. Applause drowns out any protests Joaquin may have had, the crowd chanting his name one last time as Principal Contreras ushers him off the stage. The heat of Anna's eyes boring into me mixed with Joaquin helplessly wading through the crowd make the room spin. With the lights back off and the music blasting, Contreras begins to panic, signaling for us to restore order before he loses control of the student body.

Luckily only one of us is midspiral. Anna flicks the lights back on and turns the music to a more respectable volume. Contreras gives us a grateful nod, clearing his throat until he has everyone's attention again.

Anna slowly swivels her chair around to face me, like a movie villain. "Care to explain what that was?"

Even if I wanted to, I don't think I could. Excuses and lies bubble up inside of me, and for a split second I wonder if I'm going to blurt all of them out at once. The door to the booth bursts open, startling both of us so bad we screech in unison.

"Whoa, whoa, it's just me!" Joaquin waves his arms until we settle down, closing the door gently. "What happened back there?"

Their eyes shift to me.

"I, uh . . ." Glancing at Anna for backup is a mistake. She makes a face that would send a saint to hell. "I forgot to tell Anna!" The words tumble out of my mouth before I can properly think things through. "I got distracted by a light board malfunction and missed your signal, so Anna just turned the lights off, totally my fault."

Anna throws on a stiff smile as I silently beg her to co-sign the lie. "My bad," she says through gritted teeth.

If Joaquin sees through my bullshit, he doesn't let it show. He slumps against the light board, wearing a devastated frown. "It's okay. Guess it's back to the drawing board."

"We'll think of something," I say, wincing internally at the unintended *we*.

Joaquin gives me a small nod. "Marco's for lunch?"

"Sure." He gives me a fist bump before trudging out of the room to rejoin his teammates. The tension he leaves behind is as thick as summer air. I've barely moved toward Anna when she throws up a flat palm.

"Don't," she snaps before I can even open my mouth.

"I di—"

She hisses like a cat until I back down. We let the quietness settle for a few seconds before I try broaching the subject again.

"I just don't want him to get hurt," I whisper. "You've seen what Tessa does to people. She's brutal."

It's low, picking at the scab that is Tessa and Anna's former friendship. But covering up your bad choices requires making more bad choices.

Anna's brow furrows as she tucks a loc behind her ear. "Is that it?"

The question catches me off guard, and the tone of her voice does too. Soft and gentle. Very unlike the Anna that hissed at me moments ago. My voice is caught in my throat, unable to come up with an answer that'll satisfy her. However long passes, her patience runs out. She grabs her things and heads toward the door, pivoting at the last second to face me.

"Think about what you really want out of all this—helping Joaquin and whatever you think you just did," she says before walking away.

She slams the door behind her and leaves me reeling. Alone,

my brain becomes a jumbled mess of questions, excuses, and panic. While my classmates cheer and spill out into the halls, I bury my head in my hands and struggle to get it together before the janitor kicks me out of here.

Even though my brain is like a freshly shaken snow globe, one thought comes through loud and clear.

I can't let Joaquin go to prom with Tessa Hernandez.

CHAPTER EIGHT

DETENTION SERIOUSLY CRAMPS YOUR social life. Not that I have much of one, but still. After the pep rally, the rest of the student body gets to go free and rain chaos on Elmwood while I have to stick around for another hour in an uncomfortably warm classroom. The guy from the cafeteria glitter bomb incident and I are the only unfortunate souls who managed to land themselves detention on a half day. Both of us for promposal-related incidents.

By the time we're finally set free, campus is a ghost town. Nothing left of the pep rally madness except for crushed energy drink cans in the parking lot. I head toward the bus stop on the opposite side of campus, freezing when the only car in the lot beeps at me.

"You leaving me hanging?" Joaquin shouts as he sticks his head out the window. In my post-detention funk, I'd completely missed the tin can of a car and the iconic license plate that gave Herbert his name—HR83RT.

The guilt that gnawed at me through detention fades at the sight of Joaquin's smile, and relief takes over. Because I have a ride, because he's here, because he doesn't hate my guts.

Yet.

"You didn't have to wait for me," I say once I've made myself at home in the passenger seat.

"I promised I'd buy you lunch for a week, didn't I?"

Technically, yes, but he knows damn well that he doesn't need to promise me anything for agreeing to help him.

"Sure, but you didn't have to waste a whole hour waiting for me."

"Who said he wasted it?" a tinny, unexpected voice calls out from the dashboard.

I whip around to find Isabella waving at me from where Joaquin has his phone mounted beside the steering wheel. He wraps an arm around my shoulders, pulling me across the console until I'm squished into his tiny FaceTime frame.

"Look who finally decided to answer her phone," Joaquin says to me with an unusual snip to his tone.

Isabella doesn't grace him with a reply, just her middle finger.

"Shouldn't you be in class?" I ask her with a raised brow.

"Oh, young child. That's not how college works," she sing-songs, twirling a lock of her newly dyed bright red hair. "My next class isn't until four." She rolls onto her stomach, propping her phone up on a pillow. "Heard you got busted."

"Yeah, because of *him*." I pinch Joaquin's arm.

"Next time my brother's being a useless simp, you should—"

"*Anyway*," Joaquin interjects, releasing his hold on me. "Isabella was just saying that she'll be home in three weeks."

"Freedom!" Isabella exclaims. "Don't worry, I'll be back just in time to embarrass the two of you on your way to prom."

"Gee, thanks," Joaquin replies. "Don't you have new people to terrorize?"

"Nope." She pops the *p*. "You're top of my 'people to annoy' list."

"Bye, Iz," Joaquin says in a deadpan voice. "Tell Mami I'll talk to her later."

"Byyyyyye. Don't get any more detention for acting like a—"

Joaquin hangs up the call before Isabella can finish. I note a photo of him, Isabella, and Mrs. Romero at the beach last summer, each with a Fudgsicle, on his home screen. Up until they both left last summer, he'd always kept his home screen as whatever the default option was. In the upper right corner is a widget counting down to his flight to San Juan. Fifty-seven days to go.

He catches me holding back a laugh. "Don't."

"Well, maybe next time don't try to prompose to Tessa with highly flammable substances and your sister won't have any ammo to use against you."

Instead of cracking a joke, he keeps his eyes on the road as he pulls out of the lot. Tension simmers between us, something I'm definitely not used to. We can both take a joke, and the rose incident is fair game . . . right?

Then why does it feel like I just slapped him in the face?

Guilt comes rushing back in the silence. I should tell him. Be honest about what happened at the pep rally even if I'm not ready for the inevitable questions he'll ask. Like why I did it, and why the thought of him and Tessa together makes me nauseous.

"Are cupcakes flammable?" he asks finally.

"What?"

His brow scrunches in thought, one hand staying on the wheel while the other rubs his chin. "What if I did something with cupcakes? Like . . . spelled out 'You + Me = Prom' or . . . something better. No way that'll catch on fire, right?"

"I mean, not unless you put candles in it," I reply, earning me an appreciative nod. "But someone tried asking her with cookies on Tuesday."

Anything involving food has been done. Including an assortment of candy apples spelling out Tessa's miles-long full government name. Joaquin groans, turning his attention back to the road. For the rest of the drive, I let him use me as a sounding board, throwing out idea after idea and me throwing out problem after problem, my stomach sinking with each one I shoot down.

His ideas aren't terrible per se. I just can't shake the nagging voice telling me that Joaquin going to prom with Tessa is a monumentally bad plan. I've been possessed, a voice that sounds eerily like mine killing all of Joaquin's ideas like pesky flies. By the time we make it to Marco's, he's so drained from brainstorming, he flops into our favorite booth like he's nothing but dead weight.

"You kids are out early," Jenny, Marco's oldest waitress, says as she sets down place mats and utensils in front of us. "If you're playing hooky and need an excuse for your principal, just give me the word," she adds with a wink. After over a decade of us coming here, Jenny is basically family. Joaquin and I are both too straitlaced to cut class, but it's good to know we have an ally in delinquency if we need one.

"Half day," I explain. Joaquin, still catatonic from all the brain power he exerted on promposal ideas, stays slumped in his seat.

"The usual?" Jenny eyes Joaquin suspiciously. "Extra bacon?"

"Yes, please," I respond on our behalf. Maybe some extra strips of crispy bacon are what he needs to get back his strength. "Coffee instead of slushies today, though."

We could both use some caffeine.

When Jenny comes back ten minutes later with our breakfast sandwiches and coffees, Joaquin doesn't immediately lunge for his and wolf it down in less than a minute like he usually does. Things are *dire.*

"Wanna try hitting that slushie place in Hamilton that we missed? I've got a few hours until I have to head in for my shift," I propose around my first ravenous bite. Unlike him, I can't control my hunger. "Our brains need a break."

"Can't," he replies with a genuine frown. "I've gotta head back for practice in an hour."

My brow furrows. After-school activities on half days should be outlawed. "I thought Coach Mills was taking it easy on you guys?"

Joaquin shakes his head and pulls out his phone. "Now that the pep rally's over, we're going into hardcore training mode." Sure enough, the calendar he's just opened is packed to the brim with three hour-long practices every weekday up until the championship in three weeks.

"This seems a little excessive." I examine the calendar more closely, realizing he's also scheduled for morning training sessions with Coach Mills. Guess I can kiss my ride to school goodbye. "Okay, *very* excessive."

"It's the first shot the team has had at a championship title in, like, a century," he insists as he tucks his phone away. "This is our last game as a team—my last game *ever.* If we have to live and breathe baseball for three weeks to be champions, then I'll live and breathe baseball for three weeks."

Doña Carmen might argue that he already does that, but I can't blame him for giving in to Coach Mills's over-the-top schedule. Baseball is a part of the Romero family legacy. Long before Joaquin came along, his dad was the type of one-of-a-kind player they still talk about at his high school in San Juan. Apparently, they still have a photo of him hanging in the entryway. Mrs. Romero has been shuttling Joaquin to games since he could hold a bat, and I've been sitting in the stands ever since. He's worked hard for his legacy. Who wouldn't want to go out on the highest note?

"What about after practice?" I suggest. "I get off work at—"

Before I can finish, my phone buzzes several times in a row.

Going to meet up with Carlos at Boner Grill after work tonight. Sent you some money for dinner—lmk if you got it

*Boner Grill

BONER

CARAJO!!! BONEDRY GRILL!!!

Watching my mom struggle over her phallic autocorrect should be funny, but it only sparks a white-hot flame.

K.

"Scratch that. My mom's going on yet another date tonight, so I'm on dog duty." I toss my phone into my backpack with a sigh. "Again."

"Damn," Joaquin says around a mouthful of his sandwich. "That's like the third time this month."

"Fifth," I mutter bitterly.

Joaquin gives me a sympathetic knee nudge under the table. "At least your mom's getting some."

I shudder. "Please don't ever use the words 'your mom' and 'getting some' in the same sentence ever again."

"My bad." Our usual teasing banter falters as he stares at me like a puzzle waiting to be solved. "You know we can talk about it, if you want?"

"My mom getting some?" I reply sarcastically.

He snorts, tossing a wadded-up napkin at me. "Let me be real for a minute, geez." His smile fades, and I'd laugh at his ultra-serious PSA-worthy expression if I didn't know what was coming. "About . . . y'know. The whole her dating again thing."

Joaquin and I share everything. Candy and toys and secrets and more memories than I could ever count. But I am still hesitant to talk about Mami around him. Not because I don't trust him, but because it feels weirdly . . . selfish. Sure, I barely see my mom these days because of her work schedule and love life, but at least she's around. Complaining about only seeing Mami once a week would probably feel like a slap in the face to someone who doesn't get to see theirs outside of a screen.

I toy with my necklace, avoiding Joaquin's eye.

Joaquin takes my nonresponse as an answer, swiftly moving on. "Let's do a rain check on the slushies, then. How about next Friday, after my practice?"

While I appreciate the topic switch, it's another gut punch. "I'm closing next Friday, too."

Joaquin lets out a low whistle. "Are you gonna be free anytime in the next century?"

I groan. "Probably not. Once we open up the outdoor seating area, things always get super hectic, so my tío needs all the help he can get." I cross my arms, leaning back until I'm staring at a concerning brown stain on the ceiling. "I don't even know if I'll be able to make it to Dino World this year."

Dino World is a forty-five-minute drive away from home. It's the dinosaur-themed amusement park of my and Mami's adrenaline junky dreams.

Joaquin hisses, knowing how much the loss must sting. He leans over to rest a consoling hand on my arm. "If I wasn't going to San Juan this summer, I'd offer to take you to that death trap you call entertainment."

I rest my hand on top of his, his skin warm to the touch. "That's very touching, thank you."

That's not even me being a snarky dickbag—I'm genuinely moved. Joaquin despises roller coasters. Anything that goes higher than twenty feet in the air is a definite no for him.

With his hand in mine, sitting across from each other in our favorite place, it's hard to ignore the ache in my chest. Life these past few months has been nothing but change. Mrs. Romero and Isabella leaving. Seeing Nurse Oatmeal more than I see Mami. My dream of Sarah Lawrence fading each time I open my inbox. The possibility of joining most of my class at Rutgers is looking more like a reality with every passing day.

Gazing into his eyes, honey brown and as captivating now as they were when I met him, it's impossible not to want to hold on to him, to us, for as long as I possibly can.

"Post-it Notes."

Joaquin's brow furrows in confusion, his hand pulling out of mine. "Uh . . . what?" Internally, I'm asking the same question.

"Yeah . . . You can cover Tessa's car in Post-it Notes," I say, actually using words this time. "Which has been done before, I know, but you can personalize it! Spell out something interesting or write things you like about her on each of the notes."

And, most importantly, it'll be easy to tear apart. Maybe all Joaquin needs to break the spell Tessa has on him is a cosmic sign from the universe that asking her to prom is a seriously bad idea. Since I don't have time to wait for the universe to get its ass into gear, I'll take the liberty of delivering the message myself.

Joaquin's eyes light up as he mulls my suggestion over, finally taking a bite of his sandwich, temporary depression cured. "That's a good idea." Another bite. "A *great* idea."

My chest swells with a dangerous combination of glee, nerves, and acid reflux. "I could set it up after last period on Monday," I propose, everything starting to come together in my head as I finish off the last of my sandwich. With Tessa and Joaquin occupied with changing for their respective cheerleading and baseball practices, I should have enough time to set things up for (controlled, nonflammable) disaster.

Joaquin shakes his head. "No way, you've already done too much for me. I can set it up."

Now is not the time for him to be selfless.

"I want to," I say. And it's true. This is one of the few things I *do* want to do.

My reply startles him, his sandwich frozen halfway to his mouth. "Seriously?"

I nudge my leg against his. "Seriously." His smile makes me warm all over, and for a few moments, the noise around us falls away. The sizzle of the grill, the staticky radio, the whispered conversations of other Marco's patrons. It's just me, Joaquin, and this small piece of the world we've carved out for ourselves.

"What'd I do to deserve you?"

A backstabbing excuse of a friend who wants to sabotage your one chance at love? the devil on my shoulder taunts.

"You probably had terrible luck in a past life." I snag a piece of bacon off his plate. "This is the universe's way of paying you back."

And if I play my cards right, the universe will be sending him a very important message soon: Give up on Tessa Hernandez.

He rolls his eyes dramatically before leaning in across the table, as if he's about to tell me a secret. "I think I got pretty lucky in this lifetime," he says, leaning forward.

Part of me wishes he'd back up so he won't hear how fast my

heart is beating. Part of me wishes he'd come even closer. Part of me wants to scoot out of this booth.

But I stay, like I always do, and meet his lingering smile with one of my own. A smile that's soft and easy, like everything we do together.

His eyes drift away from mine, toward my lips. I reach up to dab at the corner of my mouth, expecting to wipe away a glob of mayo but finding nothing. He laughs quietly, so close I can feel the subtle vibration in his shoulders and reaches for my hand. Warmth trickles into my cheeks.

Then a chime pops our bubble, every hair on my body rocketing to attention at the sound I assigned to incoming emails. Breaking eye contact with Joaquin feels like ripping off a Band-Aid, stinging as I scan the email preview on my lock screen.

SARAH LAWRENCE OFFICE OF ADMISSIONS
An update to your admissions status has been made.
Please check your portal.

"Holy shit," I whisper.

"What? Everything okay?"

"It—it's an update from Sarah Lawrence," I manage to choke out.

Joaquin pushes my phone toward me. "Then open it!"

My hands are shaking so hard I don't think I could type even if I wanted to. I've been constantly refreshing my inbox for days, and now that it's here, I can't bring myself to log in. Because at least right now I still have the luxury of hope. As soon as I check the portal, it could be over. My daydreams crushed.

"What if it's a rejection?"

My voice is barely loud enough for me to hear over the din of the radio, but Joaquin still comes rushing to my side of the booth. He takes my shaking hands in his, waiting until I meet his eyes to speak.

"If it is, then screw them. They're passing up on a future Tony Award–winning set designer."

I snort at his optimism, and he tightens his grip on my hands, as if to emphasize his point. "Seriously, Ive. If they don't know how incredible you are, then that's their problem."

The sincerity in his voice, and the way his eyes gaze so deep into mine make the nerves fade. Not entirely, but enough for me to find that flicker of hope again. I nod, keeping my left hand in his as I pick up my phone and sign into the Admissions portal.

Decades pass as the web page loads. Normally Marco's shitty Wi-Fi is something I'm willing to put up with for the god-tier food, but every second that goes by feels like a blow to my chest. Joaquin's grip on my hand tightens with anticipation, holding on to me so tightly I'd wince if I wasn't so consumed by my own panic. Our breath hitches as the page loads, coming out as gasps when we take in the first word at the top of the page.

Congratulations!

"I got in!" I shout, my voice high-pitched enough to summon Nurse Oatmeal.

"You got in!" Joaquin echoes, slamming his fist on the table.

He leaps out of his seat, pulling me up with him. "My best friend just got into her dream school!" he announces to the restaurant, getting the attention of everyone who wasn't eyeing us already.

"Wepa!" Jenny exclaims, bustling over to us to pull me in for a hug and a kiss on the cheek. "Congratulations, mija." She leans in to whisper, "Lunch is on me today."

One of the line cooks starts a round of applause, Joaquin encouraging the crowd to make some noise as he pulls me into a crushing hug. "You're amazing," he whispers before pressing a kiss to the crown of my head. A shiver runs down my spine, but I'm too shocked by the *Oh my God I got in* moment to process it. With my heart lodged in my throat from the best combo of excitement and nerves, all I can wish for is to hold on to this feeling—this person—forever.

When I meet Joaquin's eyes again, something new unlocks inside me.

Suddenly, I'm back at the optometrist's office when I was seven, putting on my first pair of glasses and blinking in utter awe because I never knew the world could be such a vibrant place. Because that's the thing—you don't realize what you're missing until you finally see things in focus.

And now I see him in focus.

The way my body leans into his, like a well-loved sweater. The smell of him—sofrito, sweat, and sunscreen—that feels more like home than any place in this town ever has. The urge to vomit whenever Joaquin and Chelsea sucked face in the cafeteria. That nameless feeling in the pit of my stomach whenever he brings up Tessa or prom or promposals.

I'm not afraid of Tessa taking my place at prom, or getting her own mix CD, or taking up so much room in his heart that there'll never be enough space left for me. I'm afraid of *him*. Of his smile. Of his touch. Of the way he says my name like it's something worth savoring.

I'm afraid of Joaquin Romero because I'm in love with him.

CHAPTER NINE

"DOES THIS FEEL DANGEROUS to anyone else?" I ask as someone wearing a full beekeeping suit steps into the cafeteria, carefully contained beehive in hand.

Anna stiffens uncomfortably. "If that thing even comes close to opening, I'm out of here." We make note of the exits on either side of us before keeping a watchful eye on the beekeeper's movements while Joaquin focuses on the stack of Post-its in front of him.

The beekeeper taps a girl from my AP Lit class on the shoulder. She lets out a stifled gasp when she turns around to find a cluster of a hundred angry-ass bees in a glass container. Her suitor sets the hive on the ground, flipping it around to reveal a message written in a font designed to look like dripping honey.

WILL YOU BEE MY DATE?

Before the beekeeper's target can make her decision, murmurs break out across the cafeteria as someone in a Shrek costume enters the lunchroom, carrying a poster board reading:

SOMEBODY ONCE TOLD ME YOU NEEDED A DATE TO PROM.

"Dear God," Anna mumbles as the ogre gets down on one knee in front of Tessa.

Tessa beholds her latest suitor with a sigh. The cafeteria falls silent, hanging in suspense as she gives him her usual pitying smile. "Somebody lied."

Tessa's turned down enough promposals by now that no one loses their mind when she shuts them down, but Shrek is still met with his fair share of supportive cheers when he slumps away. It's only after everyone's turned their attention away that Shrek removes his foam head, revealing a devastated Hank Azario.

"Gotta give them props for creativity," I say as Shrek/Hank tosses his poster board in the trash and the beekeeper storms out of the cafeteria, bees in tow.

"Slow day," Anna says once this afternoon's main characters have exited the room.

Most days we're lucky if we can get ten minutes of peace without a promposal interlude. The cafeteria has essentially become Prom Central. When we're not being bombarded by promposals, it's a prom court nominee passing out buttons with their face on it, asking for votes like they're running for president of the United States. I've gotten six YOU KNOW YOU WANT YESENIA buttons since the pep rally. Wear the wrong prom court button and you might get blocked from using the good vending machines. The madness doesn't stop at the race for prom court, either. Last week, a few people started selling some viral mascara that's impossible to get in stores or online anymore at twice the retail price.

Cutthroat stuff.

With today's double feature wrapped up, we turn back to the task at hand.

"This is impossible." Joaquin groans before letting his head hit the lunch table with a *thwack*.

I nudge my shoulder against his. "Chin up, soldier, we're almost done."

We're most definitely not almost done. There's only ten minutes until the bell and we still have about a hundred Post-its left to cover with compliments about Tessa. It's a testament to my acting abilities that he doesn't see how nervous I am too. Both because of my startling realization of "holy shit, I'm in love with him" at Marco's on Friday, and because we're nowhere near done.

Drama club has clearly rubbed off on me.

Joaquin runs his Sharpie-stained fingers through his tousled curls. "I'm running out of things to say."

"She's a Gemini moon," Anna offers, glancing up from her own batch of Post-its. "And a Pisces rising," she adds when we give her blank stares.

"I don't know what that means," Joaquin replies.

She grumbles something under her breath before scribbling *nice hair* on her next Post-it instead.

Joaquin looks forlornly at the endless stacks of multicolored notes taking up our table. We've been working on these since first period, and it feels like we've barely made a dent.

"She's half Dominican, half Italian, right?" Joaquin asks, scratching his head with his pen. "Is there something there?"

"Dynamically Dominican and exquisitely Italian," I throw out.

Anna snorts, her loc cuffs clanging together as she shakes her head. "Please. Tessa's as Italian as Olive Garden."

Joaquin shrinks, curling into his hoodie like a petrified turtle. I glare at Anna, but she's too busy writing *flawless skin* to notice me.

"What about personality stuff?" I propose, which gets Joaquin to come out of his metaphorical and physical shell. "You're the one who's into her—what about her drew you in? Was she funny? Easy to talk to?"

Asking feels like pulling teeth, especially when I know I don't want to hear his answer. But I trample my emotions down. This whole "realizing I'm in love with my best friend" thing couldn't have come at a more inconvenient time, considering he's already got his heart set on someone else.

Joaquin shrugs, gesturing to a crumpled stack of Post-its to his left. "I tried that. But it just felt . . . weird." He uncrumples the one closest to him, smoothing it out until we can see the *makes me smile* written on it in Joaquin's signature chicken scratch. "Like I wasn't really talking about her, y'know?"

"Then who were you talking about?" Anna asks, arching her brow.

Joaquin clams up, retreating into his hoodie again and concentrating on the task at hand. "No one," he mumbles.

The first bell breaks up any lingering tension at the table. Panic is written all over Joaquin's face as he ogles our puny completed pile and mountainous unfinished pile. "I can work on some of these during French. And then finish up the rest after bio, and maybe some during—"

"Quin," I interrupt, gripping his arm tight enough to get him to hold still. "I've got this."

His expression softens, tension melting off him. "You sure?"

"I'm sure," I reply with a nod. "I have a free period after this."

He doesn't appear convinced, peering over my shoulder at our cluttered workspace. "Isn't this supposed to be from me, though? Does it feel insincere if I let someone else do it?"

In theory, yes. But in practice, none of these compliments are going to matter by the end of the day. Not that he knows that. "It's the thought that counts."

"But you came up with this . . ."

He's got me there. "But *you* thought to come to me for help. That counts for something, right?"

He ponders that for a moment. "You're right."

"As usual," I taunt, turning him around and pushing him toward the exit.

"I double owe you, don't forget that," he calls out to me before jogging to his French class.

"I won't!" I call back in response, turning around to find Anna waiting for me with crossed arms.

"What now?"

She uncrosses her arms and glances over at where Joaquin

went. "Is this even worth it? Seems like a lot of effort for two people who might not even like each other."

"They like each other," I insist, turning my attention back to my Post-its. "She winked at him once and said hi to him in the hall the other day. That's basically a declaration of love from her, right?"

Anna sighs.

"Tessa likes it when people compliment her nose," she says, an unexpected sadness to her tone. "She got it done in seventh grade after a cheerleading accident and never liked the way it turned out. And talk about her eyes. They're her best feature."

Before I can thank her for the tip, she walks off, leaving me and my hundreds of Post-its.

Thanks to my free period and an online thesaurus, I'm a compliment machine by the time the final bell rings. Doesn't matter if any of them are true, just that they're done.

Curiosity gets the better of me, and I peek at the few that Joaquin managed to finish during lunch. Most of them are vague (*nice smile*, *shiny hair*) and even the more specific ones (*fun to talk to*) aren't very inspired. I'm not sure how I feel about it, though. Honestly, I'm not sure how I feel about anything anymore.

Friday was . . . a lot. Realizing you're in love with someone should be exciting, but instead it felt terrifying. Joaquin and I have been best friends practically since we could talk. I can barely imagine a life where I'm two hours, and a state, away from him—what the hell would I do if he shot me down and things were so awkward between us that we never spoke again? Or, even worse, he feels the same way, only for us to break up like every other high school couple and bitterly despise each other for the rest of our lives? Just look at my parents—they haven't spoken in over a decade.

Joaquin and I may be best friends, but we're not meant to be. Just like with me and Danny, the popular guy and unpopular girl never last long.

I gather up my treasure trove of Post-its proclaiming Tessa as everything from "magnanimous" to "perspicacious" into my bag and bolt for the parking lot near the baseball field. Time is of the essence if I want to pull off my plan.

Fighting off the guilt took up more time than I'd anticipated. My complicated feelings for Joaquin may be locked up in a box in the back of my mind, but that doesn't mean I'm suddenly okay with him and Tessa as a concept. An uneasy feeling is still swirling in the pit of my stomach as I head outside, but the thought of Tessa waltzing into my life and pushing me out of Joaquin's keeps me grounded.

Because if Tessa agrees to go out with him, I can kiss any future moments with him goodbye.

I only have a fifteen-minute grace period before Mr. Cline, the detention supervisor, marks me absent. The last thing I need is another week tacked on to my sentence. As expected, the lot behind the baseball diamond is packed with cars. Most of the seniors sticking around for practice move their cars over during lunch to avoid the twenty-minute trek from the senior parking lot to the field. One of the few times Cordero's massive, sprawling campus has come in handy.

Scanning the lot, I quickly spot Tessa's black Prius and her signature hot-pink steering wheel cover in the prime spot in front of the vending machines. Now I just need to scope out a victim. Another black Prius—not this year's model, like Tessa's, though—is parked on the opposite end of the lot.

A countdown rings in my ears as I get to work, plastering as many of the Post-its onto the car as I can. My hands are a blur of pinks, blues, and greens as I rush to spell out the word *PROM?* before anyone can spot me. I have about ten minutes before the cheer team starts filing out of the locker room and onto the field for their practice. With my luck, I have five.

Compliments blur my vision and my fingers have never felt so disgustingly sticky, but I find my rhythm. Blue for the *P*. Green for the *O*. Pink for the rest. Soon enough, I have control over my body again, pinning the notes in place like a well-oiled machine. Nearly finished, I dart out of view, hiding behind a neighboring car, when I hear someone approach.

"Yo! Check this," a voice shouts. DeShawn is the first to take in my handiwork with wide, amused eyes.

I'm a regular fixture in the stands and on the field, so my presence wouldn't seem out of the ordinary to any of Joaquin's teammates, but it does ruin the illusion of romance if they catch me setting up a promposal for him.

DeShawn calls out to his teammates one more time, "Bruh, you've gotta see this!" before disappearing into the locker room to rally the troops.

Shit. Less time than I thought.

Whispering a Hail Mary under my breath, I throw on a few last-ditch Post-its, half of which don't stick for longer than five seconds, before darting across the lot to safety behind the ticket booth.

DeShawn is back with half the team moments after I make it to my hiding spot. I'm too far away to make out what they're saying, but they're clearly amused—slapping each other on the back, taking pictures and videos.

Weird . . .

Promposal season is like Oscars season. A few Post-it Notes on a car is hardly video worthy. Best-case scenario I just Post-it'ed some cheerleader's car and saved her lazy jock boyfriend from having to put any actual effort into his own promposal. Or, worst-case scenario, I stuck them on one of Joaquin's teammates' car, and he'll brush it off as a prank.

The possibility of accidentally having Joaquin propose to some unsuspecting dateless cheerleader also crossed my mind. Though, *dateless* and *cheerleader* don't usually belong in the same sentence. I wouldn't put it past him to get down on one knee and ask out someone he barely knows—not that he and Tessa know each other *that* well—but anyone is better than Tessa.

The rest of the baseball team and some cheerleaders come spilling out of the locker room, the crowd surrounding my slap-dash masterpiece getting rowdier by the second. I can't shake the gut feeling that I may have just seriously messed things up.

And not the way I'd hoped to.

Joaquin comes tumbling out of the locker room with pink

cheeks and fear in his eyes. His jaw drops as he takes in the Post-it-covered car, making him stand out against the backdrop of his amused teammates.

Once he's able to pull his attention away from the spectacle, he searches the lot.

Searches for me.

Our eyes lock for a fraction of a second, his finding mine after I step out from behind the ticket booth. Time moves in slow motion as he mouths, *"What did you—"*

I glance back at the car. Half the notes having fallen off by now, spelling out *P OM* instead of *PROM?* Not crowd-worthy if you ask me, but maybe the bar for entertainment is astoundingly low.

Then I spot it. A bumper sticker on the back of the car that reads ELMWOOD'S #1 COACH THREE YEARS RUNNING.

Fuuuuuuuuuuuu—

"All right, very funny," Coach Mills bellows, starting a slow clap as he steps out onto the lot.

Joaquin rockets to attention, like a soldier awaiting command. The bright red whistle around Coach Mills's neck glistens in the sun, blinding me even from twenty feet away. "Got your laughs in?" He halts in front of the car, arms crossed sternly. "Now, who did it?"

Snickers and giggles break out among the crowd, but no one steps forward. Tessa stands at the center of the cheerleading pack, covering her giggles behind an immaculate French-manicured hand.

"So, think you're slick enough to pull this stunt but not own up to it?" Coach Mills taunts, making sure to stare directly into the eyes of every single member of his team as he scans the crowd.

A hush falls across the lot. I hold my breath as I watch Coach Mills examine the car again and turn back to the crowd with a disapproving grimace.

"Fine by me, then. Since whoever thinks I have"—he plucks a Post-it off the car—"'thick, luscious hair'"—the team struggles to hold in their laughter as their bald-as-an-egg coach waves the slip of paper—"doesn't want to own up, how about ten laps before we get started today, huh? Seem fair enough?"

Laughter quickly dissolves into groans. Danny sucks his teeth and faces the rest of the team with a scowl. "C'mon, who did it?"

Joaquin bristles, picking at a scab on his elbow. Staying calm under pressure is supposed to be his strong suit but keeping cool on the field and keeping cool at the risk of punishment is a whole other ballgame.

Guilt guides me as I walk toward the crowd. I'm the only one who can save the team and come out mostly unscathed. Coach Mills can't rip me to shreds for screwing up what, for all he knows, was a genuine attempt at a promposal.

"Fine, laps it is, then," Coach announces before I can sacrifice myself. He blows the whistle around his neck, earning winces from everyone within a fifty-foot radius. "Let's move!"

The baseball team scatters like ants, some jogging over to the field to get a head start on their punishment laps while others go back to the locker room to finish changing.

"Sorry you had to see that, Ivelisse." Coach Mills tips his cap to me before corralling those headed to the field, alternating between clapping and blowing his whistle to get the boys into gear. I bite my lip, considering going after him and explaining before ultimately deciding to head inside to find Joaquin instead.

Before the cloud of BO and Axe body spray in the hall outside the locker room can drown me, someone grabs my arm and pulls me to safety. The familiar scent of Joaquin's Irish Spring body wash and coconut curl gel washes over me like a balm.

"I'm so sorry," I blurt out the second I'm sure we're alone, the words tumbling out of me faster than I can keep up with them. "I swear I had no idea that was Coach Mills's car. I was looking for a black Prius, and that was the first thing I saw, and . . ."

The panic and nerves are real, even if the excuse isn't. It's not a complete lie, though. I *didn't* mean to pick Coach Mills. My plan for light chaos exploded into a full-blown catastrophe.

"You missed the hot-pink steering wheel?" he asks with a frown.

"I . . . I didn't see it," I choke out. "I was too busy—"

"It's fine, Ive," Joaquin cuts me off, his voice firm but gentle. Disappointed, but still so kind I forget to feel guilty for a second or two. He sighs, brushing his hair out of his face. "It was an accident."

Right. An accident.

"It's not too late for me to go tell Coach Mills. Save you guys the extra laps."

Joaquin shakes his head. "I'm not landing you any more detention."

A promposal martyr, running extra laps in the name of saving me from spending the rest of senior year in detention. Speaking of which . . .

"I should probably go." I avoid checking the clock on the wall over his shoulder. Knowing how little time I have to make it to detention will just make me sweat more than I already am. "I'm sorry again, Quin."

He nods, mumbling a "you're good" under his breath and heading back outside to catch up with the rest of the team before he earns himself another round of laps for tardiness. Along the way, Tessa steps out from the girls' locker room, brushing right past Joaquin. Their arms graze.

"Sorry," he says.

"Don't be," she says with a small—and quite possibly flirty—smile.

But before their conversation can go any further, one of her squad mates whisks her away. Joaquin's shoulders slump, his body sagging as he walks out of the building while a rush of excitement runs down my spine.

It took a whole lot of sweat and panic, but my plan worked. Promposal attempt #3 was a flop, and the universe has delivered its message: Joaquin and Tessa are doomed from the start. I crack my knuckles and fight back a smile as I skip my way to detention.

Mission accomplished.

CHAPTER TEN

TO THINK, THERE WAS once a time when I thought coming home smelling like fried plantains every other day would be a perk.

After sitting on the bus stuck in prom season's daily "rush to the mall" traffic jam for over an hour on my way back from my closing shift, I'm so exhausted that I don't even notice the living room lights are on.

It's not until I'm wrapped in just a towel, making my way to the bathroom down the hall, that I realize someone else is in the house. Somewhere in the living room, I can hear light footsteps padding over the carpet. Breath hitching, I reach for the closest weapon I can find—a decorative vase holding a fake lotus flower—and slowly approach the intruder. I halt at the end of the hallway, holding the vase against my chest as I wait for any sign of where they might be, when someone suddenly comes around the corner.

"It's about time you—"

Mami's greeting is completely swallowed by the sound of my scream. For all my planning, I don't actually do anything with the vase, just hold it against my body and shout bloody murder until I open my eyes and realize the intruder is just my mom.

"Jesus, you almost gave me a heart attack." Mami yanks the vase out of my hand.

"Sorry," I mumble, resting a hand over my racing heart. No point in telling her I was quicker to believe someone had broken into our house than that she was home. "I thought you were working tonight?"

She groans after setting the vase aside on a nearby end table. "I had an awful migraine when I woke up, so I called in sick." That explains the sweatpants and messy bun. Even when she's wearing scrubs, Mami insists on mascara, lipstick, and hoops. "Come into the living room when you're done showering. I feel like I haven't seen you in forever."

The feeling is mutual.

Hope blooms in my chest as I give her a nod and a smile before heading into the bathroom. It's been over a month since we've had a night in together, but I don't let myself jump to conclusions. Lest we forget, last time I thought we'd be hanging out she bailed on me. After my shower, I half expect to find the living room empty and yet another frozen meal or take-out container on the dining table with a note to not wait up. Maybe a lipstick kiss on the note if she's feeling generous. Another night alone. Another night of silence.

But she's still there, wrapped in a throw blanket on the couch with Nurse Oatmeal, who's gotten ahold of poor Otis the Otter. Before Mami can notice me, I pinch the inside of my elbow just to be safe. Sure enough, it's not a dream.

"These two need to just call it quits already," Mami says, gesturing to the couple on the TV once she's clocked my presence. "They're so toxic."

Most of the couples on our latest guilty pleasure, *Married to My Ex's Ex*, would be considered toxic, but there's a special place in hell reserved for Mariana and David, who left their fiancé and fiancée, respectively, at the altar for each other.

"They do in the next episode," I tell her as I sit down beside her, Nurse Oatmeal giving up on Otis and coming over to sit on my lap instead. "Sorry, spoilers."

Mami gives me a tight-lipped smile. Was I supposed to wait for her to keep watching? Because if I did, we'd be weeks behind, and social media is spoiler central. No way I was getting spoiled.

We sit in silence as Mariana kicks David out of their apartment for texting an ex behind her back, on the edge of our seats as she sets fire to his clothes after throwing them out on the front lawn. Mami pulls me closer and runs her fingers through my damp hair, weaving it into a loose braid I can wear to bed for perfect natural curls in the morning. In between gasps, we pass a container of dumplings back and forth like popcorn.

"Work been okay?" Mami asks during the commercial break, reaching for a carton of lo mein. An incoming notification lights up her phone—a new message on one of her various dating apps. Several messages, based on the number of stacked notifications she has on her home screen. My heart clenches, ready for her to focus on them instead, but she locks her phone and turns back to me. The tension quickly melts away. She still chose me. "Tony's not driving you crazy?"

Tío Tony may have a foot in height and a hundred pounds of muscle on Mami, but I have no doubt she'd put her baby brother in his place if she needed to.

"It's been good." I can see her visibly relax at the reassurance. "And he only has one other waitress, so he can't get rid of me that easy." Without me, he'd have to wait tables himself.

Mami grins, pulling me in by the shoulder to press a kiss to my temple. "Think you'll make enough for both of us to retire soon? These overnight shifts are killing me."

I snort, leaning into her warmth and resting my head on her shoulder. The comforting smell of Chanel N°5 and Fabuloso makes my limbs heavy with an exhaustion I haven't let myself feel in weeks. "No dice. I'll be lucky if I can afford a used car this century."

Mami clucks her tongue as she waves off my concerns. "We'll find you something," she insists, and for once, car owner-ship doesn't feel like a pipe dream. If there's one thing Mami's proven after more than a decade as a single mother, it's that she can get shit done, money or no money.

"Speaking of which . . ." Mami leaps off the couch with a knowing smile and rushes to her room. She returns with a large white shopping bag filled with red tissue paper, setting it down in front of me. "I got you a little something."

I tear through the paper like a kid on Christmas Day, Nurse Oatmeal happily taking the scraps into a corner to tear apart. Beneath the paper is a carefully folded scarlet hoodie, my stomach dropping as I realize what it is before I've even pulled it out of the bag.

"I forgot that you didn't have one yet," Mami says with a squeal as I hold up the Rutgers hoodie. "And I got this one for me!" She pulls another hoodie out from behind her back, the same scarlet shade. RUTGERS MOM is written across the chest in white cursive font. "We can match on move-in day!"

Flashes of my epic Marco's celebration come rushing back, the pure elation I'd felt as Joaquin and I reread my Sarah Lawrence letter out loud to Jenny and the line cooks. I'd considered texting Mami then, telling her about my acceptance. But with her heart so set on me going to Rutgers, I knew it was the type of conversation that'd be easier to have in person. But I didn't expect three days to go by without seeing her.

I also didn't expect her to buy us matching Rutgers hoodies.

My mouth hangs open in surprise, the truth threatening to tumble out of me at any second. I can see Mami's smile and the elated glimmer in her eyes. For the first time since I visited the campus, I wonder if Sarah Lawrence is actually worth it—if making my mom *this* excited is worth more than a gut feeling. The pure joy I'd felt on Friday sours, dreams of sitting on the lawn discussing Tennessee Williams with friends in between classes morphing into nightmares where I'm somehow even more alone there than I feel here, without either of my best friends or my family to fall back on.

Suddenly, Sarah Lawrence doesn't seem so perfect.

I press my lips into a tight line, urging my confession to go right back to where it came from. This is the first normal night we've had together in over a month. Obviously, I've missed spending time with Mami, but I didn't realize just how much until I had her here, sharing dumplings and braiding my hair while watching reality TV. I can't just ruin the one night I've actually felt comfortable in my own house in weeks by telling her I might move to New York instead of staying close by like she and every other member of our family did before her. Bronxville isn't *that* far, but it's a whole hell of a lot farther than any of my tías, tíos, and cousins have gone.

Like that afternoon at Marco's, I'm pushed by an uncontrollable force. A desperate need to grip this moment before it slips away from me. I still have another two weeks until I have to send in the registration deposit to confirm my spot, I tell myself as I hold the hoodie up against my chest. Plenty of time to figure out what I want to do with my future. And when I do, I'll be honest with Mami. I'll leave the future for another day to focus on the present.

"Can't wait," I reply.

Mami squeals in delight. She pulls on her own hoodie before gesturing for me to try mine on. It's a perfect fit. She claps her hands as she joins me on the couch again, running a hand along the arm of my sweater. "We've gotta send a picture to your abuela."

We pose for a selfie, making sure the Rutgers signature *R* logo is front and center. My face feels wooden, but the filter Mami applies to the photo makes me into a perfect, dewy angel. She presses a wet kiss to my cheek after sending the photo off to Abuela with the caption *New Scarlet Knight in the family!!!!*

"I'm so proud of you, mama," she whispers, handing me the last dumpling as Mariana and David take over the screen again.

All I can do is smile and shove the dumpling into my mouth before I can ruin the moment. The pork and fried dough feel heavy as bricks in my stomach.

The only thing she should be proud of is what a good liar I've become.

CHAPTER ELEVEN

MY LITTLE STUNT WITH Coach Mills's car makes me an instant hero. An anonymous one, but a hero, nonetheless. For the rest of the week, social media is flooded with pictures and videos of Coach Mills stumbling upon the surprise romantic gesture. Sometimes the Post-its are Photoshopped to include *very* not-safe-for-work compliments, while others just zoom in on the way Coach Mills's mustache quivered when he spotted his car. It's the most anyone has ever paid attention to me since the news about me and Danny broke.

Well, not *me* directly.

Still, I'll gladly take being an antisocial outcast over being the face of Cordero's latest meme.

"Earth to Ivelisse." Anna snapping her fingers knocks me out of my zombie trance. "Keep your head up," she hisses while our history teacher has her back turned. "Unless you want to sign a lease and move into detention permanently."

Picking my head up takes a Herculean amount of effort. Between detention, frantically trying to finish sets for *Shrew*, and squeezing in closing shifts at Casa Y Cocina, I'm running on fumes. Not to mention the emotional turmoil of decoding my feelings for my best friend and trying to decide where to spend the next four years of my life. My brain is *not* a pleasant place to be right now.

"Help me, I'm dying," I mutter just loud enough for her to hear, propping my chin up on my fist and letting my eyes close for juuuuust one second.

"Hey!" Anna snaps, whacking me on the arm when my head starts to droop again. "No more mini naps."

Along with the warning, she tosses me a can of Raspberry Unicorn from her backpack. My taste buds are still recovering from the one I downed at the pep rally last week, but half-asleep beggars can't be choosers. When the coast is clear, I crack open the can and savor the sweet, nauseating taste of battery acid and caffeine.

It takes three sips to get me through our last class of the day. When the final bell rings, my entire body is thrumming like the fizz still left in the can, my hands shaking as my body pulses with an ungodly amount of sugar.

"I'll head over to the auditorium as soon as I'm free," I tell Anna as we walk toward our lockers, the words coming out a mile a minute. "We're working on the staircase today, right? Or are we doing lighting cues? Or music cues? Or we could—"

Anna clamps a hand over my mouth. "Slow down, Eager Beaver. We're not working on anything today."

A warning siren blares in my ears, the perfectionist in me

hyperaware of how many days we have until opening night (not many), and how much work we have to get done (a shit ton). "What? But we still have—"

"Plenty of time to get everything done," Anna finishes for me. "The glee club needs to use the auditorium today, so we swapped days this week."

I swallow hard around the lump in my throat. Usually, the glee club claims the auditorium on Fridays, which means Tío Tony will be expecting me to head straight to Casa Y Cocina for my post-detention closing shift tomorrow. There goes two days' worth of profits.

"But don't go landing yourself more detention," Anna adds, waving a warning finger. "You're lucky sabotaging lover boy's little mission didn't earn you another month on your sentencing."

The words are like an ice bath.

"I . . . I didn't sabotage anything," I stammer, the cold giving way to a warmth that spreads from my cheeks down to my toes. Sweat beads across my forehead as I give her my best casual shrug. "I was in a rush, and they're both black Priuses."

Her dark brown eyes narrow to slits. She pinches the soft skin of my inner arm.

"Ow! What the hell?!" I rub my reddened skin.

"Did you expect me to believe that?" she snaps. "I am *offended*." She makes sure to enunciate each syllable for emphasis.

"I'm serious!" I reply with an indignant pout. "I really didn't know it was Coach Mills's car."

Technically, that's the truth. Nonetheless, she sees right through me. Friends are overrated; you can't even lie to them.

Anna sighs, giving up on glaring at me in favor of trading books out of her locker. "Be in denial if you want. But seriously, don't get yourself any more detention."

"I'm not in denial because there's nothing to be in denial about!" I lean up against the locker beside hers. Except, y'know, that I'm in love with my best friend. But she doesn't need to know that. "You said yourself that Joaquin going to prom with Tessa would be a terrible idea."

"Yeah, because it is." She slams her locker door shut, turning on her heel and heading toward the parking lot. "But I didn't tell you to go set up all his promposals for disaster. You could, oh I don't know, have an actual conversation about why he shouldn't go with her?"

I hate when she's right.

Talking to Joaquin would save me a whole lot of effort but still leaves the very relevant problem that just the thought of talking to him about this makes me want to hurl. Telling Joaquin he can't ask Tessa out means unraveling the feelings that are sitting in the pit of my stomach like the cafeteria's questionable lunch special. Yes, Tessa's the worst. Yes, I don't want to lose my best friend to someone like her. But there's so much more to this than what's on the surface.

And I'm terrified of telling him the truth.

Touching that locked part of me means opening a Pandora's box of emotions I'm definitely not equipped to handle right now. Not when I barely have enough time to breathe, let alone "process my emotions" like a well-adjusted Almost Adult.

"It's complicated," I mumble, more to myself than to Anna while I trail behind her.

"Wow, never heard that one before." She stops in her tracks so abruptly I almost walk into her.

When she faces me, her eyes soften. "I get it, okay? The whole 'things are getting complicated with my best friend, and I don't know what to do about it' thing," she says, almost a whisper. There's a sadness to her words, something I almost never get to see glimpses of behind the tough exterior she puts up for the world. This place wasn't kind to her in the aftermath of her fall-out with Tessa. No one knows what happened besides them, but Anna's still seen as the villain. God forbid she express any type of anger, or else they'll just decide their assumptions about her are true. That she's mean and spiteful when we both know that's galaxies away from the truth. I've never met anyone more loyal and caring. I can't imagine how exhausting it must be for her. And it's just another reason why Joaquin and Tessa shouldn't be together—she let one of her oldest friends fall. Hard.

"What was it like? Losing your best friend?" I ask, taking a chance on prying a bit at the mystery shrouding her and Tessa's relationship. Not because I'm some nosey small-town teenager sniffing out the latest gossip. Deep down, I do want to know. To prepare myself, maybe, for what's inevitably going to come.

"I didn't lose her. I walked away from her," she clarifies, not meeting my eyes. "Everybody else decided they knew our story when we barely understood it ourselves. And I still don't know how I feel about it. Or her."

"It seems like you hate her."

"I don't hate her." Her reply is quick, sharp. I'm taken aback by it, and the sincerity in her eyes. She tugs at the chain of her bracelet, the star charm twinkling in the light. I always thought

Anna was past whatever she and Tessa had before. "I'll never be able to hate her . . ."

Anna takes her time finishing that thought, clearly weighing the words in her head before she finally says, "Try to be honest with Joaquin. It'll save you a lot of trouble."

Before I can reply, she heads to the parking lot and I'm left with a couple minutes to get to detention and a whole lot to process.

Detention is the perfect place to panic.

Today's riveting Thursday afternoon crowd is just me, one of the stoners from Chris Pavlenko's band of goons, the poor guy who landed himself detention through the rest of the year for whacking a lunch lady in the head with one of the MISTY WILL YOU GO TO PROM WITH ME T-shirts he was shooting out of a homemade cannon this morning, and Mr. Cline, resident sex ed teacher and detention monitor.

As always, Mr. Cline plugs in his headphones and is fast asleep within a record three and a half minutes of sitting at his desk. Which leaves me with plenty of time to stare at the empty notebook in front of me and overthink what I'm about to do.

Anna's voice rattles in my ears, possessing me like a demon and forcing me to open a notebook and write down everything I can't say out loud so I can finally exorcise myself of the guilt that's been eating at me. The caffeine from my Raspberry Unicorn keeps me so on edge my teeth start to chatter.

Be honest.

Easier said than done, I tell the specter of Anna that now haunts my brain. Coming clean is my best move, especially if I'm not as discreet as I thought I'd been about my plans for Joaquin's third promposal attempt.

At least it seems like my plan did the trick. Three whole days have gone by since The Incident, and Joaquin hasn't come up with any new convoluted plans to ask Tessa to prom. He's listening to the universe. And yet, victory doesn't taste as sweet as I hoped it would.

With Mr. Cline in dreamland, I pull out my phone and open my text thread with Joaquin.

> Good news: it's quesadilla day in the caf.
> Bad news: they're all sold out. Even better news: I snagged you one.

> Come by my free period if you want it & thank me later 😊

> Ooooookay I guess you're not in a quesadilla mood?

> Five minute warning before I eat this myself

> [photo]

> It was delicious

> Is that your abuela blasting Bad Bunny rn???

> Bc I can hear it all the way from my bathroom

> good morning my dear best friend who may be dead
> but I wouldn't know because he won't text me back!!!

It's not unusual for Joaquin not to immediately respond to a text. But these are all sitting in message purgatory—read but not responded to. Now that he has morning practice sessions with Coach Mills, I've been riding my bike to school instead of hitching a ride with him, and the lights in his bedroom have been out every night I've gotten home this week. I get that it's not like I was texting him anything important, but he hasn't so much as given any of them a thumbs-up or a cry-laughing emoji that I can roast him for because who our age uses the cry-laughing emoji unironically?

Maybe he knows. If Anna could see right through me, Joaquin would've known I was lying through my teeth instantly. And now he's super pissed and ignoring me. Ghosting our friendship like a date—or promposal—gone wrong.

I'm spiraling.

That's the last time I let Anna talk me into one of those energy drinks. Caffeine is *not* my friend.

Okay, okay, chill, Ivelisse. Deep breaths. Inhale, exhale, whatever bullshit that yoga instructor Mami dated two months ago taught her.

Once I've talked myself off the metaphorical ledge, I turn back to the empty page of my notebook. Journaling usually helps clear the mind, right?

I press the tip of my pen to the page but still can't force myself to open up, not even to this blank page. Instead, I try to go down a somewhat related route and write out all the pros and cons of Rutgers versus Sarah Lawrence. But all I've written is *Would make Mami happy* for Rutgers and *Vibes are right* for Sarah Lawrence before deciding this is too high pressure for my caffeine-addled brain to handle.

To further avoid being honest, I decide to get out all of my prom-related frustrations, inspired by Anna's classmates' Tessa-centric sonnet.

10 THINGS I HATE ABOUT PROM

10. The traffic. Going <u>anywhere</u> within five miles of the mall is a nightmare.

9. Constant—and I mean <u>constant</u>—PDA. Are seniors wearing body spray laced with pheromones?

8. There's glitter everywhere. Enough said.

7. The pressure to spend up to four figures on an outfit you'll only wear once for a grand total of three hours.

6. The lunchroom turning into a mine field thanks to prom court politics.

5. Prom dress group chats because God forbid <u>two</u> people wear a purple dress. The horror.

4. Student government allocating almost 75 percent of their budget to a dance. Why make the underclassmen suffer through a dozen bake sales just for most of their

money to go toward an overpriced undersea photo backdrop?

3. Every year someone gets paid to ask someone else out as a joke, and it's all shits and giggles until they find out and start having a telenovela-worthy fight in the senior parking lot.

2. Watching dickheads buy up all the good mascara from the one Sephora in town and selling it for double the price like some kind of makeup black market.

1. The. Freaking. Prom. Posals.

It's cathartic, writing down all of my petty annoyances to pass the time. Which, unfortunately, just confirms exactly what Anna said: I'll feel better if I'm honest.

With a sigh, I flip to a fresh page and force myself to write the first thing that comes to mind.

Dear Quin,

Decent start.

Another ten minutes go by before I can write another word. Hundreds of apologies and questions and statements flash in front of my eyes but nothing feels worthy of what I truly want—*need*—to tell him. That some days it feels like the sun rises and sets with him. That he's the only part of my life that feels safe, stable, the way it did before everything—his mom leaving, mine never sticking around, his newfound feelings for Tessa—changed.

That I'm terrified of what it could mean to lose someone like him.

The pen moves across the page in a blur, my body following some belly-deep instinct my frazzled brain can't process. Words appear on the page by divine Raspberry Unicorn inspiration.

> I'm sorry for wrecking your promposal. Twice. And for not telling you the truth about how they fell apart. Twice. I know you're really into Tessa and think this is some "made in the stars" type of love story after one memorable spring break. But—

But what? The thought of him falling for someone who hurt me stings more than the third-degree burn he accidentally gave me in fifth grade? That I haven't felt this way since I saw him making out with Chelsea? That I'm terrified of him falling for someone else when I fell for him first? This letter is about being honest, sure, but I'm still not ready to open up to him about that last question.

Thankfully, I'm saved by the bell.

An earsplitting alarm blares over the loudspeakers, a monotone male voice saying, "FIRE! PLEASE EVACUATE!" on loop.

"What the—" Mr. Cline startles so suddenly, the chair he's leaning back in topples over, his head smacking against the chalkboard with a thunk. He groans, rubbing the red mark forming on his bald spot as he stumbles to his feet. "Let's hustle before—"

Too late. Before he can warn us, the sprinklers engage, showering the classroom in a fine spray of ice-cold water. My stoned prison mate makes a dash for the door, leaving behind his bag and half-eaten Twinkie. Once the downpour starts, Mr. Cline abandons professional bravery, not even bothering to check on me or Cannon Boy before darting out of the room too.

I clutch my notebook and backpack to my chest and rush into the hallway, my stuff already soaked. The halls are thankfully dry except for the puddles Mr. Cline and Stoner Goon left behind. I'm halfway to the exit when the world turns upside down, my foot slipping and sending me hurtling toward the ground.

Before my head can crack open like an egg, something—*someone*—catches me by the waist, leaving me suspended in midair. I open one eye, a familiar face backlit by the hallway's horrendously unflattering fluorescent lighting.

"Joaquin?" I croak out. Did I hit my head and go to heaven (or hell, who am I kidding?) and this is some kind of mirage?

"Ivelisse," he responds with a sly smirk. It's not until then that I realize just how close we are, his face a breath apart from mine. My cheeks immediately flame as I realize I'm definitely not the most attractive sight to behold right now.

"What're you doing here?" I ask once he's pulled me up, discreetly attempting to flatten down any flyaways the water may have caused. His hand continues to brace my waist like I may collapse in shock. Which, to be fair, I might. The amount of caffeine and fear-induced adrenaline pumping through my veins can't be healthy.

"Saving you from 'the fire.'" The air quotes throw me off, but he answers that question before I can ask it. "Needed to break you out of detention somehow." He points his thumb in the direction of the triggered fire alarm beside the detention classroom.

"Quin!" I smack him on the arm. "What the hell?! You could get in massive trouble!"

"Relax, I'm a fire-alarm-pulling pro." When I open my mouth to protest, his arm comes up to rest around my shoulder and tug me toward the exit. "Unless you want to keep standing here and let me get caught."

Fair enough. I lean into the warmth of him, chasing away the chill from the water that's slowly soaking through my hoodie and jeans. He doesn't let go of me until we get to his car. He pops open the trunk, rooting through one of the dozens of gym bags he keeps around in case of emergencies for a spare T-shirt. He gives the handful he finds a sniff, his nose scrunching in disapproval before he ultimately reaches for the hem of his own shirt and pulls it over his head.

My face goes hot as the core of the earth. I'd scoffed at the Emilys for gawking at him when his shirt rode up, and now seeing his impressively-defined-for-a-teenager's abs on full display makes my world spin. How the mighty have fallen. "What're you—"

"Here, get changed," he interrupts, tossing me the shirt off his back and a pair of shorts from his trunk before opening the door to my illustrious changing room: the back seat.

"Why?" I ask as we slide into the car, and I shrug out of my wet clothes as quickly as I can. Thank God for tinted windows, Herb's sole upgrade. "And shouldn't you be at baseball practice?"

"Turns out Coach did go way overboard on the training

schedule. Half the team couldn't even stand up today, so we get the night off." When I focus on him in the rearview mirror, I see the dark circles under his eyes. Usually he's only this exhausted during finals week.

"Well, if you're about to go off on a crime spree, can you at least drop me off at home first? I don't trust my mom to post bail."

"Don't flatter yourself," he taunts as he flips on the radio, keeping his eyes carefully averted from where I'm struggling to pull off my damp skinny jeans. "If I was about to go on a crime spree, you're the last person I'd call."

"Excuse you!" He's lucky I'm pantsless, and therefore in no position to fight back. "I'd be an excellent partner in crime."

Joaquin scoffs, reading something on his phone that he makes sure to keep out of my line of view. "Please. You can't lie to save your life. Ten minutes into an interrogation and you'd rat me out for a cheese sandwich and a ride home."

"Well, is it a grilled cheese or a regular cheese sandwich?"

He ignores my question in favor of paying attention to whatever's on his phone. Meanwhile, I eye the damp notebook I threw onto the seat beside me, my half-written apology mostly smudged away thanks to the sprinklers. I'm a better liar than he gives me credit for, but he's not entirely off base either. I'm definitely quick to break under pressure. All it took was a few unread texts for me to start spilling my guts on paper.

"So, what *is* your plan for tonight, then?" I ask after I've finished changing.

Joaquin waits until I give him a tap on the shoulder, signaling that I'm decent again, to reply. He leans across the console to open the glove compartment, pulling out something that I narrowly catch when he tosses it to me. A black eye mask with the words SLEEPING BEAUTY written in hot-pink gemstones.

"If this is supposed to be an answer, it's not a very good one."

Rather than reply, he throws the car into gear, waiting until we're stopped at a red light down the block to face me.

"We're going on an adventure."

CHAPTER TWELVE

"THE LOST CITY OF ATLANTIS."

My latest guess as to where we're headed is met with a negative buzzer sound from Joaquin. I groan, smacking my head against the headrest like a toddler who was just denied McDonald's.

"C'moooooon, can I at least get a hint?"

"That would be cheating."

Given his insistence on the blindfold, I have zero clues as to where we're headed except that it definitely isn't around the block. At first, I tried to keep track of the time by counting how many songs played on the radio. But he's settled on a station that's more devoted to commercials than songs. I've heard Joaquin humming Whitney Houston and Celine Dion more than actual music. Not for the first time, I desperately wish Herbert had an AUX cord. I can't even switch on one of our mix CDs thanks to me being stuck in the back seat.

I slump as low as I can go, the edge of my seat belt digging into my neck. "Since when does this game have rules?"

"Since I decided it does."

"Pendejo," I mutter under my breath.

He lowers the volume on the ten thousandth commercial for Spill-E, an all-in-one cleaning device, to say, "I heard that, and I'm knocking ten points off your score."

"Wait, there are points now?"

Even if I can't see him, I can sense the joy in his voice and the laughter he's keeping in. Glad he's at least having fun torturing me.

He cranks the volume back up and I resign myself to my fate.

"The Egyptian pyramids?"

"Nope. You lose another five points."

"Oh, fuck off."

This time he doesn't fight the laughter, getting it out of his system before replying, "Don't worry, we're almost there."

By "almost there" he apparently means ten more minutes of the bumpiest drive I've ever experienced. My head almost collides with the roof as we drive over what's either the world's deepest pothole or a gap in the space-time continuum. "Sorry," he mumbles around a hiss. "Rough patch of road."

"Rough patch of road?!" I snap, my stomach bubbling like a chemistry experiment gone wrong. "I almost got decapitated by my seat belt!"

"I promise the surprise is worth having no head!" He reaches back to pat my knee.

Wherever the hell he's taking me, it'd better be made of solid gold.

Thankfully, the last stretch of the journey isn't as nausea-inducing. After one last commercial break, we finally settle to a stop, and the car switches off.

"Ready to lose your mind?" Joaquin asks. I can hear his seat belt unbuckling.

A mixture of nerves and excitement gurgle in my uneasy stomach. "As I'll ever be."

Joaquin carefully guides me out of the back seat, one hand in mine and the other steadying me by the waist. His grip shifts to my shoulders, pushing me forward a few steps before letting go. Pleased with my positioning, he whips off the blindfold with a flourish. "Behold!"

Gazing directly into the afternoon sun after almost an hour of being surrounded by darkness feels like cutting into an onion. I wince, shielding my eyes until the world slowly starts to come into view again. My other senses kick into action while my sight recovers. The sound of bloodcurdling screams whipping through the air. The smell of deep-fried, sugar-coated dough.

"We're going to Dino World?!" I spin to study Joaquin, his lips pressed into a tight line as he tries to suppress another laugh.

"No," he replies. "We're *at* Dino World."

Instead of smacking him for being a smartass, I greedily take in the neon coasters soaring above the pine trees.

"What're we doing here?" I ask without tearing my eyes away from the mother of all coasters—the Tyrannosaurus Death.

Joaquin shrugs. "Promised I'd make it up to you for helping me, didn't I?"

My heart stutters, caught somewhere between my butt and

my throat, unable to process anything that isn't the jumble of feelings this boy brings out of me. When he turns to face me, his dark brown curls glimmer in the light of golden hour.

He offers his hand. "You coming?"

It's hard to look at him, at his smile, and not wish that things between us could be different. That I wasn't falling for someone I love too much to let go. That we might be hours rather than minutes apart next year. That he wasn't falling for Tessa. But I push aside the doubts and insecurities—about me not being enough, about us and who we're destined to be to each other along with the guilt over hiding more than just my feelings from him—and I take his hand.

We both deserve a little happiness.

"No way. Absolutely not. Not in a thousand years."

Joaquin plants his feet firmly on the ground, steady as an oak tree and impervious to my attempts to tug him forward. I loop both of my arms through his crossed ones, pulling with every fiber of my strength, but he doesn't budge.

"Pretty please?" I plead, clasping my hands together and putting on my best pout.

Everyone knows that the Terrordactyl, Dino World's oldest and most iconic coaster with a record-breaking eight inversions, is best enjoyed in pairs of two. That way you don't have to spend the entire ride worried about accidentally barfing on a stranger. Anyone with an intense fear of heights like Joaquin wouldn't want to board a coaster with a 450-foot drop, but there's no way I'm leaving without getting at least one ride in.

Joaquin shakes me off to wave his arms at the coaster. "That thing has more loops in it than my signature!"

"That's what makes it so much fun!"

"That's what makes it a death trap."

I roll my eyes. "No one's died on it, you chicken."

"Yeah, and I'm not gonna be the first." Joaquin marches over to a nearby bench, plopping down and folding his arms again. "Meet me when you're done."

Frowning, I eye the single-rider line. Can't imagine anyone would be too pleased if I heave chunks of my barely digested Snickers bar all over them. My stomach is made of iron—it has to be when you're an adrenaline junkie—but the first inversion of the day always throws me for a loop. Pun intended.

After carefully planning out my next move, I pounce, sliding up to Joaquin with a perfectly crafted pout. The kind that I know always breaks him.

"Quin . . ."

"Nope," he snaps before I've even sat down, not looking up from his phone. "Put away that face. It won't work."

"What if I bought you funnel cake afterward?"

He scoffs. "You think I'm gonna want to eat after surviving that thing? Yeah, don't think so."

Dammit, good point. Despite that, I won't give in that easy. "You wouldn't want to disappoint your very best friend in the entire world, would you?"

"I don't, but I will."

All right, fine. Time to go for the jugular. "Well . . . you wouldn't want your very best friend in the entire world to accidentally let it slip to the rest of the baseball team that you still sleep with a stuffed giraffe?"

That gets his attention, eyes wide as saucers.

"You wouldn't dare," he sneers.

My pout morphs into a vindictive smirk. "Oh, I would."

Our eyes meet, locked in an unblinking war until finally, he gives in. "Fine. But if I die, it's on you."

Other parkgoers shoot us confused glances when I leap off the bench and punch the air. "I'll deliver the finest eulogy you've ever seen. There won't be a dry eye in the house, promise."

I hold up my hand both to seal our agreement with a shake and hoist him off the bench. He groans as he slaps his hand into mine, giving me the drabbest handshake ever before begrudgingly heading toward the line for the Terrordactyl.

Joaquin is as stiff as a statue as I push him through the minimal line. Usually, the summer weekend wait times can be as long as an hour per ride, but thanks to our midweek trip, we're up at the front in no time.

"Ready for the ride of your life?" I tease, whipping out my phone to film him as the ride attendant straps him in, his tomato-red face buried in his hands. He responds by flipping off the camera.

Strapping me in is a significantly easier process since my arms aren't locked in front of my face. Joaquin is trembling like a leaf by the time the rest of the car is loaded up, biting down on his thumb so hard he'll probably draw blood if he doesn't let up soon.

"I hate you I hate you I hate you," he chants under his breath as the car sets into motion, slowly climbing toward the sky for our initial ascent, leading to a hundred-foot drop that goes straight into our first loop.

"Let's do deep breaths," I propose. We have a solid ten seconds before the drop. Maybe if I can distract him with guided meditation, he won't notice how high up in the air we are. "C'mon, in for five." I take the lead, inhaling sharply.

"Shut up," he snaps.

"Wow, okay, no need to be rude."

I spare him any more of my snark and let him live his best anxious life as we climb to the top of the peak. The wind whips through my hair as we overlook Dino World like kings and queens. Beyond the trees and clusters of mile-high coasters, the setting sun has painted the sky soft pinks and purples.

Suddenly, Joaquin takes my hand—linking his fingers through mine in a death grip that would feel painful if it wasn't so exhilarating. His lips are parted when I turn to face him, so close to mine it makes me jump.

"Don't let go," he whispers against the roar of the wind.

This high up, with this boy beside me, the world stretched out in front of us, falling almost feels like flying.

Joaquin survives his experience on the Terrordactyl unscathed, but I can't say the same about my sneakers.

A blond boy in a Power Rangers T-shirt whipped around toward us as soon as the ride docked on the platform. He gave us a once-over, glancing at who must've been his older brother before vomiting on my shoes. Rest in peace, three-year-old Adidas.

"Y'know, this never would've happened if we didn't go on that ride in the first place," Joaquin taunts before popping a piece of funnel cake into his mouth. Vomit or no vomit, I made a promise.

I stick my tongue out at him as I readjust the strap on a pair of brontosaurus-themed sandals I snagged from the gift shop.

Joaquin nudges his plate across the picnic table. "Funnel cake heals all wounds."

"You're thinking of deep-fried Oreos," I reply. No use in passing up the opportunity to annoy him.

He wrinkles his nose before yanking the plate back to his side of the table. "You have no taste."

"Fried Oreos are the most disgustingly amazing creation in American culinary history."

He leans in, eyes narrowed. "If by 'amazing,' you mean the exact opposite, you'd be right."

The last person who should be doling out unsolicited food opinions is Joaquin Romero. Arguably, his most fatal character flaw is that he hates Oreos. What teenager doesn't like cream-filled chocolate cookies? He's practically a serial killer.

Something catches my eye before I can respond to his Oreo slander.

"Photo booth!" I shout, clapping my hands in excitement.

"Photo booth?" Joaquin echoes, scanning the area in confusion.

I take his face in my hands, angling it toward the freshly vacated photo booth a few feet away from us. "Photo booth."

Finally, it clicks for him too. We rush across the dining section to the booth before anyone else can slide in. Normally I keep my expectations low when it comes to photo booths. The lines are always five years long, or the booth is out of service. There's no way we're walking away from a chance to immortalize our teenage good looks on film.

The seat inside of the booth is a tight squeeze. Joaquin shoves his hip against mine, leaving me smushed up against the opposite wall.

"Watch it!" I shove his thigh hard enough to send his never-ending legs out of the booth, his sneakers peeking out under the white curtain.

"Please, Ive, control your jealousy. It's embarrassing. We can't all have long, beautiful legs, and you just have to accept that."

Joaquin starts up the camera's timer, the countdown already down to one before I have time to refocus.

"What the—"

"Say cheese!"

The camera flashes just as I go to jab Joaquin in the shoulder, capturing the moment of calm before the storm. Joaquin loses his shit when the preview image pops up—me mid-attack and him wearing a shit-eating grin. Tears trickle down his cheeks as he cackles like a hyena, his right hand rubbing at where I sucker punched him on the arm.

When the countdown starts again, I gear up for revenge. Shoving my hand in his face, I make sure he's fully edged out of the photo while giving my most picture-perfect smile. The final product—Joaquin fully out of frame except for a single flailing middle finger over my shoulder—is stunning.

"Fine, truce." Joaquin offers up his hand once I release his face.

I narrow my eyes at him, scrutinizing every inch of him for any tricks he may be hiding up his sleeve. The flash goes off, only one picture left until we're done. Reluctantly, I slap my hand into his and accept the bargain.

"Smile!" Joaquin shouts, gripping my hand so tight he knows I won't be able to pull away. His free hand cups my cheek and pulls me in close enough to lick the other cheek, the flash going off right as I let out a squeal.

"You. Are. The. Worst," I mutter as I wipe my face with my sleeve.

"Weird way to say 'you're the best, and I'm constantly in awe of how great you are' but sure."

I huff out of the booth, swiping the two photo strips we— actually, *he*—paid an inhumane $15 for.

I'm only properly facing the camera in one panel—the one where I shoved Joaquin out of frame. But the expression on my face as Joaquin licks my cheek, somewhere between disgust and the purest type of joy, is worth the grossness. I wouldn't change a thing about it. The photo or the moment.

I can already picture it taking prime placement above the bed in my dorm room—wherever that might be. I peek over at him, knots twisting in my stomach at the thought of the future. Rutgers isn't the fresh start I wanted, but it could mean more nights like this one. More nights with *him*.

The lights across the park begin to dim, an unspoken announcement that the End of Day Lightshow is about to start. We keep quiet as the fountains before each ride entrance ignite, spraying Technicolor jets into the air, an explosion of color surrounding us. Lanterns strung along the food stands come to life, bathing our picnic area in a warm peach glow. Above us, fireworks spark across the stars to create patterns and dinosaur outlines, pulling oohs and aahs from every corner of the park.

Behind us, the speaker system crackles. The music switches from an upbeat pop track to something more familiar.

"Isn't this song—"

Joaquin cuts me off by sweeping me off my feet—literally. He lifts me up from my seat like he's gunning to be on the cover of a romance novel, setting me down gently before wrapping an arm around my waist. My head spins, our chests pressed together as he takes my free hand in his and sways to "I Want You to Want Me"—a song Mrs. Romero used to blast almost every time we got into the car.

"What're you doing, dork?" I tease, holding back a giggle as he struggles to follow a basic three-count waltz.

He beams as he guides me along. "This song demands to be danced to."

"If this is you trying to distract me so I won't make you go on the Triscareatops, it won't work."

The hand on my waist comes up to pat my head. "Shhhhh, just sway with me."

While usually I'd quip back, this time I shut up and go with it. His hand returns to my waist, our movements slowing down as we find our rhythm with one another. Cautiously, I lean my head on his shoulder—wait for him to pull away. But he doesn't flinch, just holds me tighter.

The song is as cheesy as I remember, like something straight out of the end of a '90s rom-com. And with the gentle patter of Joaquin's heartbeat against my cheek, I feel like I'm in one.

We stay there, wrapped up in one another, even after the song fades. Fireworks blend into our soundtrack, pops and explosions and cheers as the lights over our shoulders dim from one pastel color to the next. The smells of the park—sweat and popcorn and powdered sugar—fade under the scent clinging to Joaquin's collar. Irish Spring body wash, the lavender dryer sheets his abuela loves, sofrito and cilantro.

The smell of home.

"So, I was thinking . . . ," he says so quiet I almost miss it.

"Mmm . . ." I could keep my hands on his chest, lean into his touch like this, forever.

"What if I asked Tessa to prom here?"

And, just like that, the bubble bursts.

Cracks echo in my ears as the illusion I'd let myself get swept up in shatters. His hands drop, the light show comes to an anti-climactic close, and all that's left is my racing heart.

"W-what?" I ask, reaching up to rub my temple. The whiplash of the topic change leaves me with the first signs of an oncoming headache.

"DeShawn's been asking around if anyone has any ideas for what StuCo should plan for senior skip day next Friday, and I was thinking we could come here." He waves his arms toward the spectacle of rides and games and food vendors behind us. "One of the guys on the team has a cousin who works here. Maybe we could get him to take Tessa on a scavenger hunt thing that ends here before the light show. I could probably ask them to play this song over the loudspeaker too. It'd be perfect, right?!"

What hurts more than the thought of Tessa is the way he still says *we*. As if this is a joint venture, something we're both doing because we're in love with Tessa Hernandez. As if these past few days haven't made me feel like we're less of a *we* than ever. I'm not strong enough to maintain eye contact, the ache in my stomach making me slump. My gaze falls to the photo strip poking out of his pocket.

"Y-yeah. Pretty perfect," I mumble because I don't have it in me to say no. To tell him that I feel like everything is crumbling. To tell him that I'm in love with—

"Sweet," he says, interrupting that dangerous line of thought. "I'll talk to DeShawn tomorrow and see if we can make it work."

He turns away from me and takes in the park with new wonder in his eyes. Clouded by the shimmer of what must be visions of Tessa and her perfect glossy hair and perfect designer minidress kissing him as a dozen fireworks spark.

"This is gonna be epic," he says under his breath.

He's right. It would be the most epic, showstopping promposal of the year, and if Tessa said no, I'm sure half our class will claim to lose their faith in true love.

"It would be," I reply, my voice barely a whisper.

But it's never going to happen.

CHAPTER THIRTEEN

THERE'S NO RETURNING TO normal in the aftermath of Dino World. After I blamed my sudden mood shift on an upset stomach, Joaquin dropped me off at home and sped away with stars in his eyes and Tessa on the brain. With just a week until senior skip day, we've both got to kick our asses into gear. Him, trying to plan out his picture-perfect promposal, and me figuring out how to stop it.

It's impressive how much Joaquin is able to get done so quickly. I scan the itinerary he sent over last night, an hour after dropping me off at home. His plan to have Danny's cousin, Dino World's resident Diana the Diva Dino mascot, escort Tessa around the park, collecting free prizes and funnel cakes along the way, before ultimately leading her to the gazebo at the center of the light show, is pure magic.

And more importantly, it has plenty of opportunities for sabotage.

I take one last look at the itinerary, committing it to memory even though I have plenty of photos of it on my phone, and approach the boy waiting outside the second-floor bathroom for me.

"Are you Jonathan?" I ask, taking a hesitant step back when I spot the guy taking a hit off a Juul as I approach. That's *definitely* not allowed indoors.

The boy—Jonathan—nods and shoves a greasy lock of dark hair beneath his lime-green ALIENS R FOR REAL beanie. I quickly hand him the itinerary and an envelope full of the last of Joaquin's summer job money since Jonathan "doesn't trust money transfer apps." Joaquin would've delivered the goods himself if there wasn't a strict "arrive on time or run five laps" policy in place for his remaining baseball practices.

Jonathan quickly counts the stack of bills, nodding in approval before kicking himself off the wall and tossing his spent Juul pod onto the floor.

With the deal done and dusted, I text Joaquin that the plan is in motion and race toward the auditorium to work on what little set design I can now that I'm free from detention.

And almost run directly into a cow.

Standing in front of the staircase leading down to the auditorium is a real, whole-ass cow, decked out in a pink frilly bonnet and a sash that reads I'M UDDERLY OBSESSED WITH YOU.

"Promposal," Anna explains, walking out of the auditorium with an armful of used paintbrushes. I should've known.

"What's it still doing here?" The cow gives me a thousand-yard stare.

"Turns out cows can't go downstairs, so . . ." Anna shrugs. "Guess they're waiting until his real owner comes and gets him."

I'm sure "no livestock on campus" will be added to the

ever-growing student handbook by the end of the year. Right after "No T-shirt cannons or bees."

"Where were you?" Anna asks with a raised brow. "I thought detention ended ten minutes ago."

"Just handling some stuff for senior skip day," I say, convincingly enough that she doesn't see right through me. I really am getting good at this whole constant lying thing.

Anna nods, and I join her as we walk down the hall to the drinking fountain to clean off the brushes.

"Speaking of which, let me know if you need a ride. My mom's out of town for some health care conference the next two weeks, so I get the car." Anna punctuates the statement by pulling the keys out of her vintage blazer pocket, jangling them with a grin.

"You're actually going?" Not that I'm complaining about having Anna around—she's so against school-sanctioned events I wouldn't have put it past her to skip senior skip day and just stay home.

"That's breaking the cardinal rule of senior year," she says, as if it's obvious, while wiping down the last of the brushes.

"Shouldn't going to prom be the *actual* cardinal rule of senior year?" I ask as we make our way back to the auditorium.

Anna rolls her eyes. "Absolutely not. Senior skip day is a 'fuck you' to the admin while prom is just an excuse to wear overpriced clothes, eat some dry, seasoning-free chicken, and listen to an underpaid DJ play one-hit wonders from when our parents were teenagers. No thank you."

And here I thought *I* was cynical about prom. "Well, for what it's worth, we would've looked super cute."

She leans over to pinch my cheek. "The cutest." Suddenly, her smile falls. "Wait, is this you saying that you're not going to prom too?"

After all my prom-related exploits, definitely not. Dances have never been my thing, though Joaquin and I do have a number of them under our belts. The awkward pictures on the front lawn and the shoes that always pinch and the small talk with people from my classes while Joaquin, someone with actual dance moves, parties it up on the dance floor. Even if my non-existent plan comes together and Joaquin doesn't go with Tessa, who's to say he won't spend the entire night trying to woo her anyway?

Might as well save myself the nausea.

"It's looking a lot like that."

Anna nudges her shoulder against mine. "Maybe we can do something else instead. Order pizza and binge something laughably terrible."

The thought is a bright spot in the storm clouds that have hovered over me this whole week. "It'd be an honor to eat pizza and binge something laughably terrible with you."

Anna grins, tossing a loc over her shoulder. "It's a date."

With our prom night plans in place, we focus on bringing the town of Padua to life onstage. Now that there's just over two weeks left until opening night, all six of us keep our heads down and get to work. The Emilys don't even ask me about Joaquin—a first. We're able to make a decent amount of progress in the hour we have before breaking for the night, enough that I'm no longer feeling like we're in a desperate race against time to do the impossible.

"Need a ride home?" Anna asks as we grab our bags from backstage.

"Nah, I biked here so I should be . . ." I trail off as I take in the flurry of notifications waiting for me on my phone.

Tío Tony: 3 missed calls, 1 voice mail.

Mami: 4 missed calls, 2 voice mails.

Joaquin: 2 missed calls.

Tio Tony:

Are you on your way?

Is everything okay?

Your mother doesn't know where you are either—call us back.

Mami:

Where are you?

Your tío said you missed your shift and haven't responded to any of his messages

Joaquin doesn't know where you are either

CALL ME ASAP

Joaquin:

Dude are you good?

Your mom just called me freaking out

"Shit, shit, *shit!*" I yell, slamming my foot in frustration. In the madness of running off to Dino World and trying to brainstorm potential skip day sabotage, I'd completely forgotten to tell Tío Tony that I'd be at tech crew today instead and wouldn't be able to make it to my closing shift tonight.

"Scratch that, can you drop me off?" Based on how pissed Mami sounds in these messages—and I haven't even opened the voice mails—I can't waste time biking home.

Anna nods, spotting the worry written all over me, and we book it for the parking lot.

"You're amazing, I love you and owe you my firstborn!" I shout to Anna as I pull my bike out of her trunk and run toward my house.

"Hope you don't die!" she calls back, waiting until I've tossed my bike onto the front lawn and busted through the front door like an FBI agent on an arrest mission before driving away.

"Nice of you to finally join us, Ive," Mami says as I trip into the house. She's lingering by the doorway with her arms crossed, still wearing her purple scrubs. Nurse Oatmeal comes racing to the door, barking louder than ever thanks to my graceless entrance.

"I'm so sorry, I—"

Mami holds up a warning finger before I can finish. She crosses over to Nurse Oatmeal, scooping her into her arms and petting her head until she finally stops her tirade in favor of licking Mami's fingers.

"Where have you been?" Mami snaps as soon as the barking subsides.

I'd called and attempted to explain myself during the car ride over, promising that I was safe and heading home, but I guess I'll have to start over again. "I'm sorry, Mami. Our rehearsal schedule got switched up and I forgot to tell Tío Tony."

"What has gotten into you lately?" She plows right past my explanation. "You don't answer my calls, you're replying with one-word answers to my texts. Then your tío tells me you have *three weeks* of detention? You've never had detention before, Ive!"

So much for keeping that from her. Annoyance surges through me like an electric current, my fingers clenching into fists, my teeth grinding together as I use every ounce of my energy not to unload. Telling her that this is only the second time she's been around when I got home in a month isn't going to help my case. Though the fact that she might only be here because she thought I'd disappeared does hurt enough to make my eyes start to burn with unshed tears.

"I'm calling your tío," she says before setting down the dog and grabbing her phone. "I can't have you working until ten o'clock at night when you're distracted like this. School comes first."

The threat of losing my only source of income creates the first crack. "Mami, please, I need this job," I plead, rushing to stand in front of her, anger cooled now that I have to beg her for mercy. I'm not above getting onto my knees if I have to. "The detention thing was just a misunderstanding, I swear."

She raises a micro-bladed brow. "Oh, so they're giving out detentions for misunderstandings now?"

"It's not . . ." I exhale sharply, willing my voice not to crack despite the tightness in my throat. "I took the fall for a friend so they wouldn't get an even harsher punishment."

The explanation softens her expression slightly, but her mouth is still pressed into a tight line. "You shouldn't be putting yourself in those types of situations in the first place, Ivelisse."

How the hell was I supposed to know Joaquin's innocent promposal was gonna catch on fire?

"You can't start getting into trouble this close to the finish line," Mami continues. "What if Rutgers heard about this? You don't just have a free ticket to act up; there can still be consequences."

"I don't want to go to Rutgers."

The words slip out without me even realizing I've said them, so quiet I wonder if I just imagined them. But Mami's expression is definitely real.

"What?"

Immediately, I regret saying anything. Especially now. This is a conversation I knew we'd have at some point, but did I really have to blurt it out while she's already pissed as hell?

"I . . . I don't want to go to Rutgers," I choke out. I urge myself to calm down before continuing, my voice surer this time. "Because I got into Sarah Lawrence."

Days of confusion and guilt fall away when I say the words out loud. I don't want to go to Rutgers. I've known that since the day I got in, but I was too afraid to face it. For once, I want to take a risk. It could be lonely, and hard, and not at all what I pictured, but I'm willing to try. Because I'm tired of fading into the background.

Mami appears completely perplexed. Which, fair. I definitely threw a curveball at her. "That's great, Ive, but why are you just telling me about this now?" She rubs her temples. "Isn't the deposit due next week?"

"I tried to tell you, but . . ." I can't find the right words to soften the blow.

"But what?" Mami snaps when I take too long to respond.

"But you're never here!" I finally say, the words pouring out of me like water through cracks in a dam. "You've been blowing me off to go on dates for *months*, and then when you're actually home you spring this Rutgers merch on me, so I didn't say anything because I didn't want to get into a fight the one night I had with you!"

Mami takes a step back, as if I pushed her, her face a mixture of shock and anger. Nurse Oatmeal attempts to keep the peace, standing directly between us.

"You don't understand how hard I work," Mami spits out, voice low and hard and bitter. "To pay for this house, for food, for you to be able to even go to college. I have *always* put you first in everything that I do."

"I never said you don't work hard," I reply quickly. And I never would. Mami has always been the hardest-working person I know but that doesn't change what the real problem is. "If you weren't home because of work, that'd be one thing, but I've been eating dinner by myself for weeks because you're meeting Doug or Paul or whoever the hell it is this month. I'm not distracted. I'm *tired*, Mom. I'm tired of running around every day, trying to make everyone happy, and feeling like I'm failing instead. I'm tired of wondering if I'm ever going to see you.

And I'm really effing tired of coming home to an empty house. *That's* why I don't want to answer when you call. Because you're just gonna tell me you're not coming home. Again." She opens her mouth, probably to scold me, but I plow through to my next thought. "And even if I *was* distracted, how would you know? It's not like you're ever here to find out anyway!"

My body heaves, loaded with all the things I haven't said yet and the weight of the things I have. I half expect her to whip a chancla out of thin air and throw it at me like every Latina matriarch, but Mami stays quiet, stunned. Staring down at me with something in her eyes that I can't read. Something far worse than disappointment.

"Don't ever speak to me that way again. I'm your *mother*," she spits, literally, and points a pink fingernail at me.

Common sense tells me to play nice and beg for forgiveness. I can't take back what I've already said, but I can stop myself from saying anything else I regret. But I don't, I just let out another bitter, hollow laugh. "Yeah, well, it definitely doesn't feel like you are anymore."

I regret it the second the words leave my mouth, my shoulders hunching forward as if to snatch them back and swallow them down. But it's too late, they've left their mark on Mami like a slap across the cheek.

And the worst part is, a part of me likes it.

"You get back here right now!" Mami shouts at me when I turn on my heel and head for my room. I don't stop. I just need to close the door and she'll leave me alone. I don't even process the squeak of her sneakers against the floor until she grabs me by the arm and whips me around. "You don't walk away when I'm speaking to you!"

"No!" I wrench my arm out of her grip. Tears cloud the shape of her, but I can picture her clearly. Red in the face, wavy flyaway hairs breaking free from her bun, her lips slightly parted like she's going to break out into a scream. "You don't get to decide you want to bail on being a parent five nights a week! That's not how this works. It's not a part-time job."

"Enough!" she shouts so loud her voice makes the ceiling lamp rattle. "You don't understand what it's been like for me since your father left. How lonely it's been."

"He left me too!" The tears fall freely now, streaming down my cheeks, clinging to my chin. "And I always thought things were fine because I still had you. But these days it feels like you can't wait to leave me too."

With that, I close the last of the distance between me and my room and slam the door with all of the anger I have left.

CHAPTER FOURTEEN

I DON'T BOTHER TO lock my door. Not that it matters since Mami doesn't come after me. The silence hurts the most—that she has nothing left to say to me. The house is eerily quiet. The same as it's been for months, but this time Mami is just down the hall.

Listening to music helps. I'm too emotionally fragile to focus on homework, so I bury my face in my pillows and listen to "Can't Take My Eyes Off You" enough times that I can easily sing along with the lyrics before I move onto the digital version of Joaquin's "Driving with Ive" mix CD (the only music we listen to in the car that's from this decade) and lose myself in the memories of a thousand car rides.

A flash of light snaps me out of my daze, so bright I wince. The ray is gone as quickly as it appeared, only to reappear seconds later. And then disappear just as quickly. And then reappear. On repeat, four times.

I dig myself out of my blanket cocoon and walk on my knees

over to the window beside the edge of my bed. Across the darkness of our backyards, Joaquin waves from his bedroom window, flashlight in hand.

"What're you doing?" I mouth. He makes a gesture I don't understand before sighing and showing me his phone, pointing to the screen.

Vaguely getting the message, I reach for my phone, waving it for him to see. Within seconds, I have a new text.

sorry thought you might be grounded

wasn't sure if you had your phone

I snuggle back under the covers, letting myself get comfortable before replying.

nope, still a free (wo)man

For now, at least.

why did you think I was grounded?

Three dots pop up more times than I can count. I'm prepared to call him out on it when a response finally comes through.

macaw

Oh shit. It's been at least two years since Joaquin pulled the macaw card—a secret code word we came up with when we were ten because we thought it sounded funny. Macaw means you drop everything, no questions asked. We each get one a year—a rule we came up with to stop ourselves from abusing our respective macaw privileges. I already used mine on one of the many nights I came home to discover an empty house, a note on the kitchen table from Mami telling me not to wait up, and her room a disaster of abandoned date-night outfit options.

I type out *you okay?* before realizing that's against the macaw rules. You don't have to have a reason for using macaw, and that's half the beauty of it. If he wants to tell me, he will.

> all right, what's the plan?

His reply comes almost instantly.

> meet me outside in 10

Double shit. I'm not officially grounded, but I might as well be. Either way, sneaking out definitely won't help whatever Mami and I have going on between us right now. But . . . you don't say no to a macaw text. It's against the Joaquin and Ivelisse Code of Ethics. Freshman year, Joaquin left midway through one of his baseball games to come meet me after I used my macaw on figuring out a way to keep Mami from finding out that I'd flunked my first ever midterm.

We always show up. *Always.*

Wiping off my cheeks and running a comb through my hair,

I grab my purse and an emergency bag of candy—you never know what you'll need when a macaw text comes along—and crack open my window as delicately as I can. I don't make a habit of sneaking out—mostly because I hardly have anywhere to sneak out to—but the window is my safest bet. Mami is hopefully asleep, and I just have to make sure I don't accidentally step on one of the neighborhood raccoons.

As promised, Joaquin is waiting for me in his driveway, leaning against the hood of his car. He's dressed up, by his standards, wearing a pair of black jeans and an open flannel as opposed to sweats and a muscle tee. Suddenly I feel underdressed for the occasion in my knock-off Lululemon tights and purple hoodie.

"So, I was thinking—"

I press a finger to his lips, hushing Joaquin and pointing back at my place. The windows are still dark. If Mami heard us, she's not coming to get me . . . yet.

Joaquin nods in understanding, opening the passenger side door for me.

"As I was saying," he says once we're in the insulated safety of Herbert, Janet Jackson playing on Joaquin's go-to '90s radio station. "Slushie time? We still haven't tried out that place in Hamilton."

"Your wish is my command . . . or, well, your command since you're the one driving . . . but yes. Slushie time." Another rule about the macaw card—the card puller gets final say. Even if I wasn't in the mood for slushies, I wouldn't have the right to tell him. Tonight is about Joaquin and whatever emotional turmoil he's going through.

Huh. Two breakdowns in two different houses on the same night? I'll have to ask Anna if there's a planet in retrograde or something.

We're quiet for the short drive, Joaquin insisting we blast the CD of my favorite songs even though this is *his* crisis outing. The bright red date on the dashboard clock glares at me. One week until Joaquin attempts to prompose to Tessa for the fourth time and I still haven't thought of a way to stop it, other than loosening a screw on the Ferris wheel and causing mass hysteria. I rest my head on the window, away from the clock. My eyes close, and I try not to let the thought of Tessa taking my spot in the passenger seat consume me.

A knock on the window jolts me back into consciousness.

"C'mon, sleepyhead." Joaquin opens the door carefully, making sure I'm not going to slump out of my seat. He turns around once I'm out of the car, offering his back for a ride.

"I can walk on my own, Quin."

"Don't care. This is my macaw day, and I demand that you let me give you a piggyback ride."

I let out a sound somewhere between a scoff and a laugh. "Whatever floats your boat, weirdo."

Joaquin snaps his fingers, urging me to hustle. "Let's go, I'm not getting any younger."

I roll my eyes and pick up the pace. I wrap my arms around his shoulders, waiting until I'm sure my grip is solid before leaping the rest of the way. His hands catch me halfway, hoisting me up by the backs of my thighs.

"Satisfied?" I whisper once we're settled, my chest flush to his back, our cheeks pressed together.

"Extremely," he replies, and I can feel his lips tug into a smile.

Being the generous, and very strange, soul he is, Joaquin does me the honor of carrying me up to the to-go counter of Blastoff Burger. Once the cashier returns to their post after handing off an order, I tap Joaquin to put me down.

"Nope, you go ahead and order from here," he insists, tightening his grip on my legs.

My cheeks flare at the thought of human interaction while wrapped around my best friend like a spider monkey. "What? Why?"

He grins mischievously. "Because I think it's funny."

I go to jam the heel of my foot into his side, but he readjusts me before I can, tossing me into the air like a sack of flour and catching me just as easily.

"Hi!" Joaquin greets the cashier while I'm disoriented. "My friend here is ready to order." He pinches the side of my leg with a smirk so cocky it should be illegal.

I sigh. "Can we get two large slushies, one blue raspberry and one lime? And mozzarella sticks."

Joaquin gawks at my having the audacity to order his two least favorite slushie flavors, and least favorite side. "You dare disrespect me like this? On *my* macaw day?"

I ignore him and hand over my debit card. "Not my fault you're so picky."

"Blue raspberry isn't even a real flavor. Something can't taste blue."

I brush off his protests with a smirk of my own. "Guess you should've ordered, then."

Instead of admitting defeat like a mature eighteen-year-old would, he lets go of my legs and drops me like a hot potato.

Like a fish gasping for air, I cling to Joaquin for dear life. He stumbles back just as my legs hit the ground, our limbs tangling together as we struggle to get our footing. We never do, both of us tripping over ourselves until we collapse on top of each other.

On top of each other. As in me on top of him. Horizontally.

His arms are locked around my waist from where he grabbed me as we fell, flipping us around so he took the brunt of the impact, his fingertips uncomfortably close to the edge of my hoodie.

I brace my hands against his chest, my heart racing as we both blink rapidly through the shock. Our chests rise and fall together, our breath mingling in the barely-there space between us. Close enough for me to smell his peppermint ChapStick.

His eyes find mine, wide and filled with something that might be terror. His lips part, but the words are caught in his throat. Everything I should say has gone out the window, and everything I want to say feels too dangerous to utter out loud.

It'd be so easy to close the distance. To do the one thing my heart wants, but my brain won't let me. It would only take one inch to change everything.

"Can y'all move?"

The cashier pokes his head out of the to-go window, pulling off one side of his headset as if that'll help him glare harder at us.

Joaquin and I go as red as the bag in the cashier's hand, jumping to our feet so quickly it makes my head spin. "Sorry, yeah, thanks," I mumble incoherently as I struggle to wipe dirt and grass off my hoodie and grab the slushies at the same time.

A twentysomething couple hovering beside us cover their grins behind their hands, waiting patiently until we've collected our order and left the cashier a ten-dollar bill as a tip to step up and place their order.

"You okay?" Joaquin asks as we head back to his car.

"No, I'm mortified," I say with a groan. "This moment is going to come back to haunt me in the middle of the night for the next forty years."

"I meant, did you get hurt?" he clarifies with an unusually somber expression. "Like, in the fall."

"Oh." The lack of humor on his face throws me for a loop. Normally he'd quip back with some one-liner about how I have worse things to be embarrassed about. Which I do. "'M fine. You?"

"Probably a bruised butt, but I'll live." This time there's a hint of humor, and the pressure in my chest eases up.

We sit cross-legged on the hood of his car, spreading our bounty between us. Joaquin pokes at the blue raspberry slushie like it's a suspicious unlabeled package before taking a cautious first sip. His entire face screws up like he just swallowed a dozen lemons.

"Disgusting. Absolutely disgusting."

"You're such a baby," I tease, knocking my knee against his and swiping the cup out of his hand.

A piercing, sour taste rushes through me the second the slushie hits my tongue. My face scrunches up just like his, unable to resist the shock of the unexpected flavor. "Okay, never mind, you're right. That's vile."

Joaquin waves his arms in a way that screams "I told you so" without actually saying it.

We set aside the noxious blue raspberry in favor of the lime—which, somehow, is nowhere near as sour as the blue raspberry is. Even combining our slushies together doesn't do anything to save the overpowering flavor of the blue raspberry. Definitely not shimmy worthy.

"All right," I announce after we've taken a few sips, pulling out my phone and opening the Notes app. "What's your ranking?"

Joaquin takes one more sip before making his final judgment, swirling the plastic cup around like a sommelier. "I'm feeling generous. Four."

"Very generous indeed," I reply, adding Blastoff Burger to the location column, and adding Joaquin's rating to his column. I reach for his cup, taking another sip to be sure before giving my ranking. "The blue raspberry is trash, but the lime isn't half bad. And I've gotta give 'em props for having this many flavors. Four and a half."

Joaquin nods in agreement as I add my own rating to the final column. "Sorry this place turned out be a dud."

I shrug. "I mean, it probably would've been better if I ordered flavors we actually like." He lets out a soft, quiet laugh.

"And *I'm* the one who should be sorry. We wasted your macaw on a place that kinda sucks." I hold up a rubbery mozzarella stick with my phone-free hand. Neither of us are huge fans of deep-fried cheese, but these are thin, chewy, and an insult to mankind.

"Okay, now that we've sampled all our contenders, the winner is . . ." I scroll through our list. "Marco's. Shocker."

Iggy's Ices put up a commendable fight, but no one stands a chance against Marco's—the only establishment we gave tens across the board. Sure, it's probably the sentimentality speaking, but it really is a damn good slushie.

"All hail the champion," Joaquin says with a smile as he leans back against the car's windshield, gazing up at the full moon. After a beat, I join him, carefully situating myself so I'm not leaning against Herbert's wipers.

"Can I tell you a secret?" Joaquin asks once I'm settled.

"You're a flat earther?" He gives me a confused frown. "What? That's exactly the type of thing you'd want to keep a secret."

He rolls his eyes. Then he stays quiet for so long I start to wonder if he's actually waiting for permission to tell me, or if I've ruined the moment by making a joke out of it. I open my mouth to apologize when he finally speaks up again.

"I heard you. And your mom. Earlier." The words come out in clipped staccato, as if he's measuring out each syllable before he says it.

An uncomfortable chill runs through me at the thought of anyone, but especially him, hearing my blowup with Mami. "How much of it?" I ask, not that it matters. The entire debacle was a shitshow.

"Most of it," he answers sheepishly. "I got back early from practice and saw you throw your bike down out front. I thought something might've happened since you weren't answering your phone, or you needed help, so I came running over, and . . . well . . . your voice, uh . . . carries."

"Oh." So much for keeping my baggage to myself tonight.

"If you don't want to talk about it, forget I said anything," Joaquin offers quickly, waving his hands in the air like he's sweeping away the fact that he even brought this up in the first place. "We can go back to roasting these shitty slushies."

He says that last part a little louder than he should. Over his shoulder, the cashier narrows his eyes. Guess the cashier must be the manager—who else would care about some teenagers not liking your product? Joaquin must feel them boring into his back, making him turn with a wave. "Food's great!" he calls out, as if that'll make the situation any better.

It does make me snort, though.

"Guess Abuela has a point about me not having an inside voice," Joaquin mumbles as he turns back around.

"Well, you know I can relate," I reply. Apparently, my voice is loud enough to carry outside of an entire house.

Joaquin scoots closer to me, the two of us pressed shoulder to shoulder. "You sure you're okay?"

I nod. "Yeah." The thought of the argument threatens a fresh wave of tears—seems I'm not as cried out as I thought I was—the memory of Mami, heartbroken and furious, swimming through my blurry vision. "I just lost it."

My voice cracks on the last syllable, and I use every ounce of strength I have not to let the tears fall this time. Not here, not now, not when this entire outing is supposed to be about Joaquin. "Things have been . . . a lot lately. With things at home and school and work and . . . y'know."

No need to mention the emotional whiplash of trying to help him orchestrate his fairy-tale ending with Tessa while I grapple with my own complicated feelings about him. And, thankfully, Joaquin doesn't press.

"You deserve a break," he says, reaching over to take my hand and squeeze it. "Think you can survive two more months of school? Then it's slushie adventures and day trips to Marco's for three full months, baby," he sings with a pleased smile and a wave of his hand. "And then you'll abandon us small townies for New York."

The absurdity of his voice keeps the tears at bay, a watery laugh bubbling up inside of me. "Says the one who's abandoning *me* to live your best life in San Juan."

Joaquin stiffens at the mention of the trip, his cheeks visibly pink even in the darkness. Suddenly, he's become fascinated by the moon again. "I'm not going to Puerto Rico," he says.

"What?! Did something happen?" I gasp. "Wait. Is your abuela okay?" I whisper as quietly as I can, as if speaking the words out loud will manifest something terrible into existence.

"Everything's fine," Joaquin reassures, his tone casual enough that I release the tension in my shoulders. "It's . . . not a good time. Isabella just found out she got this internship she applied to, so she's going to stay in DC over the summer. Plus, Abuela's vertigo has gotten worse this year, so we don't think a three-hour plane ride would be the best idea and leaving her here alone isn't really an option . . . Maybe next year."

He tries to shrug it off like it's no big deal. Except I know him. That he's valiant, and selfless, and puts everyone and their mother before him. It doesn't matter that he's been excited about this trip all year—so much so that he has that countdown on his phone—or that things haven't been the same for him since his mom and Isabella left.

"But my mom and I can keep an eye on her!" I offer, already brainstorming how we could watch Doña Carmen over the summer. Sure, Mami and I might not be on speaking terms right now, but nothing mends bridges like banding together to take care of your favorite viejita. "My mom can check on her before work, and I can when I'm back from my shifts. Nurse Oatmeal's useless, but at least she can keep your abuela company during the day too."

It's not a perfect plan, but it's solid. We may not be Doña Carmen's doting, beloved grandson, but we're a second family.

"I can't ask you to do that," he says with a shake of his head. "Not after everything you've already done for me."

Over the past fifteen years of knowing each other, we've done a thousand favors for one another. He's sat through dozens of plays and musicals, let me sit on his shoulders at every parade we've been to, and stayed up until 2:00 a.m. making me a three-layer cake for my quinceañera after the allergen-free baker we'd hired dropped out the night before the party. And I've made him flash cards for midterms he was sure he'd fail, sat in the stands of every one of his games, and driven two states over and back just to get him a pair of sneakers he'd desperately wanted for his birthday.

I'd do all of those things again, and a thousand more, if they made him smile.

"But you're not asking me to do anything," I tell him. "I'm offering, huge difference."

"Thank you, but it's fine, seriously." He turns his head, raising a brow. "Unless you're just desperate to get rid of me this summer?"

I throw my hands up in defeat. "You got me."

He chuckles softly, ramming his shoulder against mine hard enough that I nearly topple off the side of the car. Before I can fall, his arm wraps around mine and narrowly guides me away from the edge.

"You'll be hearing from my lawyer," I mutter in mock outrage once he lets go, his fingers leaving an explosion of goose bumps where they brushed against my bare skin. "Will Isabella at least come home for the beginning of her summer vacation? Prom wouldn't be the same without her roasting you for whatever you decide to wear."

My laugh dies when Joaquin shakes his head. "She starts this week," he mumbles.

"Well . . . what about for your game next week? That's on a Saturday, she can just come for the day."

He shrugs sheepishly. "Guess she forgot. I didn't really mention it either, since she's been busy with . . . y'know. College stuff. Hanging out with her friends down there." He peeks up at me from beneath his miles-long lashes. "Promise you won't forget me when you have all your cool Sarah Lawrence friends?"

He tries to keep his tone light, but the hurt in his voice is so strong it cuts right through me. There's no world where I ever forget him, no lifetime where he's not at the center of mine.

"I could never forget you."

I'm not sure about much of anything when it comes to the future, but I can be sure about that.

His smile is warm but fleeting, and I fight back the urge to hold his hand. As he turns away from me, I realize Isabella staying in DC means no one from his family'll be at the championship game. Doña Carmen would go if she could, obviously, but she's at an age where she can't handle sitting on those rock-hard bleachers for an entire game. How can the star that led the team to the championship look out into the crowd and not see any of his family there? Some last hurrah.

"Is that why we're here?" I ask before I can stop myself, breaking macaw rule number one—no questions asked.

Joaquin doesn't answer immediately, shaking his head before replying. "No." I wait for him to elaborate, and when he doesn't, I shift onto my back, ashamed for asking.

"I thought you could use it," he says several seconds later.

For what feels like the hundredth time tonight, I turn to him in shock. "What?"

He shrugs. "After the whole thing with your mom, I thought you could use a night out. If you weren't grounded for life."

The sweetness of the gesture flies over my head, my pea brain only able to focus on the sanctity of this silly tradition we came up with when we thought bird sounds were the height of comedy. This is who Joaquin is. He'll give up anything if it makes someone else's life easier. If it makes someone else happy. "But you only get one—you can't waste it on me!"

"I didn't waste it, Ive." He leans in, eyes on mine, and tucks a stray piece of hair behind my ear. "I got to spend tonight with you."

His hand lingers on the nape of my neck for a moment. Before I can speak, he reaches for the blue raspberry slushie and leaves me breathless and shivering. His face contorts for a second time, his tongue now stained blue.

"Nope. Still tastes like battery acid."

While he dumps the rest of the slushie onto the ground—carefully out of the cashier's line of view—I'm left with the enormity of what just unlocked inside of me.

That I don't care if what I'm feeling could ruin anything. That all I want is to take his hand and hold him close and lose myself in his eyes. That I love him in a new way.

And I think I'm ready to tell him.

CHAPTER FIFTEEN

I COULD'VE TOLD HIM then. I *should've* told him. If there's anything that's ever screamed "Joaquin and Ivelisse's perfect moment," it's us sitting on the hood of his car in a parking lot
critiquing slushies. It could've been a fantastic metaphor for our
entire friendship: how Elmwood is as dull as dirt, but having
Joaquin here makes it worthwhile. That, when we're together,
watching cars head somewhere more interesting can feel exciting. Like the best kind of adventure.

But I didn't.

I thought I was ready, the words locked and loaded, but I
couldn't find the strength for that final push. The doubts that've
been swimming through my head since that afternoon at Marco's
came back full force. Thoughts about how Joaquin doesn't feel
the same, or how we'd never work out as more than friends, or
how the Joaquins of the world never wind up with the Ivelisses.
How, even if we might work out, we're doomed for disaster once

I'm two hours away. I already have one failed relationship with an uber-popular guy under my belt—do I really want to lose the most important person in my life for a chance at a second, probably short-lived romance?

It took the rest of the week and a mental slap in the face to get out of my head. I can't keep acting like a baby, running away from my emotions. If I'm brave enough to uproot my entire life for a gut feeling and a chance to start over with a clean slate, I can be brave enough to do this. Start taking chances now, instead of just in the fall.

Clearly these feelings aren't just fading away like I was hoping they would, and unless I want to spend my last few months with Joaquin feeling like I'm on the brink of exploding, I have to be honest with him.

And now I have approximately twenty minutes to either get my shit together and tell him how I feel or watch him prompose to Tessa in front of the entire senior class and every patron of Dino World.

I leap from my seat on the bench across from the employee area when Jonathan finally appears, decked out in his Diana the Diva Dino costume, sans the head. It'd be an unsettling image if I wasn't on a mission.

"Hey!" I call out to him, not getting his attention until I'm blocking his path.

"Oh." He glances up from his bag of Takis. "Hey. I'm going to meet that Tessa chick, like you said."

"Great. There's been a change of plans, though. Joaquin needs you to bring her here instead." I pull a map of Dino World out of my pocket, opening it and pointing to the bright red circle I marked on the far-right edge. "Tell her to go through the whole thing, and he'll be waiting on the other side."

"Uh. Okay."

While my gut doesn't totally trust Jonathan not to screw this up, I don't have time to hold his hand and make sure he gets Tessa to the Haunted Hadrosaurus, all the way on the opposite side of the park from where Joaquin'll be waiting. Even if she speed-walks through the warehouse outfitted to look like a pre-historic nightmare, it'll buy me at least an extra half hour.

Wasting Joaquin's money on a promposal that's bound to be ruined does make the guilt harder to swallow. I try to tell myself it'll be worth it as I head back toward the bathrooms, where I told Anna I'd meet her after I conspicuously slid away while she waited in line for a turkey leg. Tessa will get the scare of her life, and if I don't make a total ass out of myself by telling Joaquin how I feel, he'll still walk away with a prom date by the end of the night.

Except I still have no idea what to say.

"So," I say to my reflection in the bathroom mirror. "I know we're best friends and that this might complicate things a little bit. Or a lot. But I . . . like you. I mean, of course I like you, you're my best friend, I mean I love you—like, romance movie love, not cousin love. Not that I think you're like my cousin, I mean—"

No. Nope. Terrible. I take a breath, tap the ELMWOOD SUCKS sticker on the corner of the bathroom mirror twice for luck, and start again.

"Joaquin. Good evening."

Fuck no. I sound like a Victorian vampire.

My entire body slumps until my forehead quietly thumps against the mirror.

This is impossible.

How do you sum up over a decade of friendship and two weeks (or, possibly even longer—who knows how long this has been just sitting inside of me) of not-just-friendship feelings into a succinct monologue that's swoony, complimentary, and not completely embarrassing?

A slam makes me jump, and I momentarily wonder if the answer has come to me via an indoor bolt of lightning. But nope, it's just a middle-aged blond woman and a toddler with puke down their shirt. I rub at the red spot on my forehead from where I was pressed up against the mirror, suddenly regretting getting that close to it. Nothing in an amusement park is sanitary.

I wait on a bench outside the bathroom for fifteen minutes until Anna returns, turkey leg in hand. "You throw up?" she asks in between wolfish bites.

"No, I'm fine."

"You sure?" She raises an eyebrow before waving her turkey leg at me. "You don't exactly look it."

Fair point. Between running around looking for Jonathan and panicking about having to confess my feelings, I'm not exactly at my best. And since I don't carry makeup around with me like a rational teenager, and Anna's on an all-natural kick right now, I'm stuck the way I am. Frizzy baby curls galore thanks to the unexpected spring humidity, and ghostly pale due to my lack of appetite this morning.

You can't blame me, though. Confessing your love for your best friend is a lot to deal with on a Friday night.

"I'm fine, promise," I reassure her, wiping my clammy hands on my jeans. "Have you seen Joaquin?"

My texts letting him know we were here went unanswered, which I'd half expected. Joaquin made plans to head over early with the rest of the baseball team to scope things out—serve as the unofficial welcome wagon for any Cordero senior brave enough to skip class.

Anna shakes her head, both of us scanning the crowd. She offers me a bite of her turkey leg, which I decline. Taking a hunk out of a massive piece of roasted meat probably isn't in my best interest right now.

"Let's go on some rides first. The lines always get super packed before closing," Anna proposes, jutting her chin toward the growing line for the Brontosoarus. "We can meet up with him later."

"No!" I reply too urgently, her sauce-stained mouth tugging into a suspicious frown. Jonathan's probably almost done with Tessa's mini-tour of the park, which means Joaquin must be getting into position at the gazebo. I recover quickly, gesturing to Anna's half-eaten turkey leg. "Finish your meat leg. I'll find Joaquin and be back in twenty." Or less. Or more. Depending on how things go.

Anna shoots me a questioning gaze. "First off, I could finish this in two minutes. Tops. Second of all, what's up?" She crosses her arms, careful to keep her turkey leg a safe distance from her mustard-yellow MERCURY IS IN GATORADE crop top.

"Nothing's up," I insist. My attempt to walk past her is swiftly blocked by her standing in my path.

She waves her turkey leg like a weapon, preventing me from making a run for it unless I want to take a bone to the head. "You've been acting like you're a minute away from passing out since I picked you up."

I exhale slowly. "I need to talk to Joaquin about something."

Anna's lips part, and her grip slackens so much her turkey leg almost tumbles to the ground. "You're gonna tell him," she says, breathless. Before I can ask what she means, her eyes bulge to the size of the $10 lollipops in the gift shop. "Holy shit, it's finally happening!"

"What're you talking about?"

She shoves my shoulder gently. "You're finally telling him you're in love with him!"

"I . . . I . . . What? How did you know?" I ask in as quiet a whisper as I can muster, worried that one of our classmates overheard her.

"Uh, hello, it's obvious."

When I don't respond with anything except a puzzled expression, she takes the liberty of explaining. "Say whatever you want about how 'you really are just friends' and 'you'd never thought of him that way until now' or any of the hundreds of other excuses I'm sure you're trying to come up with right now but know this . . ." She pauses for dramatic effect. "Whether you knew it or not, you have been head over heels for that boy since the day I met you."

My throat goes dry as the Sahara Desert, unable to choke

out the dozens of questions I have for her. "Why didn't you say anything? If you knew this whole time?"

"Because that's not my business," she replies casually. "Don't you watch rom-coms? No one ever tells the protagonist they've got it bad for the love interest. They have to figure it out for themselves. Or else, where's the fun?"

"So you waited *four years* for me to figure it out?"

"To be fair, I didn't think you were going to figure it out until after college," she says. "Do the whole 'see other people, go through your own heartbreak, then find your way back to each other over the summer' thing. Very cliché. Very Hallmark."

While the reassurance that my emotions aren't just some jealous, spiteful part of me trying to sabotage Tessa at the expense of my friendship is validating, it doesn't ease any of my nerves. If anything, it makes them worse. We've already dated different people before. Sure, both instances were brief and not exactly sweeping romances for the ages, but why didn't we find our way to each other then, if that was all we needed to realize who was standing right in front of us? More importantly, if it's always been this obvious how I feel, does Joaquin know too? And if so, that opens a door to a nebulous world of possibilities.

Mainly, that he doesn't feel the same way about me.

The thought of Joaquin shutting me down makes my knees weak, a startling cold seeping through the humidity and deep into my bones. Anna notices the shift in my posture, the way I hunch in on myself.

"This is a good thing," Anna reassures me, gently gripping

my shoulders. "Being honest is *always* a good thing. No matter what comes next."

I want to ask her how she knows, but a piercing velociraptor roar startles us both. The roar subsides, a cheery voice blaring through the PA system to announce that the light show will begin in fifteen minutes.

"It's go time," Anna announces, taking my hand and pulling me into the crowd.

We almost lose each other in the sea of parents, children, and classmates, our hold on each other so tight Anna's violet coffin nails leave marks on the back of my hand. Like the pep rally, we're able to make it through the throng of bodies mostly unscathed but drenched in sweat. For a fleeting instant, I almost wish I'd taken a shot of Raspberry Unicorn for strength. Anna hops onto a nearby bench, shielding her eyes from the glare of the setting sun as she scans the crowd.

"Found him!" She lets out an excited squeak before hopping off the bench and bustling me toward the right side of the park. It doesn't take long for me to see Joaquin too. Alone, solid as an anchor as crowds come and go around him, in front of the Ferris wheel instead of at the gazebo like he'd originally planned. He's dressed up for the occasion, wearing black jeans and a white button-down rolled up to his elbows. His jaw seems sharper, too, more defined. Like he was carved by the angels themselves. I swallow hard. He's unbelievably beautiful, and I can't believe it took me this long to notice.

"Maybe I shouldn't do this," I mumble, already prepared to head back the way we came.

"Oh no, no, no." Anna hooks an arm around my shoulders, yanking me forward before I can make it more than five feet. "No chickening out."

She tries to push me forward, but I'm rooted in place, terror keeping my limbs locked. "What if he doesn't feel the same way?" I ask under my breath, a question I don't expect her to have an answer to but need to purge from my brain regardless.

"Then he doesn't," she replies calmly. "But at least you'll know."

I could remain standing here and try to decode the sadness in her voice, the way her hands tighten around me as she says it. But this isn't about prying truths out of her, and with every minute I waste wondering if this is the right decision, I'm one step closer to losing my chance for good.

"Okay," I say after what feels like an eternity of watching Joaquin scour the crowd for someone I know isn't me and start heading toward him.

Each step feels like a thousand miles. Closing the short few yards of distance shouldn't take as long as it does, but the voice that's plagued me since Joaquin came home from spring break ramps up to full volume as I let my body carry me forward. *This is a mistake, he'll never feel the same way, if he did he would've told you by now, he'll be happier with someone else.* Taunts and doubts on loop, overlapping one another until I can't think straight. But when he finally turns to see me, my mind goes quiet.

"Hey." A smile breaks out across my face as our eyes meet, the worry melting off me. It's impossible not to feel weightless when he looks at me, my body rushing to close the last bit of distance as I wait for that same smile to take over him too. The one that feels like he's reserved just for me.

But it never comes.

His lips tug into a frown as I finally reach him, his sharp jaw clenched as if he's been gritting his teeth. Everything about him becomes startlingly unfamiliar. The balled fists and locked shoulders, his warm brown eyes turned dark and cold.

"Are you okay?" I ask, quickly scanning him for any signs of what might've gone down.

He doesn't respond, shifting his steely gaze away from me to somewhere off in the distance. "Did something hap—"

"You told Jonathan to take Tessa to the Haunted Hadrosaurus?" Joaquin cuts off my question with one of his own.

The harshness of his voice catches me off guard, the boom of it knocking me back like a shove. "How did—"

"He just told me he left her there," Joaquin finishes for me. Across the crowd, I spot Diana the Diva Dino slipping a vape pen beneath the edge of her oversized head.

Every part of me goes into hyperdrive, my body trembling from the effort of keeping myself upright. Tears burn my vision before I can even open my mouth, the guilt I've been swallowing for so long crawling up like bile. "I . . . I . . . I'm . . ." Everything I come up with falls short of everything I want to say, and the things I can't explain. Because what am I? Sorry? A liar? A shitty excuse for a friend? All of the above?

"I . . . I'm sorry, Joaquin," I eventually manage to stammer out.

"So you did it on purpose?" he snaps, the tears clouding my vision answering that question for me. "What the hell, Ive?!"

"I didn't . . ." Again, I can't find the words.

"Didn't what?" His voice is harsh in a way I didn't think was possible from him. Not to me. This is what I've made him—angry and bitter and cold. Suddenly, his expression shifts as something clicks inside him. "Wait . . . is this why all of my promposals went sideways? Were you just sabotaging all of them?"

"No!" I reply quickly, as if that makes what I did any better. "Not the whole time."

"How long?"

"Just since the pep rally."

He runs a hand down his face, massaging at the tension in his jaw. "Fuck, Ive. Seriously?"

It'd be easy to break down and sob, beg for forgiveness. Standing my ground is harder. "I'm so sorry, Quin. So, *so* sorry."

He plows right past my apology. "So, the whole thing with Coach Mills's car . . . you did that on purpose?"

I shrug, the movement making me ache. "Kind of. I promise I didn't know it was his car specifically, though!"

Joaquin gazes somewhere beyond the trees, so deep in thought his face has become unreadable.

"Why?"

I wish he'd asked me anything else—how I did it, how I planned it—anything except why. The truth I'd carried in my heart when I got here, a wish for a future with him as sweet as the funnel cake we'd eaten together last week, turns sour on my tongue. I may not have understood how I felt when I made the first move, but there's no way I can tell him the full truth now. Even if he never speaks to me again. I won't tear myself open, pour myself out to him, give him the rawest and most vulnerable part of myself in the same breath I used to tell him I'd sabo-taged him.

We won't get our happy ending, but he still deserves better than that.

"Because it was her," I mutter, the lingering bitterness I thought I'd squashed coming back with a vengeance now that the walls I built around my feelings have crumbled. Not the whole truth, but it's not a lie either.

"For real?" he scoffs. "Danny's a shithead for what he did to you, but you can't put all the blame on Tessa for something *he* did."

"It doesn't matter!" I snap. "They hurt me—*she* hurt me. You saw how terrible I felt after that. How I blamed myself and al-ways felt like I wasn't good enough—"

"You've always been more than enough—"

"It doesn't matter!" I interrupt, ignoring the sincerity in his voice. "I've been afraid of love for *years* because the one guy who actually seemed interested in me only cared about me for two weeks, and threw me to the curb once someone better came along. And now I'm losing my best friend to her too."

"You were never going to lose me, Ive," he says, his voice tense, caught somewhere between frustration and sadness.

"Well, it feels like I already did!" I shout, tears stinging my eyes. "All we talk about is Tessa, about prom, about all of these promposals. And can you blame me for not wanting to see my best friend get publicly humiliated like every other Cordero High dope because he decided to ask out someone who gets off on crushing people like cockroaches?!"

He crosses his arms, voice quiet as his gaze falls down to his sneakers, unusually shy considering how fired up he'd been seconds ago. "It would be different."

"What if it wasn't?"

"Then it isn't!" The vulnerability is gone as quickly as it appeared as he throws his hands into the air and lets them fall limply back to his sides. "And that's my choice to make, not yours."

"I . . . I know, but—"

"But nothing." He stomps his foot as if to punctuate the statement. "You don't get to do this, Ivelisse. You don't get to be a freakin' puppet master, pulling the strings on my love life."

"I wasn't . . ." I exhale sharply, cutting myself off as I pivot from excuses to focusing on what's more important: apologies. "I said I was sorry, Joaquin. And I'll say it a thousand times, and then another thousand more if you need me to, but please, let me—"

"Just stop," he says, his tone clipped and to the point, a sense of finality to it. He turns his back to me. My fingers twitch, resisting the urge to wrap my arms around him. Cling to him one last time. Inhale and try to remember the scent of home before it walks away from me for good.

"You don't get to do this," he says again, his voice quiet but rattled, like it's taking everything in him not to shout instead. "Not after I poured my heart out to you, and you pretended it never happened."

"You . . . what?"

But he never hears my question, already gone by the time I'm able to squeak it out through the fog of confusion. I have no idea what he meant, and I guess now I won't know. Again, I'm rooted in place, unable to chase after him even though every part of me screams at me to do it. But I can't. I've hurt him enough for one day.

So, I let him walk away, likely to find Tessa, leaving me with a thousand questions.

CHAPTER SIXTEEN

IF LIFE WITH JOAQUIN was Technicolor, life without him is gray. So dull and boring that the first two days back after the weekend bleed together with the same, draining monotony. Wake up. Go to school. Detention. Build sets. Work. Bed. Repeat.

My life is bleak in the aftermath of senior skip day. Some might even say it's in shambles. Mami avoids me like the plague, and my best friend acts like I don't exist. There's no solace from my mistakes, no safe space where I can simply exist aside from behind the stage with Anna. I have to face the consequences of my terrible choices every day. First, in the kitchen at night, which is as empty as ever but without the lipstick kiss notes from Mami. And again, at school, watching Joaquin laugh and joke with his baseball friends while he ignores me every time we see each other in the halls. It's like I'm a ghost, doomed to float through life without meaningful contact until I wither and die for real. Or run away and start a new life in some far-off place, like Alaska or Norway.

At this point, I'm counting down the days to Sarah Lawrence move-in. It should've felt exciting, sending in my deposit to my dream school using my meager Casa Y Cocina tips. And while part of me is still excited about the chance at a fresh start in August, the other just feels alone.

And the worst part is, I have no one to blame but myself.

"How's it feel to be on the brink of freedom?" Anna, the last person in my life left standing, nudges her elbow against my arm until I give her a forced grin. "C'mon, give me something bigger than that. This is your *last* day of detention, get hype!"

While her attempts at forcing me out my slump are appreciated, they haven't been that effective. Fortunately, I haven't had to elaborate on my disastrous conversation with Joaquin. One look at me at Dino World and she immediately knew whatever went down between us didn't end well. Thank God she knows how to read the room.

"Yaaaaay," I say weakly, throwing in a finger twirl for pizazz.

Anna nods appreciatively. Either the twirl does the trick, or the bar is extremely low.

"Here's the tech schedule for the rest of the week," Anna says, pulling a sheet of paper out of her binder. "Consider it a last-day-of-detention gift."

A gift indeed. Just the sight of the detailed schedule, ready and waiting to be color coded and annotated, makes my type A heart soar.

I rest my hand on Anna's shoulder. "You're a true friend."

She grins, tossing a loc over her shoulder. "I know."

Carefully, I tuck the schedule into my binder, feeling a

glimmer of joy for the first time in days. "Think we can start adjusting the spotlights tomorrow? I know we're not supposed to work on that until Thursday, but I'd rather get a jump on it since we're so behind on the second-floor setup."

Anna stiffens, the playfulness faltering. "I, uh . . . have plans tomorrow, actually."

"Oh. That's cool, I can just ask one of the Emilys to help me with the ladder, then."

My response is calm, but she's tightly wound, arms crossed and biting her lip like she's about to burst.

"Are you o—"

"I'm going to prom," she blurts out, almost shouting, earning her some weird glances from a passing group of hockey players.

"Congrats!" one of the boys calls out, giving her a celebratory fist bump before rejoining his pack.

"Oooookay," I reply slowly, allowing myself time to process why her going to prom is such a massive concern that she had to blurt it out like she's just confessed to high treason. "And is that a bad thing?"

"Well . . . no. Sort of?" She sighs, pinching the bridge of her nose before starting over again. "I made a big show of not going, and then you weren't going, and I said we could do the whole 'fuck prom' thing at my house and, well . . . I felt shitty about bailing on the plan *I* came up with. Especially with the whole . . . y'know." She waves her hand in the area between us to, I'm assuming, demonstrate my fragile emotional state.

"Anna, it's fine," I reassure her, waiting until she peers up at me instead of down at her shoes to continue. "You're allowed to go to prom even if you think it's pro-capitalist bullshit."

She softens, tugging at the end of a loc. "You're not disappointed?"

In truth, a part of me is. Anti-prom with Anna was one of the few things I still had to look forward to. Prom is a little over two weeks away, and while a part of me hopes that things between Joaquin and I will have changed by then, realistically that's not going to happen. Without me in the way, he's free to orchestrate the promposal of his dreams for Tessa and sweep her off her size 6 feet. I'm sure their pre-prom photoshoot will be outrageously beautiful and shot by a professional photographer in Tessa's impeccably maintained backyard.

Either way, my disappointment doesn't mean Anna should stop herself from having fun. I've spent enough time this semester ruining someone else's happiness for my own selfish interests.

"I'll be even more disappointed if you don't send me pictures of your dress."

That gets her to duck her head sheepishly. "That's where I'm going tomorrow, actually. My mom found a place two towns over that has some not-outrageously-terrible last-minute options. All that's left at our mall are those weird neon cheetah-print cutout dresses with the rhinestones on the neckline." We both shudder at the thought. "Those should be illegal. It's inhumane to cheetahs, and my eyeballs."

"Thoughts and prayers to the cheetahs," I say through a giggle at the thought of Anna wearing an animal-print gown. "What made you change your mind?"

Her expression is distant, but there's a light in her eye when she replies. "Someone convinced me."

My gasp is cut off by the sound of the final bell. Unless I want to tack on another day to my sentencing when I'm steps from the finish line, I need to get to detention ASAP. But the rosiness in Anna's cheeks and the newfound shyness has me rooted in place.

"Anna! Oh my God!" I shout, whacking her arm with my binder. "Why didn't you tell me you were talking to someone?!"

She shrugs. "It's not *official* official. I still have to ask her." She sheepishly peeks over at me. "I was wondering . . . do you think you could help me pull a few strings? Nothing that'll get you more detention, I promise."

"Duh, of course." While I'd love to stand here and grill her about her new romance until she spills every detail, detention waits for no one. Reluctantly, I start to back away, making a V with my fingers and pointing them at my eyes before pointing them at her. "You're telling me everything tomorrow. No excuses!"

The massive grin on her face betrays the seriousness of her eye roll. "Don't you have somewhere to be?"

"I'm serious! Details. Tomorrow. And if you don't send dress pictures by ten tonight, I'm sending Nurse Oatmeal after you!" I call out, waiting until she waves in reply before I turn around and run to detention.

Sliding into the room with a minute to spare, I expect to see Mr. Cline, and maybe one of the stoners who are in their usual detention rotation.

I definitely don't expect to see Tessa Hernandez.

Even in an empty room, she manages to be the center of

attention. Seated in the front row, bent over a notebook, she tosses the glossy curtain of hair shielding her face from view over her shoulder. Her honey-blond highlights catch the mid-afternoon sun streaming through the window, giving her an effervescent glow.

Being in her presence makes me feel like a potato.

"Thank you for joining us, Ivelisse," Mr. Cline says in his usual drone. "Please take a seat."

Choosing somewhere to sit shouldn't feel like an AP-level math exam, but it does when Tessa Hernandez is a factor. We're the only two people in detention today, which means my choice holds an annoying amount of weight. Sitting too far away makes it seem like I'm avoiding her. Sitting too close looks as if I *want* to be near her.

Or I'm completely overthinking this and she probably hasn't even noticed my existence yet and never will.

Banking on the latter, I opt for a seat closest to the windows. Having a view—even if it's of my classmates having fun while I'm trapped inside—helps the time go by. Once I'm settled, Mr. Cline comes over with the sign-in sheet. Tessa's name is already written at the top of the page in bright pink gel pen.

"Congratulations on making it to the end," Mr. Cline says after I've signed my name below hers. "Most kids stop showing up after week two."

Hold on—was not showing up an option this whole time?

"They take the demerits instead," he says, reading my mind.

Mr. Cline sets down two slips of paper on my desk when I hand him back the clipboard. A slip of paper certifying that I've served all three weeks of my punishment and a coupon for free chips and guac at Chipotle that expires today.

"A parting present," he says without a hint of humor before returning to his desk.

I tuck the confirmation slip and coupon into my wallet and set to work on annotating my tech schedule. I'd be lying if I said I wasn't just sliiiiiiightly terrified of how much we need to get done before opening night next week. Listing out everything we have left to build, rig, or paint alone takes up the back of an entire page. The president of the drama club has been side-eyeing me every time she gets to a *Shrew* rehearsal only to find a half-built set and a nonexistent lighting setup, and I can't even blame her. Shakespeare would *not* be proud.

Tech week is always hell. For the rest of the week, our small but mighty tech crew will run on Red Bull, iced coffee, and fear of aspiring actors. We'll spend all of opening night next Monday hoping and praying that everything comes together before crashing for the best eighteen-hour sleep of our lives and doing the whole thing again for a full week of performances. But this'll be a special brand of panic. Mami didn't make good on her threat to call Tío Tony and tell him to take me off the schedule, but I did give up all of my shifts next week anyway. Unless I want a balcony to collapse on Petruchio mid-monologue, I need to get my shit together.

Besides, preventing mass thespian casualties will be an excellent distraction from the fact that my best friend in the entire world, rightfully, hates my guts.

My last hour of detention goes by without incident. With ten minutes left, Mr. Cline startles himself awake with a sneeze so loud it could be heard down the block. Something unspeakably gross dribbles out of his nose as he settles down from the aftershock of the sneeze, quickly covering his face with his hand and rushing out of the room when he realizes there are no tissues on his desk. I'm focusing on the last of my tech week notes and struggling to forget the sight of whatever was dangling out of Mr. Cline's left nostril when a shadow stretches over me. I peek up, jumping back in surprise at the sight of Tessa Hernandez sitting at the desk in front of me.

"Hi," she says, all light and casual, like this isn't the first conversation we've had in . . . well, ever.

"Hi?" I didn't intend for it to come out as a question, but the shock gets the best of me.

"You're Joaquin's friend, right?" she asks with a raised brow. "Ivelisse?"

"Yeah," I mutter bitterly. Much like Chris Pavlenko, yet another person who has been in the same class as me for almost a decade can't confidently pick me out of a lineup. Great for the self-esteem.

"I'm sorry," she says, a sentence so startling I have to do a double take to make sure I didn't just imagine hearing it.

"For . . . ?" It comes out slowly, begging for her to interject with an explanation, but instead she chews on her glossy lower lip and gazes out the window, doubling as an ethereal fairy.

"Joaquin and I hung out a bit over spring break." She pauses, as if to let me process that information like it hasn't been haunting me for the past month. "He's a really good listener."

"He is."

She nods, her lips turning upward into a small, shy smile.

It feels strange to see her act so unassuming, like she doesn't crush people's hearts on a near daily basis. "He talked about you. A lot."

That shouldn't make my cheeks burn like I've suddenly come down with a 101-degree fever, but it does. The thought of Joaquin talking about me in any context makes my heart race, but the thought of him talking about me with Tessa is especially nerve-wracking.

"We were hanging out at lunch the other day and got around to talking about you again, and . . . your ex, Danny." Her smile drops. "And I wanted to tell you that I'm sorry."

Ho-ly shit, I did *not* have Tessa Hernandez apologizing to me on my bingo card for this year.

"Oh . . . uh . . . thank you?" I stammer, unsure how to respond.

My reply doesn't seem to register with Tessa. Her brows knit together as her eyes stay focused on something outside, her lower lip quivering into a frown.

"I'm not sure what Danny told you about that night . . . ," she says so quietly I almost miss it.

"That you asked if he wanted to hook up."

She winces before nodding. Honestly, I wasn't sure whether or not to believe Danny. It's surprising that what he'd told me wasn't entirely off base. The crushed fourteen-year-old freshman who still lives inside of me seethes, relishing the vindication of knowing my dislike of Tessa was justified. But the present me doesn't get any satisfaction out of the truth—it only makes my stomach twist uncomfortably.

"I was a dumbass freshman year," she finally says, toying with her oddly familiar moon charm bracelet for so long I assume she's not going to continue. "My dad had gotten this new job and he was flying to conferences all over the place every few weeks. We hardly ever saw him, and when I did, all he'd do was nag me about grades, and extracurriculars, and all that bullshit you need to get into a good college. God forbid he actually ask me how my day was going."

Well, I never thought I'd find something Tessa Hernandez and I could actually relate on.

"I started doing stuff I knew would upset him. Going to parties, smoking, hooking up with strangers. I don't know what the point of it was . . . to get his attention, I guess. Make him stay, even if it was for whatever sucky reason I'd come up with," she whispers, her voice so unlike the biting one I'm used to, she seems like an entirely different person. "It was my idea to hook up with Danny, yes, but he told me you two were over. I swear. Still . . . I'm sorry. Deep down I knew he was probably lying, but I felt like shit, and honestly, I didn't care much about anyone but myself back then, so . . ."

That shouldn't shock me. Danny and I weren't together long, but it didn't take much time for me to realize he wasn't the doting boyfriend I'd always dreamed of. And maybe part of me always knew that—that Tessa was never to blame for what happened between me and Danny. Maybe it was just my insecurity, a raging beast that bubbled to the surface the second Joaquin announced he wanted to ask her to prom. A fear that I'll never be enough compared to girls like her. And bitterness, from the way my classmates made me a target because I was an "imperfect" girl with a "perfect" boy.

"I regret a lot of things I did freshman year," she continues, eyes fixed on her perfect gel manicure. "I ruined things for my sister—Dad cracked down on both of us after he had it with me, even though she never did anything wrong. She never does. And I ruined things with someone else I really cared about . . . so, yeah."

With the ball back in my court, I have no fucking clue what to do. I've spent so long thinking Tessa was the villain that seeing a vulnerable side of her feels like stepping into an alternate universe. Just because she's apologized doesn't mean I have to forgive her, but it feels hard not to consider it. Not when I spent the past three weeks making terrible decisions because I wanted to hold on to the one part of my life that hadn't fallen apart.

"Thank you for telling me," I finally reply. "I . . . uh . . . can sympathize," I tack on. The last person I want to talk to about how I self-destructed my relationship with Joaquin is the one who got between us in the first place, but I'm not so heartless that I'd leave her hanging.

Like that afternoon at Marco's, I'm seeing another person I've known almost my entire life in focus. Tessa, a girl I've always assumed had everything and who ate people's hearts for breakfast, is apologizing to me for something I'd assumed she never cared about.

We sit there avoiding each other's eyes for a beat, neither of us sure where to go from here. There's barely five minutes left of detention but there's enough unraveled truths between us to discuss for days.

"Joaquin is super into you," I say, trusting my normally untrustworthy gut. Talking him up to Tessa is the least I can do after everything. Just because he and I can't be friends doesn't mean he shouldn't still get his happy ending with her.

My attempt at playing his wingwoman makes her smile, but something about her energy still seems distant. "I know," she says plainly. Not exactly the reaction I was hoping for.

"I might be biased," I begin, leaning in as if I'm sharing a secret. "But he'd be a really solid prom date. Parents love him, *and* he already owns a suit. Truly the whole package."

Tessa breaks out into a laugh, which is either mortifying or excellent news. Jury's out.

"Joaquin's sweet, but not my type."

Anger sparks in me on Joaquin's behalf. The man is a saint with a million-dollar smile and a heart of gold—how could he *not* be someone's type?! Especially with Tessa's ultra-strict dad, he's sure to be an easy parent pleaser.

"He's the best, though, I swear! Even our dog loves him, and she hates everyone! Plus, he actually showers every day, so he doesn't smell like BO twenty-four-seven, and I know his car looks like it's about to disintegrate, but it's got good bones, and he's planning on upgrading to something from this decade once he—"

"Thanks for the endorsement," Tessa interrupts, clearly amused. "But I already have a date to prom."

That saps the wind right out of my sails. How is Tessa saying yes to a promposal not front-page news? Unless she accepted minutes before heading into detention, there's no way I wouldn't have heard about it through the grapevine by now. "Oh. Congratulations."

Suddenly, her cheeks flush a pink as subtle and rosy as her lip gloss. "Thanks," she murmurs, tucking a strand of hair behind her ear, her moon charm almost catching on her helix piercing. "Joaquin's a great guy, but I'm not really interested in being anyone's rebound."

Huh? Unless Tessa thinks Joaquin hasn't healed from the wound of Chelsea dumping him sophomore year, she's most definitely *not* in rebound territory.

"He's been single for, like, the past two years," I say with earnest conviction, as if that'll sway her into dumping her date for him.

"Aren't you two . . ." She makes a gesture with her fingers that I realize with slowly dawning horror is supposed to imply that he and I are together.

"Oh, we're not—" I wave my arms in front of my face. "No, definitely not anything. Just friends."

Tessa nods slowly, seemingly unconvinced. She's not the first person to make that assumption. It took months for me to convince the baseball team's wives and girlfriends that I wasn't still one of their ranks after Danny and I broke up. Even after four years, I still have to explain to the newer WAGs, *No, I'm not going to the games to ogle my partner's butt.*

"Seriously. Just. Friends," I reiterate, punctuating each statement by tapping my finger against my desk. Just friends. That's all we've ever been and all we'll ever be.

"Sure," she replies, though it's quite obvious that she doesn't believe me.

I can't help wondering if there's a reason she thought we were together—aside from us always physically being together.

If maybe Joaquin said something that might make her think we are more. But I quickly shut down that line of thought.

Before I can continue to plead my case for why Joaquin and I are totally 100 percent platonic, and she should give him a chance if her mystery date doesn't work out, Mr. Cline's alarm goes off, signaling the end of my last detention.

"Sorry, sorry!" Mr. Cline shouts as he comes stumbling into the room, a bloody wad of tissue held up to his nose. "You're free to go!" He turns off the alarm and rushes out of the room again without ever glancing over at us.

So much for a meaningful goodbye.

Tessa returns to her original desk at the front of the room and gathers her things. With the spell of our brief interaction lifted, I shove my stuff into my bag and head for the exit. By tomorrow, I'll either find out this was some exhaustion-induced fever dream, or we'll return to the status quo of never speaking to one another.

We head out, Tessa a few steps ahead of me. She halts in the doorway, one hand on the knob. She whips around so quickly her hair smacks me across the face like a eucalyptus shampoo–scented fan.

"Joaquin really likes you," she says while I rub my cheek. "I wasn't kidding when I said he talked about you a lot. Like *a lot* a lot."

The thought of it makes me warm all over, but reality crushes that flicker of hope. Even if he did spend his spring break hyping me up to Tessa Hernandez, any fondness he had in his heart for me must be long gone by now.

"I don't think he likes me very much right now." Saying it out loud burns like the sting of a freshly pulled Band-Aid, but a part of it is soothing. To finally say it instead of bottling it up.

Tessa nods, her face still wildly beautiful even when she's somber. "I fucked things up with my best friend once," she whispers, a real secret this time. "And it took years for me to un-fuck things between us. Years of wishing I'd just been honest with myself from the start instead of pushing away someone I really trusted." My heart races at the thought of Anna, of how she just said those words to me less than a week ago.

Tessa pauses for a beat.

"I don't know what happened between you two," she says, her piercing brown eyes locking with mine. "But take it from me, un-fuck things now. Worst-case scenario you spend a whole lot of time feeling bitter and angry that you lost your best friend. Best-case scenario, you figure things out."

With that, she turns on her heel and leaves me behind in a haze of confusion, wonder, and the scent of her eucalyptus shampoo.

CHAPTER SEVENTEEN

IT TAKES THE ENTIRETY of my thirty-minute bike ride back home for me to process what the hell just happened. I had a conversation with Tessa Hernandez. A civil conversation that started with her telling me the truth about the Danny situation and ended with her telling me to make things right with Joaquin.

What the fucking fuck?

Hardly ever interacting has left little space for a good impression of Tessa to expand. I know she's been a jerk and that she did something to make Anna despise her; that was enough for me to form my own conclusions.

But . . . what if Joaquin was right? What if she really *is* different and I was too caught up in my own misplaced anger and jealousy to see that? Could she really be that bad if she's the apple of literally everyone's eye? Sure, a fat bank account and a face that plastic surgeons dream of catapulted her to the top of the social hierarchy, but people wouldn't be throwing themselves over one another to try to ask out someone who's a massive asshole, right?

As soon as I open the door, I'm greeted by Nurse Oatmeal. She follows me into my room, barking her little lungs off. She gives up once I've flopped onto my bed, turning her attention to one of my chewed up chanclas while I stare at the cracks in my ceiling and let my head spin.

Joaquin talked to Tessa about me. A lot, apparently. Enough to make her think that we were a thing—which, to be fair, isn't unusual. The WAGs are convinced that we've been secretly hooking up for years, but that doesn't mean anything. *Shouldn't* mean anything. But I can't help holding on to the hope that it does, or did, once upon a time.

I open my text thread with Joaquin. We haven't said anything to each other since Dino World, even though I considered reaching out. Apologies over text don't hold the same value, and he's mastered the art of avoiding me at school. With the championship game this weekend, he's hardly ever home, either. Closing our text thread, I scroll through my camera roll instead. It's like a time capsule, documenting our finest moments from across the years. Joaquin beaming at me from the baseball field after he hit his first home run of the season. The two of us Lady and the Tramp-ing a ramen noodle after we were too cheap to buy our own $32 bowls at the new trendy place downtown. Walks through the park with Nurse Oatmeal, her always with a stick or some type of debris in her mouth. Us on my most recent birthday, him attempting to smash cake into my face while I held up Otis the Otter to protect me.

Speaking of which . . . where is Otis? I scan the collection of stuffed animals on my bed, but there's no sign of him there or on the floor. My mind whirrs—I swear I saw him recently. I check behind my desk and even my hamper but don't spot any stuffed otters. Then it clicks. Glaring at Nurse Oatmeal, I head out to the living room and find her collection of destroyed treasures. Sure enough, Otis is at the bottom of the pile, his head mostly chewed off and his chest leaking cotton. Poor guy.

I hold him to my chest, nuzzling him even though he smells like dog slobber, as if that'll bring me a little bit closer to Joaquin. Now I regret ever letting Nurse Oatmeal get anywhere near Otis. I should start keeping my stuff in a safe.

Something sharp pokes into my chest. I wince, pulling Otis back and expecting to find another one of Nurse Oatmeal's treasures stuffed inside him like some kind of dog toy Frankenstein, but find the corner of a piece of card stock instead.

Reexamining Otis, I realize he has a pouch in his back, with a zipper going from his head to his tail. Guess I would've found this out sooner if a certain goblin canine hadn't stolen and destroyed him. On the floor, next to where Otis was, I spot an OPEN ME! sticker with patches of Otis's fur still stuck to the back. So much for that.

Carefully, I pull the slip of paper out through the gash in Otis's back. It's a letter, folded in half with my name on the front in handwriting that I'd know anywhere.

A letter from Joaquin.

I run my fingertips along my name, my heartbeat thrumming. This must've been in there since he gave Otis to me four months ago . . . whoops.

Curiosity wins over caution, and I tear open the letter.

Clutching a piece of Joaquin in my hands, a chance to hear his voice, even if it's only in my head, is like a rainstorm in a drought.

Dear Ive,

The same words I'd written to him just a short time ago. Something as simple as a greeting shouldn't make my vision blur with an onslaught of tears, and yet, here we are. Two words into the letter and the Joaquin-shaped hole in my life aches with relief and sadness. There's a part of him left for me to discover.

Setting the handwritten letter back down again, I wipe the tears gathered in the corners of my eyes. Waiting until I'm clear-headed enough to keep reading.

Happy birthday!

I know you probably wish this was a key to a new Mercedes or something, but bear with me, I'm only one dude, and I can barely afford Herb.

I've spent a lot of time trying to figure out what I want to say, and even though this is draft ~~sixteen~~ seventeen, I'm still not sure I'll get it right. But you should be grateful either way—I almost went with interpretive dance, and that would've been awkward as hell for both of us.

So . . . you're my best friend. And you know that. Or, I hope you do. If not—hi. I'm Joaquin, you're my best friend, and I hope I'm yours too. And because you're my best friend, what I'm about to say is really complicated, and might make things weird or awkward, since you're most likely going to be a whole state away soon. It's totally fine if we're not on the same page about this but, as the millennials say, you only live once. And I'm really tired of keeping this one in.

I think you're amazing. The bees knees. Peanut butter to my jelly. Well, not literal peanut butter, because that would kill you, but you get the idea. You've been a part of my life for so long I can't remember a time when you weren't, and all my happiest memories end with me next to you. I know we've never said this before because it's kind of mushy, but I love ranking slushies, and going to Marco's, and cuddling Nurse Oatmeal, and doing nothing with you. But more than any of that, I love you. In a friend way, and in a not-friend way, and in so many different ways I don't really understand what I'm feeling half the time.

All I know is, you're my favorite person. And I want every single one of my memories, from when we were ten to when we're eighty, to end with me next to you.

Quin

PS—Try not to let Nurse Oatmeal get her hands on this lil guy.

I read the letter again, and again, and again, until the words start to blur together. My heart is pounding as I hold it against my chest. The words rattle around inside me like a pinball, lighting up everything it touches. *I love you, I love you, I love you.* Words we've said in passing on birthdays and holidays taking on new shape and meaning.

The missing pieces of the puzzle click into place. The last

thing he'd said to me before he stalked off at Dino World was that I'm the one who crushed him first and pretended it never happened.

I can see the whole picture now.

There's no time for me to dwell on the what-ifs—what if I'd found the note earlier, what if I'd never found it, what if Joaquin never feels the same way again—all that matters is finding him, telling him that I know everything now. Reading the letter isn't superglue. It won't fix what I've already broken, but I can't let him think I saw this four months ago and chose to ignore it.

Nurse Oatmeal and I bolt outside to the treehouse, her sitting patiently on the grass while I head up. Scaling the ladder at record speed, I delicately step around the fallen pieces of the ceiling and reach for the box of abandoned toys. The walkie doesn't flicker on when I flip the switch, sputtering out static for a few seconds before turning off entirely.

"C'mon, you piece of junk!" I grumble, slapping the walkie's battery pack a handful of times before it suddenly crackles back to life.

Most of the treehouse floor is covered in dust and woodchips, but splinters and dirty jeans are the last thing on my mind as I crawl over to the window. The wood buckles and creaks under my weight, and I slow down carefully. One wrong move could leave me crashing through to the ground, and I definitely can't pull off a neck brace.

Joaquin's room is bathed in a soft orange light, slowly fading into a pretty mauve when it suddenly flickers on and off for half a second before abruptly switching to an offensively bright neon green. Shadows dance along the wall as Joaquin storms out of his desk chair to kick at the light strip. Whatever he does sets off a chain reaction that leaves the lights blinking and jumping from color to color every few seconds like the world's saddest nightclub.

Stifling a laugh, I wait until he's managed to get the pulsating rave situation under control to hold down the talk button on the walkie.

"Joaquin . . . I know you probably don't want to hear from me right now, but if you're hearing this, can you pick up? Please?"

With his window closed, it's impossible to make out his face, or whether he heard me. No signs of movement, just the outline of him hunched over his desk. He could be wearing headphones, and Joaquin's basically dead to the world as soon as he pops in earbuds. But maybe he isn't. Maybe he heard me loud and clear and decided not to pick up anyway.

"Joaquin? You there?" I try one more time, leaning almost entirely out of the window as I wait and hope for the sound of his voice.

But the walkie stays quiet. The shape of him shifts, getting up from his desk and disappearing from view. The lights stutter one more time, switching from pink to yellow, then off completely.

And they don't turn back on.

CHAPTER EIGHTEEN

SENIOR LOCK-IN IS AS terrifying as it sounds.

Everyone gathers in the gym after school on a Friday, armed with sleeping bags and their cutest pajamas to spend the night locked in a room that smells like feet. Which is exactly why I'm leaving as soon as I'm done helping Anna.

"Places, everyone!" I announce with a clap as Anna puts the finishing touches on her ensemble for the occasion—a silver sequined dress with matching crescent moon clips woven through her locs.

"Seriously?" she replies dryly.

"Just because this is a one-person performance doesn't mean we can't take it seriously."

She fidgets with the star charm on her bracelet as she peeks out from our hiding place in the equipment closet to get a glimpse of the steadily growing crowd. "This isn't a performance."

"All promposals are performances," I reply indignantly. "Or at least the good ones are."

I sound like I drank the Cordero Prom-Craze Kool-Aid, but the point remains. If anyone deserves the picture-perfect promposal, it's Anna, and I'm here to make sure that happens. It already took twenty minutes of pleading—and fifty dollars—to let us dip out of tech week rehearsal early so we could make it here in time to set things up, but Anna is well worth the emotional labor (and cash).

Even if I have no idea who she's actually asking.

Anna's been so tight-lipped about this new development in her love life, you'd think she was sworn to silence by the CIA. Still, helping her pull off her down-to-the-wire promposal has been a welcome distraction and a good way to free myself of the negative prom-related karma hanging over my head.

"She here yet?" I ask, peeking over her shoulder to scan the room despite not knowing who I'm looking for.

Anna slams the door shut like she just saw a ghost, leaning against it with an expression that screams pure terror. "Mmm-hmm."

"You okay?"

Anna nods, biting her lip so roughly it creases the purple lipstick she spent ten minutes perfecting.

"You sure?" I reach out to rest a hand on her trembling shoulder. "Because you seem lik—"

"I'm asking Tessa," she blurts out with so much force it makes the basketballs behind us wobble. "To prom. Right now."

It takes my brain several beats to process what she just said, leaving me standing there open-mouthed. "Tessa?" I choke out, picking my jaw off the sticky floor. "As in Tessa Hernandez?"

Anna nods again, and I almost short-circuit from the effort

of understanding how Anna, Tessa, and prom wound up in the same sentence.

"I know I should've told you when I first asked for your help, but I panicked. I thought it might make things weird, or you'd be pissed and wouldn't want to talk to me again, and I realize how screwed up that is and I'm sorry," she rattles out at top speed, careful not to step too close to me despite the cramped space we're sharing.

Anger is the last thing on my mind, but I can't blame her for not wanting to tell me. Especially after I spent almost a month sabotaging a slew of promposals meant for Tessa. I hadn't planned on prepping for a real one. "Didn't you two hate each other, like, five minutes ago?" I could've sworn I saw her scowl at Tessa in chem last week.

She shrugs, running her hands down her arms like she's fighting off a chill. "We started talking again two months ago. Our parents made us go to this college networking thing. It was just a bunch of wannabe politicians handing out their business cards to anyone who'd give them the time of day. Unless we wanted to listen to someone give us their ten-step plan to eliminate world hunger, our only option was to talk to each other."

Reconnecting while avoiding strangers—the world's most relatable love story.

"It . . . didn't really work out, at first. We went through too much shit for things to go back to normal overnight. I said some stuff I really regret over break, about how she can't just waltz into my life again like nothing happened. And then you said something may have happened between her and Joaquin over break, and that drove me nuts, even when I knew it shouldn't. But . . .

she didn't give up. Every night she'd text me, telling me she wanted me in her life, even if it was just as a friend. And eventually that turned into something more."

Suddenly, Joaquin's story about spring break with Tessa makes a whole lot more sense. Him finding her crying on the boardwalk. Anna's subtle prying about their relationship, and her general irritation toward his promposal attempts. "Why didn't you tell me before I agreed to help Joaquin ask her?" Knowing Tessa was spoken for would've saved us a whole lot of time, money, and heartbreak.

Anna is ashen, and I immediately regret not watching my tone. "Because I didn't understand what was going on!" she replies, throwing her hands up in the air. "One second, I couldn't stand her, and the next she was all I could think about. I told myself I wouldn't get in deep if she didn't feel the same way—not after what went down before—but things are different this time around. She can date now, for one, and her dad isn't as much of a hard-ass as he used to be. But by the time we figured that out, you were getting ready to tell Joaquin how you felt, and I thought everything would just fix itself. We'd both end up with the right people."

While I still have questions, my last—and only—conversation with Tessa cuts the line to the forefront of my mind. "She said she already has a date," I say quickly. "She was at my last detention, and I tried to convince her to give Joaquin another shot, but she said she'd already found someone."

A smirk tugs at the corners of Anna's lips, the twinkle in her eyes giving her secret away.

"She was talking about *you!*" I whack her arm. She's been

Tessa's prom date for days, and I had no idea. Either they're phenomenal actresses, or I need to be a more attentive friend.

"She asked me. I said yes. She wanted to keep it low-key. She's gotten enough proposals already anyway. But . . ." Anna trails off, a faraway look in her eyes and a smile playing at her lips. "We spent the past four years ignoring each other. We can't make up for lost time, but we can make new memories while we can."

I nod, weighing my next words carefully. "So . . . what happened between you two? Before high school, I mean?"

She sighs, her silver nails tugging at a loose piece of string at her hemline. "It's a long story," she replies, and I'm prepared to drop the topic when she continues. "We fell for each other before we even knew what it meant to love someone the way we did. And aside from her dad, we weren't ready for it then. Her especially." Anna's smile blossoms as she tugs at the end of her star charm bracelet one more time. Suddenly, I make the connection. That was why Tessa's seemed so familiar—they're part of a matching set. "But I think we're both ready now."

A dozen emotions rush through me, each one punctuated by another dozen questions. I still want to know every detail of what led Anna and Tessa back to each other, but for now, I pull her into a hug. She's stiff in my grip at first, arms locked at her sides for a few seconds before wrapping loosely around my middle.

"I'm really happy for you," I whisper into her shoulder.

Her sniffles are muffled against the fabric of my sweater. "Thank you for everything."

"Don't thank me yet," I reply when we pull apart. "I could still blow this whole thing up. I'm kind of a pro at the whole sabotaging promposals thing."

She shoves my shoulder as we both break out into giggles, my body feeling lighter with every breath. It feels good to laugh about it, even if a part of me aches from the guilt.

But it sounds like I have one last shot at making sure a promposal for Tessa Hernandez doesn't end in catastrophe.

"You ready for showtime?" I ask as I crack my knuckles and limber up like I would before any performance.

Anna inhales sharply, nodding before throwing open the storage closet door. "Let's do this."

Once Anna's texted me that she's reached her mark, I set things into motion. With the push of a button, the entire gym is flooded in darkness. Screams echo through the room at first, along with a few cheers at the prospect of privacy. We only have a small window before tonight's chaperones—Coach Mills and Mr. Cline, who's surprisingly alert tonight—spring into action to shut us down. I move as fast as I can in the darkness, hanging the centerpiece of Anna's promposal on the hooks we'd spent the entire morning installing. With everything in place, I get out of the way and text Anna that she's clear for takeoff.

"Hey, Tessa," Anna calls out into the darkness.

Panic in the room mellows out. Now that we're past the height of promposal season, the fatigue of constantly witnessing romantic spectacles has worn off enough for there to be genuine excitement buzzing through the room.

Once Anna has everyone's full attention, I reach into my pocket for the remote that brings the neon sign hanging on the wall behind her to life, her declaration written out in cursive hot-pink lights.

It's Always Been You

"You free next Friday?" Anna finishes once the sign has flickered to full brightness, bathing the gym in a soft rosy glow.

Tessa steps out of the crowd and into the light, wearing a light pink slip gown, her hair weaved into an intricate braid crown. The sound of her footsteps against the waxed floor echoes through the dead-silent room, and my heart pounds louder with every step she takes toward Anna. I can barely make out the eager faces surrounding them, but what matters is the way Tessa stares at Anna like she's the only girl in the world.

"I think I might be free that day."

And Anna, defying everything I've known about her for the past four years, beams so wide she could light up the sky with her smile.

The entire auditorium erupts into cheers that could be heard in Antarctica as the overhead lights flip back on, Coach Mills already barking at everyone to control themselves. In the midst of the chaos, Tessa pulls Anna in for a sweeping kiss. To avoid getting caught red-handed near the light switch, I rush into the crowd for cover, clapping and shouting until my throat starts to protest. I jump onto the balls of my feet to get a better view of them, accidentally stepping on the foot of the person beside me.

"Sorry, I—" My apology cuts short when I realize I've locked eyes with Joaquin, skin damp like he just finished a workout. He must've just come from baseball practice. "H-hi."

It's the first time I've seen him up close since senior skip day. I'd run away if I wasn't stuck in the middle of a crowd. I half expect him to do the honors of leaving, but he stays, as rooted in place as I am, neither of us finding the courage to look at each other directly.

"Hey," he replies quietly, glancing over his shoulder at where Danny is loudly brainstorming what Tessa and Anna's couple name will be. Tessanna seems to be the front runner.

"I didn't know they were together. I swear," I say without thinking. Very smooth first thing to say post-argument. I'm pretty sure *no one* knew they were together, but I can't have him thinking he and Tessa couldn't get their happy ending because I was trying to protect someone else's. Things fell apart because I wasn't honest with him, but this isn't something I ever would've hidden from him.

"I don't think anyone knew," he says with a shrug before turning back to look at them. "Makes sense, though. They *were* best friends."

Despite my best efforts to stay in the moment, my mind starts to scour my recent memories for signs I could've missed, anything that could've explained how I didn't see this coming. But maybe that's the point. Love is unexpected. And I know as well as anyone, that falling for your best friend—even an old one—is easy.

When I turn back to Joaquin, he's been whisked away by his friends. Gone before I could even wish him luck on the championship game tomorrow. Watching him disappear into the crowd hurts more than not seeing him at all. But watching Anna and Tessa hold one another in the soft pink glow, Tessa cradling Anna's jaw like she's the most precious thing on this earth, it's impossible not to believe in second chances.

CHAPTER NINETEEN

AT APPROXIMATELY 3:30 IN the morning, an idea comes to me.

It was born out of a nightmare. I'm in the stands, watching Joaquin at his championship game, except there's no roar of the crowd or cheers from the entire student body. It's just me, alone in an empty abyss watching Joaquin scan the crowd for a familiar face. His eyes glaze over me each time, never seeing me even though I'm the only person in front of him.

I wake up in a cold sweat, Joaquin's name on my lips, but I'm able to hold in my scream before I wake up the entire house with my lovesick nightmare. The red numbers on my alarm clock swim in and out of my vision as my eyes adjust to the dark. My heart is pounding, my skin drenched in sweat, but when the fear subsides, something new is born.

I glance over at my alarm clock again—four more hours until it's a socially acceptable time to call anyone. Nine hours until the championship game. Any lingering anxiety from my nightmares melts away as my brain switches gears into planning mode. There's only so much I can do at three in the morning, but I grab my laptop and start typing up a plan anyway.

That nightmare may have been rooted in my own fears about the future, but it held some truth too. That, today, at the most important game of his life, Joaquin won't have any family in the stands to look for.

Unless I can pull this off.

"C'mon, pick up, pick up," I mumble to myself as I pace my room.

Isabella is a notoriously heavy sleeper. Her junior year, Joaquin and I had to bang pots and pans to get her to wake up in time for the SAT. And it is *seriously* messing with my mission right now.

"Hey, it's Izzy! Leave a message after the—"

"Goddammit," I mutter, immediately hanging up the call and sending Isabella one or two chill texts.

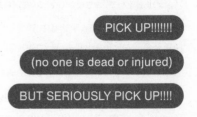

I desperately need her to wake up, but I also don't want to scare her into thinking someone's dead or her house is on fire.

Sure enough, text number eleven does the trick. Just a few

minutes after I hit send, a photo of Isabella and Joaquin before her prom lights up my screen.

"Hey!" I answer, sounding out of breath.

"W's happening?" Isabella slurs, sounding as if her face is still half buried in her pillow. Which it probably is.

"Are you doing anything today?"

"Uh, I'm going to brunch with some friends . . ."

"Can you move it?"

"Ummmm . . . I guess . . ."

"Great. Then I'm coming to get you."

Before she's even replied, I kick into action, grabbing my bag off the floor and heading for the living room. I've already wasted enough time waiting until almost ten for her to wake up and answer.

"Wait, what?" Isabella asks, her voice suddenly alert. "Coming to get me for what?"

"Today is Joaquin's championship game," I explain.

It takes Isabella several seconds to process. "Shit . . . ," she mumbles after I hear her nails clacking against the speaker, probably checking her calendar app. "I completely forgot . . ."

My reply comes out a mile a minute. "He didn't remind you because he's a selfless little angel who never wants to impose on people. But your abuela can't go because metal bleachers aren't good for her back, and obviously your mom won't be there, and he can't just not have anyone in the stands for him at his last game ever."

"But won't you be there?"

I swallow hard, hand stilled on my bedroom doorknob. I

figured I might have to tell Isabella the truth about what happened between us. But a phone call isn't the place to do it. Not unless I want to waste fifteen minutes on backstory when we're already running tight on time. "It would mean a lot to him if you were there," I say, almost a whisper. "Joaquin misses you both so much. Maybe he doesn't act like it because he's trying to put on the whole 'macho boys don't cry' charade, but he does. He had this countdown thing on his phone until the trip, and he even changed his phone background to a picture of the three of you. And he's *never* changed his phone background before."

I can hear shuffling on her end of the line, the sound of a sniff followed by a stifled yawn. "Okay," she says finally, her voice still thick from sleep. "But can't I just take the Amtrak or something? You don't have to drive all the way out here."

"The cheapest ticket that'll get you here in time is almost three hundred dollars," I reply quickly. She's working an unpaid internship, and I'm on a waitress' salary—needless to say, we don't have three-hundred-dollar train ticket money to spend on a sentimental high school baseball game. "If I leave now, we'll get here with plenty of time to spare. Even if I hit traffic."

I'd already called Tío Tony this morning to ask if I could borrow one of his cars for the day. Thank God my uncle is a fanatic car collector, because I can't imagine Mami would just hand over the keys to ours when we haven't been speaking.

"O-okay," Isabella replies, more shuffling as I'm assuming she gets up and starts to force herself to wake up. "I'll be ready. Text me when you leave."

I give her my word and end the call, throwing my bag over

my shoulder and rushing out of my room to head to Tío Tony's when I'm stopped by an unexpected sight: Mami, waiting for me in the living room.

She jumps up from her spot on the couch as soon as I come out of my room, her cheeks unusually flushed. "Hi!" she says enthusiastically, as if she hasn't spent the past two weeks avoiding me.

"Hi . . . ," I reply cautiously. I'd been banking on her being asleep until at least noon after last night's shift so I could head out of the house without questioning. If this is some kind of prank show where I'm about to get my ass handed to me by a D-list celebrity, I'm not afraid to jump out the window, die, and haunt my mother for the rest of her life.

"I thought we could sit and talk." She gestures to the couch where Nurse Oatmeal is passed out on a chewed-up throw pillow.

"I was about to head out, actually." I point my thumb at the door.

"Oh . . ." Mami's voice is a hollow echo. Everything about her seems on edge—the usual confidence she exudes as she floats from room to room stripped down to a person I haven't seen before.

When she doesn't say anything else, I try taking a step toward the door, but her voice halts me in my tracks.

"I broke up with Carlos," she blurts out unexpectedly.

Unsure of what kind of reaction she wants, I give a noncommittal shrug. "That sucks," I say, even though I have no idea who Carlos is. Her dates have blended together.

She steps away from the couch to approach me, slowly at

first. When I don't lash out, she closes the distance, not touching me but holding me in place with the intensity in her eyes.

"I broke up with all of them, Ive. Deleted the apps, blocked the websites. All of it."

Now it's my turn to respond with a hollow "Oh." Moments ago, I'd been dead set on getting out of here, but the plan falls away when I *see* Mami. The lack of makeup and flair, the dark circles under her eyes. "Why?" I ask before I can let hope spark in my chest.

She takes another step forward and reaches for me, slowly enough to give me a chance to pull back. At first, I want to. While guilt about the way I shouted at her has been eating away at me, I'd be lying if I said there isn't a small part of me that is still angry. Sure, I could've found a gentler, more civilized way of telling Mami how I felt, but that doesn't mean those feelings weren't valid. I resist the urge to run away from her, to slam the door and leave and go finish mending one bridge before facing another, and let her take my hand.

"Because you were right." She holds my hand in both of hers. "When I asked you if you were open to me dating again, I said I would take things slow, and I didn't. I got wrapped up in the thrill of men being interested in me again that I lost sight of what was always most important to me." She inhales sharply, her lower lip quivering. "I didn't realize that I was hurting you. You should've been my first priority."

The sight of Mami on the brink of tears makes my entire body clench up. It's not the first time I've seen her cry, but knowing it was because of me digs the wound deeper. But it comes with relief too. A calm in knowing that I wasn't off base in getting upset, and, more importantly, I have hope. A tiny seed planted in the pit of my stomach at the thought of having my mom back again.

The Very Adult thing to do would be to say something profound and wise that would both impress Mami and convince her to forgive me for the shitty things I'd said.

Instead, I start bawling.

Mami jumps back and lets go of my hand like I'm a ticking time bomb. "Mija, what's wrong?" she coos from a safe distance, carefully resting a hand on my back when I double over from the sheer force of my sobs.

Once the floodgates open, they're impossible to close. Every bottled-up emotion from the past three weeks spills out and I have to wrap my arms around myself just to keep steady. Pain and guilt and fear pour down my cheeks, my entire body shaking as Mami pulls me in for the type of hug I've needed for months. Warm, and soft, and comforting. A piece of my life I thought I'd lost.

"Things are so screwed up right now," I choke out between sobs, burying my snot-covered face in Mami's hoodie.

"Oh, Ive," she whispers into my hair, rubbing slow, soothing circles along my back.

My concept of time vanishes as Mami ushers me back toward the couch, the urgency melting away as we sink onto the cushions. Mami doesn't push, running a hand through my hair as I let out the last of my wails, my shoulders vibrating with each wave. I release everything, sobbing until my body has been bled dry of moisture. My cheeks are damp, my throat is raw, and my eyes feel swollen to the size of golf balls, but it's the best I've felt in weeks. With Mami's fingers playing with the ends of my hair, and the smell of her perfume on the collar of her hoodie, it's impossible not to feel safe here. And maybe that's what I've been missing this entire time, why I felt so lost and angry and bitter.

I'd lost my safe spaces.

"You don't have to talk about it if you don't want to," Mami begins when my sobs have simmered down to sniffles. "But I'm always here to listen if you do. Always."

I nod, wiping the snot from my face with the back of my sleeve.

"It's kind of a long story," I mumble. Way to make Mami's apology about me and my baggage instead. *Great job, Ivelisse. You're really learning how to not be a self-centered individual.*

Mami smiles, leaning in closer to take my hands into her lap. "I've got time."

I don't. But I tell her everything anyway. From Joaquin telling me he wanted to prompose to Tessa to the ways I made sure his plan would fall apart to finally finding the courage to tell him how I felt, only for everything to crumble before I could even get the words out of my mouth.

"Wow . . . ," Mami whispers once I finish the story with a shaky breath. "You've had a busy month."

That's an understatement.

"Things with Joaquin will sort themselves out," Mami continues, smoothing my hair. "I know you two have never dealt with anything like this before, but you're best friends. You've known each other your whole lives—you don't just throw that relationship away over one argument."

"But it's bigger than that," I protest, hands trembling at the thought of never getting to tease, laugh, or drive somewhere pointless with Joaquin again. "I was selfish, and I ruined his big chance at asking out the girl he likes because I couldn't be honest about how I felt. Best friends don't do that."

Mami nods solemnly, patting my hand. "You're young, Ive. I know it seems like this one mistake is going to define you, and I'm not saying what you did is okay, but you have a lot of growing to do. If you knew about the tontería I got up to when I was in high school . . ." She whistles. "Trust me, it's a long list of foolishness, and none of it is pretty."

While her reassurance is comforting, the same fear that's kept me from entertaining any thought of romance doesn't fade—if Mami and Papi couldn't make it work, why would anyone else? If anything, the fear festers and swells. Growing and growing until the words are tumbling out before I can stop them.

"But what if it doesn't work out and we end up like you and Papi?"

I clamp my hands over my mouth, wishing I could scoop the words back up and shovel them down my throat. Mami and I finally decided to bridge the gap between us, and I take a sledgehammer to everything we'd built.

"I'm so sorry, I didn't mean it like that, I—"

Mami raises her hand, cutting me off before I can finish my rambling apology. She can probably hear the thud of my heart as she lets go of my hand, the kindness I'd seen in her eyes a minute ago replaced by that same vacant and hollow sadness that haunted her the year Papi left.

Just like that, my huge mouth has ruined everything again.

"Your dad and I were never perfect. But we knew things weren't working for a long time," Mami says after what feels like a thousand years of silence. "And we danced around it for years, thinking about what'd be best for you, and hoping we could change things, but . . ." She sighs, shrugging helplessly. "I guess he got tired of waiting for something to be different."

Her voice is so small it makes me want to hug her tight and never let go, but I'm worried even the lightest touch will break her.

"Relationships take work, but no two are the same. Yes, we met when we were young, too, but that doesn't mean anything for you." Tears glaze her brown eyes when she faces me. "Not if you don't let it."

Hesitantly, I embrace her, waiting until I'm sure she wants me that close. It's meant to make her feel better, but the warmth calms my racing heart.

"I'm sorry," I say again, steadier this time. "For the way I lashed out at you, and for being moody and sulky instead of telling you what I was thinking before I let everything blow up. I missed you. And I should've simply said that."

Mami shakes her head as she dabs at the corners of her eyes. "You were right, though. I'm the parent, and your dad didn't hurt just me by running off. It's my job to take care of you, to make sure you're okay. I lost sight of that, and I'm sorry." She leans in. "But that's gonna change now. Okay?"

"Okay," I whisper.

Before I can launch myself into her arms for another hug, she holds up a finger and starts backing away. "I got you something."

My brow furrows as she darts behind the couch, reemerging with a white paper bag—a sense of déjà vu washing over me. Once again, I'm unwrapping something covered in tissue paper, but this time the contents don't make my stomach drop.

Because it's a Sarah Lawrence hoodie.

"Ta-da!" Mami exclaims before whipping off her zip-up hoodie to reveal a green SARAH LAWRENCE MOM T-shirt. "We can still match on move-in day!"

This time, I don't hesitate, and throw myself right into her arms.

CHAPTER TWENTY

THE UPSIDE OF THE timing of my reconciliation with Mami is I'm able to borrow her car after all. Driving our Subaru is a much better option than cruising down to DC in Tío Tony's spare neon-red '90s Mustang. The downside, I immediately hit traffic. Why the hell did everyone in the tristate area decide to drive down to DC at 11:00 a.m. on a Saturday?!

After sitting in gridlock traffic for almost an hour, I finally make it to the New Jersey Turnpike, just to—you guessed it—sit in even more traffic. The car fan is blasting cool air directly onto my face but I still feel white-hot all over. If I don't start moving soon, there's no way I'll be able to make it to DC and back in time for the game. If I'm lucky, maybe we can catch a portion of it. But that depends on whether any of the cars in front of me move sometime this century.

Just when we *finally* start to move, my celebratory dance is cut short by a jolt of surprise when my music cuts off and a call from Doña Carmen comes in.

"Hello?" I answer quickly, worried that something may have happened while I've been gone.

"So, I hear you're on your way to DC," she replies in lieu of a greeting.

"Well, right now I'm stuck in traffic, but in theory, yes. How did—"

"Isabella just told me," she answers for me before I can finish. "This is very sweet of you, Ivelisse, but is everything all right?"

My fingers freeze on the steering wheel. "Y-yeah. Everything's fine," I stammer, keeping my eyes on the road as the flow of traffic starts to pick up.

I'm not sure how much Joaquin has told her about what went down between us—clearly not everything. I'm not even sure if he told her about his plans to woo Tessa, and there's no way I'm getting myself into even more trouble with him by spilling about his love life to his grandma.

"I've just noticed Joaquin has seemed a bit . . . off lately."

I swallow hard around the lump in my throat, unsure how to respond. "We . . . uh . . . had a . . . disagreement, I guess."

That's putting it mildly.

"About?"

"Stuff." Very convincing. "I've been having some . . . complicated feelings," I finally manage to answer.

Doña Carmen may feel like family, but she's Joaquin's actual blood. There are invisible lines drawn on the table between us that I can't cross. Not if I don't want to risk ruining things more than I already have.

"About Joaquin?"

I don't need a coherent reply, the way I stammer says enough.

She hums in thought while I sit on eggshells, tapping the steering wheel as I slowly glide down the turnpike.

"I had plenty of boyfriends when I was your age."

I choke on my own spit. The last thing I expected was for Doña Carmen to come out swinging with that one.

"Boys from school. From the next town over. Gringitos who just came to visit. One boy even drove all the way from Caguas to take me dancing—very romantic. Terrible breath, though," she continues when I finally get my choking under control. "But they all came and went. Some never called again. Some went off to the States and promised they'd come home someday, but they never did . . ." Her voice trails off.

"You and Joaquin are special, mija. If he didn't have you when his . . ." She cuts herself off again, the wound of having their family split in two still too fresh for her to touch. "People come and go. Friends, boyfriends. Sometimes even family. It takes work, *love,* to hold on to the ones that matter. Don't let go."

Don't let go. The same words Joaquin whispered to me before we plunged hundreds of feet on the coaster, but with entirely new meaning.

But I'm not the one wielding that kind of power.

"What if he wants to let go?" I ask, my voice strangely hoarse.

It'd be a clean break. Me heading away and him staying here. We may be neighbors, but he at least wouldn't have to face me most months of the year. Maybe the distance I'd been so worried about is exactly what he needs.

Doña Carmen doesn't respond at first, the pause long enough that I start to worry. "He doesn't," she finally says.

And, strangely enough, I actually might believe her.

I make it to Isabella's dorm with no time to spare.

"Get in and let's go!" I shout as I pull up in front of her building, throwing the passenger side door open like I'm the getaway driver in a bank heist.

Isabella knows time isn't on our side. My reunion with Mami set me back half an hour, plus the extra hour and a half of sitting in traffic. It's already almost three, and the game starts at five. She hops into the car, throws her bag into the back seat, and we are on the road in ten seconds flat. Thankfully, the traffic isn't as horrendous heading back to Elmwood, but we'll still be cutting it close unless I drive twenty miles over the speed limit the entire way. I want us to get there on time, but I want us to get there in one piece even more.

"Think we'll make it in time?" Isabella asks, glancing at where the map on my phone says we still have three and a half hours to go until we're back.

"Definitely not for the first few innings," I reply, breathing a sigh of relief at the clear expanse of highway—not a lick of traffic in sight. "But we can probably make it before the seventh inning."

Isabella nods, twirling a lock of her now-hot-pink hair around her finger while biting down on her thumb on her other hand. A habit that runs in the family.

Unlike her abuela, Isabella doesn't see right through me and my intentions. Joaquin and I have a history of kind gestures, and for all she knows this is another one. Nothing unusual or strange about this mad dash to cross state lines. Once I give her control of the AUX cord, she's fully content with vibing to her music while I focus on driving as fast (and safely) as humanly possible. We chat about her new life at American, about the boy she's been talking to for weeks and the girl she hooked up with last week and which one she should pursue (the girl, the guy sounds like a dud), while I carefully avoid the sordid details of my own private life.

"Whatever happened with Quin and that girl he was trying to ask out?" Isabella asks, and my heart stutters.

"They . . . uh . . . didn't work out." Vague enough, no need to wade any deeper. "She's with someone else now."

Isabella frowns. "That sucks—seems like he really liked her."

I shrug, and I make the mistake of attempting to glance at her for her reaction, only for our eyes to meet for a flash of a second. My cheeks ignite as I focus on the road, hoping she doesn't see the blush spreading down to my neck like a terrible rash.

If she does, she doesn't comment on it. But I don't miss the smile tugging at the corner of her lips as she turns to look out the window.

We fly through the last of the drive, chopping off a solid twenty minutes thanks to a shorter route Isabella knows to get us to Elmwood more directly. We're still too late to catch the beginning of the game, but with something this down to the wire, every minute matters. The game is well underway by the time we pull into the Cordero parking lot, but the tailgate party is still in full force out here.

"You'd think they were playing in the World Series," Isabella says as we make our way through the parking lot. She narrowly manages to dodge a beefy guy I can't believe is a teenager tossing a hamburger bun across the lot like a frisbee.

To be fair, this *is* the World Series of high school baseball. Especially for the seniors—this is basically our last sports hurrah. Unlike Isabella's graduating class, we actually have a shot at the championship title.

"Watch your head," I warn her as another bun comes flying our way, both of us narrowly ducking in time.

"God, I do not miss this place." She scowls right after she steps on a ketchup packet, sauce oozing beneath the soles of her sneakers.

Once she's wiped her shoe clean, we brave the crowd and head for the bleachers. The sea of fans decked out in Cordero T-shirts, hats, and sweatpants isn't any less rowdy. Popcorn and gummy worms litter the concrete as we scan the crowd for empty seats.

We manage to find two spots way up in the nosebleeds. Navigating our way up there is trickier than expected, with people getting knocked over or forcefully throwing debris every which way. I give the WAGs a polite wave as we walk past their premium seats close to the field. For once, I was hoping they'd welcome me into their midst, but all they give me are tight-lipped smiles as they huddle closer together in their seats. Guess they noticed my platonic separation from Quin, and a good view is reserved for *true* WAGs only.

Isabella and I link hands as we narrowly squeeze past a group of rowdy boys from the lacrosse team to take the seats beside them. Whatever happens on the field sends the lax bros jumping up in excitement. I watch in horror as one of their hot dogs goes flying into the air. Isabella, struggling to regain her balance after the boys nearly sent her flying into the seats below us, is standing directly in the flying hot dog's path.

Without thinking, I reach out and pull her out of the line of fire by swapping our places, pushing her toward my seat and taking relish, mustard, and a half-eaten wiener right to the face.

"Oh shit, my bad," the boy apologizes while sauerkraut drips down my cheek and under the collar of my sweater.

Somewhere behind me I can hear Isabella gasp before starting to curse the boy out in rapid Spanish.

"It's fine," I say with a plastered-on smile, accepting the napkin he offers me and returning to my seat.

"You sure you're okay?" Isabella does her best to help, swiping the napkin from my hand and dabbing at the gunk caked on my cheek and neck.

"Mmm-hmm," I mumble, and it's actually not a lie. I'm here, covered in sauerkraut and sitting in awful seats, but the fact that we made it at all is a miracle. It's not what I pictured when I woke up soaked in sweat at three in the morning, but it feels pretty perfect.

Everything except for the score.

"We're down by two?!"

I whip around to glance down at the field, Isabella seemingly as shocked as I am.

"He must be off his game," she mumbles, going back to biting her thumb.

Even from high up in the stands, I can see the sweat dotting

Joaquin's forehead. The easy confidence that carried him through the season is long gone, replaced by pinched brows and a tight-lipped frown.

"Get your head out of your ass, Quin!" Isabella shouts, and I pinch her arm, even though there's no way he can hear us from all the way up here.

"You're supposed to be a surprise!" I hiss as she drops back into her seat with a groan.

"Well, the surprise won't be good if he doesn't win."

A fair point. My plan isn't contingent on Joaquin winning the championship, but realizing his sister is here to watch him lose the final and most important game of his high school career won't exactly be the heartwarming moment I want it to be.

Things aren't much better going into the eighth inning than when we got here midway through the game. The only minor improvement is that we manage to snag ourselves some snacks before they sold out. Cordero is down by one, and Joaquin is definitely off his game. Hits he should've been able to catch in his sleep go whizzing past the tip of his glove, and his usually razor-sharp instincts fail him, leaving him scrambling to pivot and run in the correct direction. Watching his frustration boil over to the point that he starts taking it out on himself is a cruel sort of torture. If I wasn't at risk of being booed by everyone within a five-mile radius, I'd sprint onto the field after he earns his third strike, and the team their second out for the inning, and hug him so hard he'd have no choice but to unclench his fists.

But seeing me would likely make everything worse.

The self-centered part of me that landed us in this situation wonders if he wouldn't be in a slump if his best friend hadn't wrecked their friendship a week before the championship game. While I'd gladly take the blame for him, thinking this is about me is flattery. Nothing else.

"Come on, man!" Isabella shouts as Cordero's next at bat earns himself a swift first strike. "This shit's painful to watch."

I nod in solemn agreement. It *is* painful.

Every Cordero fan is on the edge of their seats as the game heads into the ninth, and final, inning. I'm chewing solemnly on a chicken tender and Isabella's downing her inhumanely large cup of Diet Dr Pepper. Tension hangs over the crowd as storm clouds start to rumble above us. Even the threat of a downpour can't pull eyes off the field. Either the game's gonna get rained out or Cordero is going to lose its first shot at a championship title in a century. Both would be equally catastrophic.

We all release a quiet breath of relief as the away team earns a swift three outs, maintaining their one-point lead. Whatever went down in the Cordero dugout between innings, it worked. There's a sureness in their movements when they step back onto the field, running and leaping and catching with an intensity I didn't see in the innings before this one. If the pressure is this stifling in the stands, I can't imagine what it must be like on the field. They know this is their last chance to save their asses.

It's too much to ask for the miracle of a home run. Joaquin's one of their most promising hitters, and even that's not really his strong suit. DeShawn manages a decent enough hit to make it to first base, but when their second hitter lands them a swift three strikes and first out, dread layers the crowd like fog. No one in our row dares move a muscle as we watch each pitch and swing like our lives depend on it.

"Let's go, that's what I'm talking about!" Isabella shouts as Danny manages another hit, him and DeShawn now holding down second and third base. It's the first time I've felt grateful for Danny in years.

We follow the crowds lead and leap out of our seats to cheer and stomp our feet in excitement. Everyone around us goes wild as the next batter steps up to the plate, a lump lodging in my throat as I lean onto my tiptoes and spot Joaquin.

A cheer breaks out among the stands, the same one from the pep rally—a cry of his name, breaking it out into two syllables. Growing louder and louder with every step he takes toward home plate, breaking out into a full-on frenzy when he turns and gives the crowd a sheepish wave. Hope. Joaquin's given them— *us*—hope.

My heart swells with a deadly combination of pride and panic. The lone chicken tender sitting in the pit of my stomach threatens to make a reappearance as a hush falls over the field when Joaquin takes his place. It's not on him to bring home the win, but it is on him to keep them in the game. Three wrong moves and he's out, and they can kiss the championship trophy goodbye.

Isabella's hand reaches for mine. I swallow hard, squeeze her hand, and pray for that miracle.

You can hear the popcorn machine whirring in the parking lot as the pitcher winds up, the ball moving through the air in slow motion.

Joaquin swings.

And he misses.

"Strike!" the umpire calls over the roar of groans in the stands.

The same rowdy group that spilled their hot dog on me starts heckling Joaquin at the top of their lungs, calling him a punk and telling him to get his head out of his ass.

Isabella seethes with rage, vibrating with annoyance as she glares at the boys like she's trying to make them burst into flames. "Only I'm allowed to say that shit," she grumbles under her breath as the guy closest to me calls Joaquin a loser.

If we weren't surrounded by our classmates, this guy would have his ass kicked into the next millennium.

Instead, I commit his face to memory and tuck it into the back of my mind for whenever I can extract my more setting-appropriate revenge. Once I figure out who he is, an expired hot dog will find its way into his locker.

Back on the field, Joaquin jumps in place before resuming his stance. Again, the world goes silent, so silent I can only hear the creaking of the bleachers and the pounding of my heart.

Everything happens in a fraction of a second. My eyes water from the stress of forcing them open long enough not to miss a single moment. The pitch. The swing. The crack of the bat making contact. The ball flying through the air.

The shortstop makes a dash for the ball, confidently extending his arm where the arc should land, right in the middle of his glove.

Except it doesn't.

The ball goes flying past the shortstop and tumbling into the grass of the outfield. The world becomes a blur of screams—mine and Isabella's bleeding together with those around us into one deafening cry. Hands tremble and voices crack as DeShawn and Danny sprint as far as their legs can take them. A fresh wave of cheers break out as DeShawn clears home. In the mad dash of watching the runners make their way around the bases, I forgot to pay attention to what's going on in the outfield. My throat tightens as the ball comes flying back through the air toward home. Danny makes a break for it, sliding down onto the dirt to avoid getting clocked in the head and skidding the last of the way to home plate.

And he's . . .

"Safe!" the umpire shouts into the stands.

The roar of the crowd leading up to this moment is white noise in comparison to the absolute pandemonium that takes over after the umpire's final call. Popcorn and hats and pom-poms are thrown into the air in celebration, tears streaking red-painted cheeks, jerseys being waved like flags.

Because of Joaquin.

Every member of the Cordero team comes rushing onto the field to surround him. It's the kind of moment you see in sports documentaries—sans a jug of Gatorade to dump over his head. His freckled brown skin glistens with sweat in the glow of the sunset, his glossy white uniform stained with streaks of dirt and grass. I spend an embarrassing amount of time gazing at him like the marvel he is, wishing he'd turn and see me.

But I have a mission to complete.

"C'mon. Coach Mills said we could meet down by the dugout,"

I shout over the screaming crowd to Isabella. I had the foresight to email him before leaving to pick her up, and thankfully he was open to the idea of letting her onto the field to congratulate Joaquin—assuming they won, of course.

Isabella nods, and we carefully head out of the stands. As promised, Coach Mills appears at the field entrance in an energized flurry, dripping with sweat and wearing a smile I didn't even think he was capable of.

"You ready?" he asks in lieu of pleasantries. He gestures for her to follow him toward the door that leads to the dugout but Isabella whips around to face me first.

"Aren't you coming?"

The joy inside me flickers like the light strip in Joaquin's room. Bright, jubilant yellow fading to dull, muted blue. "Nah. This moment's just for you two."

Isabella crosses her arms and gives me the same glare she'd given our rowdy seat neighbors.

"It's fine, I swear!" I insist, throwing in a laugh for good measure. Over her shoulder, Coach Mills taps the nonexistent watch on his wrist. We're already running on a tight schedule and getting down here from the stands was more of a process than we'd thought.

"Go be with your brother before we get kicked out," I say quietly enough that Coach Mills can't hear before turning Isabella around and pushing her toward him.

She groans but doesn't protest this time, and jogs to catch up with the others. "Don't think this means you're getting out of coming to the celebration dinner!" she calls over her shoulder.

"We'll go to your uncle's place—so you don't have any excuse for skipping!"

I roll my eyes and wave before they disappear behind a door marked TEAM ONLY. There's no point in telling her Joaquin won't want me around for this moment, and definitely not for a celebratory dinner. Tonight is about him, about them, about basking in the glory of the moment he's worked his entire high school career for. Not about us—if there even is an us anymore.

Fighting against the swarm of people trying to head out early to avoid the inevitable parking lot traffic takes more out of me than I would've expected. By the time I make it back to the stands, snagging a free seat closer to the field, I'm dripping sweat and the Diet Coke someone spilled on me. I'm just a walking Happy Meal today, aren't I?

As Coach Mills and Isabella appear on the opposite end of the field, I press myself up against the railing separating the stands from the field, ignoring the burn of the sun-warmed metal on my palms. The celebration is going just as strong as it was when we left, the entire Cordero team huddled together at home plate bouncing and screaming and jumping over one another until Coach Mills appears from the shadows, carrying a trophy the size of my entire body.

Finding Joaquin in the sea of white uniforms is easy, even without the extra few inches he has on the rest of the team. My eyes lock on him in time to see his mouth gaping as Isabella races toward him. His teammates part like the Red Sea, letting Isabella launch herself at her brother.

He's unsteady on his feet, stumbling under her weight as she wraps her arms around his neck. The team helps keep them up, clamoring to get their hands on Joaquin's back and push him upright. He still seems paralyzed by shock when Isabella lets him go, whispering something to him that I can't make out. When she finishes, cupping his cheeks and smiling at him, he lunges at her this time, burying his head so far in her neck I can't see anything but his curls.

It feels intrusive, watching him unravel in his sister's arms, tears streaking their cheeks. I don't even realize tears have started trailing down my own face until someone hands me a napkin.

There's not much that I'm proud of from the last month, but at least I can be proud of this. Creating a perfect moment, captured by the photographers buzzing across the field, for the most perfectly imperfect boy.

Dabbing my cheeks, I head back to the parking lot.

This moment is exactly the way I'd planned it. Like with *The Taming of the Shrew*, I busted my ass to pull the strings and set the scene for something beautiful, knowing I'd hide behind the curtain when the spotlight turned on. That's what I'm good at. Crafting the happy ending for someone else. Joaquin got the reunion he never saw coming, and a memory he'll hopefully cherish forever. A memory that won't involve me.

If I thought the party we'd walked into earlier was a rager, it's nothing compared to the absolute madness at the end of the game. Boys with shaved heads and red-painted faces sing the Cordero anthem at the top of their lungs while music blasts from a dozen different speakers. Grills are lit up again for a second round of burgers and hot dogs, with people passing brown paper bags that I'm sure aren't hiding juice boxes or Red Bull.

"Good Lord . . . ," I whisper to myself as the boy next to me rips off his T-shirt, revealing a Cordero Ram painted onto his chest.

Clearly, the Cordero student body doesn't know how to do anything low-key.

It's a struggle to make it to my car at the farthest end of the lot. While the excitement is infectious, a part of it is also unnerving. Boys who didn't even know I existed yesterday urge me to join them for Jell-O shots while girls who have gotten my name wrong on multiple occasions pronounce my name correctly for the first time in years. It's as if the shine of a championship win has mended any old wounds. Petty fights and breakups and cheating scandals are forgotten in the name of getting sloshed in the parking lot.

Tessa sits primly in the open trunk of her car, watching the pandemonium unfold in front of her like a queen overseeing her kingdom. She takes a careful sip of her drink—a green smoothie in a hot-pink tumbler—and straightens the bow holding her ponytail in place. Her uniform is still pristine and there's not a drop of sweat on her even though she was doing backflips less than twenty minutes ago. She's as beautifully otherworldly as always.

I linger on her longer than I should, but for once it's not because of some spite from freshman year holding me there, wishing my glare could wither her into a husk. It's because of her smile, soft and easy as she teases her friends and laughs after one of their jokes. No biting comments or tearing people down. Just being a regular ridiculously cool, attractive teenager.

Her eyes catch mine before I can turn away, the corners of her lips twitching into a small smile. She gives me a wave, earning the attention of her gaggle of friends as they stand on their tiptoes to see who she's gracing with her attention. The fourteen-year-old trapped inside me yells to flip her off and move on, but I don't listen to that part of myself anymore. So, I wave back.

A rumble spreads through the parking lot. The music and shouts crank up to maximum volume and I can feel the asphalt vibrating beneath my feet. I quickly wonder if we're about to break into a stampede when the crowd shifts beside me. Someone grabs my wrist, a flushed and panting Danny breaking out of the throng.

What the hell?

"What're you doing?!" I snap, yanking my wrist out of his grip. It's the most we've said to each other since our breakup four years ago.

"Joaquin's looking for you," he says through labored breaths, sweat dripping from his forehead to his cheeks.

"Oh." Every part of me goes warm, and suddenly I don't mind the sweat Danny left behind on my wrist.

Maybe I misheard. The music and the excitement must have gotten to me. There's no way Joaquin's been looking for me when he's surrounded by people who want to give him a shot to celebrate or take a picture with him.

No way.

"Found her!" Danny calls over his shoulder, waving his arms into the crowd.

I swallow hard as Joaquin emerges from the crowd next, just as flushed and sweaty as his teammate.

"Thanks," Joaquin tells Danny, giving him a stiff pat on the shoulder. It's a far cry from the last time the three of us were all together—Joaquin offering to sucker punch Danny in the nose for what he did to me.

Danny gives us both a nod, eyes lingering on me for a second longer than necessary of exes before he disappears into the crowd.

I glance over my shoulder as if I'm searching for proof that this is a mirage, but when I turn around, Joaquin is still there, breathless, and not a figment of my imagination. He closes the distance between us, his lips parted. "You brought Isabella here."

My heart hammers, and my skin goes clammy under the intensity of his gaze. If I could shield myself from him, I would. But I'm trapped in his orbit. "Well, couldn't have no one from your family here for your last game, so . . ."

He shakes his head, but not with anger like I'd feared. With confusion. "Why?"

"Because you needed something good," I answer meekly. "And I know how much you've missed her, and your mom. And how much you'll miss them, if you don't see them this summer."

"But . . . how? DC is like four hours away."

"Only three. Unless you hit traffic."

When he smiles, something inside me softens, gooey as a chocolate lava cake. It's a brief moment where nothing went wrong between us, and we're just Joaquin and Ivelisse. Best friends.

I can see the gears whirring in his mind as he realizes that I must've driven her here myself, but I continue before he can interrupt with questions or concerns. "I really am sorry. For . . . well, everything. I know I said it before, but things were really heated and my point kind of got lost in all the yelling, so I wanted to say it again. I'm sorry for what I did."

The confusion is gone, replaced by something unreadable. He nods slowly, breaking our eye contact to stare at his scuffed cleats. "I'm sorry too."

I do a double take. "For what?"

"For not thinking about how you'd feel about me asking out Tessa."

"You don't need to ask me for permission before you date someone."

"Yeah, but this was different." He lifts his head and steps closer to me. "What happened with Danny and Tessa seriously hurt you, and I was too wrapped up in promposal stuff to care that this might've brought up some weird feelings for you."

Getting the apology I'd been wishing for weeks ago doesn't feel as vindicating as I would've thought. Not only did I wreck things between us, but I'd left him feeling guilty over something I should've just been honest about from the start.

"It's fine." I shrug. "You were right, though. She has changed."

We both zero in on Tessa in the sea of dancing, over-caffeinated bodies. Pulling focus, the way she always does. "She's pretty cool," Joaquin says.

"You could always ask someone else," I blurt out. I may have screwed things up between them, but that doesn't mean he can't find his happy ending with someone new. "I can't imagine anyone'll say no to the champion shortstop."

Joaquin shrugs off the suggestion. "I'm good."

"Oh . . ." Relief washes over me, even though I know it shouldn't. "Are you already going with someone, then?" I ask, though it's none of my business. Barely a minute into talking to him again and I've become a mess of contradictions—my brain and my heart battling for dominance like him and Isabella warring over who controls the remote.

"Nah. Think I'll just kick it with the team and their dates. You?"

"I've got a shift. So fun." I throw in a nervous laugh that I pray will mask the obvious lie. My agenda for prom night is as barren as a desert. Even Tío Tony insisted I take the night off to "be a teenager." Nothing screams teenage loser like sitting at home on prom night eating ice cream. "Maybe order a pizza afterward, if I'm feeling wild."

This is the part where he'd usually rib me. Tell me not to get too crazy and order pepperoni, and we'd laugh until our stomachs ached. I never used to question myself before saying things to Joaquin. Now I don't even know if I should be talking to him.

A gust of wind startles us both, blowing one of the curls that escaped my ponytail free. My heartbeat quickens when he reaches out for it, easily catching the brunette lock between his fingers. I'm buzzing, waiting for him to tuck it behind my ear like he has hundreds of times before, but instead he pulls away.

"Is this sauerkraut?" he asks, holding up his kraut-stained fingers.

Mortified, I shove the traitorous curl behind my ear. "Some guy accidentally dropped a hot dog on me."

He frowns.

Behind him, the party livens up as the rest of the boys from the baseball team start spilling out into the lot. Someone dumps Grey Goose into the bowl of their oversized trophy, a "chug" chant sweeping over the lot as the team take turns sipping out of their championship goblet.

"You should go," I say, jutting my chin toward the circle that's formed around the team. "You're the reason everyone's celebrating. You deserve to get in on the action."

"I'll skip that part, thanks," he replies with a shudder and a scrunched-up nose. He's never been big on drinking, and I can't imagine he'd want to chug out of a plastic trophy his friends have been slobbering on. "And it wasn't just me, the whole—"

I don't let him finish that thought. "Don't be humble. Today's your day." I wave my arms with a flourish. "Bask in it."

He chuckles softly, glancing over at where one of his teammates is now dry heaving onto the concrete. "Well, if you insist . . ."

The way he trails off, staring back at me with a familiar warmth in his eyes, gives me pause. As if he's waiting for me to say something to make him stay, but I quickly squash that wishful thinking. Our gazes stay locked, and even as the cheers and screams around us get louder, nothing in the world matters but him looking at me. After what feels like an eternity, he turns to his teammates. "Guess I'll head back."

Because I'm still weak and selfish and want this moment to last longer, I stop him.

"Quin?"

He whips around quickly, something like hope gleaming in his eyes. "Yeah?"

I pause, the ache in my chest tightening until the one thing I'd tried to tell him weeks ago comes bubbling to the surface. "I read the letter. The one inside Otis." His lips part, but he doesn't say anything, so I continue. "Nurse Oatmeal got to him before I could find it, so I didn't read it until a few days ago . . . I'm sorry."

After a few seconds, he laughs, a sound that makes my knees buckle. "Of course she did. I had a feeling that might happen, but I just had to go the convolutedly romantic route."

And, suddenly, we're laughing together. Not hard enough that we can't breathe but harder than the joke warrants. I laugh because of the absurdity—that he hid a love letter for me inside a stuffed otter, and our dog took it for herself before I could ever read it. And with relief—that we're able to laugh together again.

But when the laughter dies down, I struggle to find the right thing to say next.

I opt for the truth. "I wish I'd read it sooner."

His lips press into a thin line as his gaze fixes somewhere past my shoulder. "Yeah. Me too."

It's not the answer I wanted, but at least it's an answer. We're not throwing our arms around one another and professing our love at the top of our lungs. It's not the beginning of a new story, but the close of another.

"Quin, c'mon!" DeShawn calls out to him, waving for him to join.

Joaquin's head swivels from his pumped-up team back to me. "Bask in it, right?"

"Right."

When he ends up choosing his teammates and rejoins them, I'm not as disappointed as I thought I'd be. Tears burn my eyes, but it's easy to stop them. Watching Joaquin get tackled by his teammates, everyone around him clamoring for a second with the MVP himself, I smile.

I've always known that he's the most incredible person in this town. Now everyone else knows it too.

CHAPTER TWENTY-ONE

IT'S SENIOR SPIRIT WEEK, and everyone got the memo but me.

"What the hell are you wearing?" Anna snaps when she spots me in the cafeteria, where all of the seniors gathered after final period to collect our yearbooks.

"What are *you* wearing?"

Anna comes storming toward me in a neon pink and purple unicorn onesie, complete with a glitter horn. "It's pajama day," she says as if it's common knowledge—which, I'm now realizing, it is.

Here I'd thought everyone had just given up on dressing presentably. Senioritis is very real and spreading faster than the freshman year mumps outbreak. With nothing but prom, finals, and one unnecessarily long graduation ceremony standing between us and freedom, the entire senior class has officially checked out. Godspeed to any teachers who are attempting to actually teach. A valiant, and quite frankly foolish, endeavor.

"This is what I wear to sleep," I reply, trying to at least save some face. No one can blame me for being in a fog today—everyone is a zombie on Mondays—but especially not Anna. Not when we spent all of yesterday in the auditorium putting the finishing touches on our Italian countryside backdrop. Nothing like spending your Sunday inhaling paint fumes.

The process was even more exhausting, thanks to the six hours I drove to bring Isabella from DC. Fortunately, she insisted on taking Amtrak home, heading back on an off-peak train that didn't cost her three figures. Plus, it gave her the chance to actually spend some time with Joaquin and their abuela. The lights at their place were off all weekend—the three of them probably adventuring while they can.

Needless to say, it's been a whirlwind of a weekend, and with four hours to go until curtain for *Shrew*, my body is officially in survival mode.

Anna doesn't buy my excuse, narrowing her eyes at me as she crosses her arms. "You wear jeans to sleep?"

I look down at my ensemble of my Sarah Lawrence shirt and paint-splattered jeans. "Sure, why not."

Anna sighs. "Try to keep up." She shoves her phone into my hand, opened to a bright red infographic—a schedule of every Senior Spirit Week event, starting with today. Pajama Day. Maybe I'll dig around in the attic for something tomorrow, which, according to the schedule, is Silly Hat Day.

The fluffy rainbow-colored tail poking out of Anna's one-sie drags on the ground as we head over to the row of tables piled high with thick, maroon leather yearbooks. The crowd parts for her now that she's half of the It couple officially known as Tessanna—a piece of gossip so unexpected it broke records. Within a whopping three and a half minutes, the entire student body knew about Anna's promposal.

Once we've forked over our paid receipts, Anna grabs two yearbooks off the closest stack and hands one to me. Mami grumbled so much about the $80 cost that I considered passing on getting one, but she insisted. In addition to my standard portrait, there'll be at least one posed shot of me with the tech crew on the drama club page that she wants to show my abuela.

"Your boy got a full-page spread," Anna says as she flips through her copy. I peek over her shoulder to find exactly what she promised, an entire page dedicated to Joaquin Romero, this year's Senior MVP.

His official baseball team photo sits front and center, with various pro shots of him midgame, and a few candids of him with the rest of the team, surrounding it like a frame. Beneath the collage, a quote is written in script so elegant it's almost illegible.

"Never let the fear of striking out get in your way." —Babe Ruth

"Oh my God."

It's horrendously cheesy, and I'm sure he absolutely cannot stand it, but I love it.

Joaquin and I are still trapped in limbo. But if we were talking, I'd text him about it right now, taking as many pictures of it as I can to make sure he doesn't vandalize it. I'd present him with a massive sheet cake with a copy of the spread on it for his nineteenth birthday, forcing him to eat his own face.

But that's another life.

"They make it sound like he died," Anna says, still scrutinizing the spread.

She has a point. All you need are some angel wings, and this would have big "May God rest his soul" vibes.

"That's what I said," a voice behind us says.

We both whip around to find Joaquin grimacing at the same page in his own yearbook.

"What's that?" Anna shouts suddenly, waving at something in the distance. "Yeah, I'll be right there!" She turns to us with a sly grin. "Sorry, gotta run. Meet me in the auditorium?"

She doesn't bother waiting for me to answer before taking off. A smart move, because if she'd stuck around any longer, I would've jabbed her with her unicorn horn. I was tempted to step on her tail and force her to stay here as a buffer, because we both know damn well no one was calling her. But when Anna has an agenda, she sticks to it.

I turn back to Joaquin, not sure what to do now that it's just us for the first time since the game on Saturday. Behind him, a clique of girls whisper among themselves while not-so-subtly ogling him. They're holding their yearbooks and gel pens at the ready, most likely waiting for me to leave so they can pounce for his signature.

"I think you've got some fans waiting for your autograph." It's meant as a playful tease, but the tension in my voice makes it sound like a barb. I wince, hoping he can see through my nerves.

"They can wait." He gives them a wave, then comes back to me with an achingly familiar smile. "I wanted to see if you'd be the first person to sign my yearbook?"

He offers his yearbook to me, Sharpie at the ready, and if my heart wasn't locked inside my chest by veins and arteries, I'd be throwing it up onto the floor.

It shouldn't mean anything. It *doesn't* mean anything. He probably wants me to write "It's been real" along with my signature and leave it at that, but it ignites a fire in me I thought I'd permanently put out. He wants me to sign his yearbook, and mundane as that might be, it's the most exciting thing he's asked me this year.

The lines on Joaquin's forehead crease deeper and deeper the longer I go without answering. "Or not, if you don't want to."

I snap back to reality, and when our eyes meet, I can't help the laugh that bubbles up inside of me. "Only if you're the first to sign mine."

He softens, the tension melting from his shoulders, his own easy smile returning. "Deal."

We exchange yearbooks and pens, me passing him one of the dozens of gold Sharpies I keep in my backpack—a good tech crew leader *always* has Sharpies on hand. Cracking the book open to the signature page, it dawns on me that I have no idea what to say. "Hey man sorry I messed up your shot at your dream girl" isn't the kind of thing I want immortalized in our senior yearbook, but it's not like I have much else worth saying to him right now. Except that I miss him, and our car rides, and slushies, and the way he always listens to the cheesiest songs possible.

And that I love him. And I'm sorry I didn't realize that sooner.

Probably a lot for a yearbook message.

The sound of Joaquin snapping my yearbook shut jolts me

back to the task at hand. How the hell did he finish so fast?! I swallow hard, realizing this means he probably wrote something super short. Most likely just his name. Maybe a "good luck next year" if he was feeling generous.

"Sorry," I mumble, sweat starting to form on my brow as I turn back to the empty page. "Writer's block."

Joaquin doesn't reply, leaning up against the nearby lunch table instead.

Thousands of ideas come to me, one on top of the other until my brain starts to operate like a greeting card factory. Writing a yearbook message shouldn't be this nerve-racking, but it's never felt so loaded before. I've only got one shot to come up with something, and I don't even have the luxury of an eraser. Something that says "I'm sorry, I miss you, please tell me we can be okay" without being longer than *War and Peace*. Or, maybe, something that doesn't say any of those things. Because how am I supposed to know what he wants me to say?

Goddammit, this is too much brain power for a Monday.

I inhale sharply, grounding myself and shaking off my doubts and panic and go with my gut. It's been pretty traitorous this year, but I have a good feeling about this one.

Quin,

You're my favorite person too.

Ive

Short, simple, and says everything I wanted to say but didn't have the courage to. Before I can overthink it, I hand the yearbook back to him before he can notice my sweaty, shaking palms. Mercifully, he doesn't immediately read the message, sparing me the mortification of having to watch his reaction in real time. Instead, he tucks it into his backpack, and I do the same with my own.

"Ready for opening night?" he asks once he's zipped his bag up.

The start of a new conversation startles me. Everything about this interaction has caught me off guard, but especially the fact that it seems so . . . normal. Like there isn't an ocean of unaddressed feelings between us. "'Ready' might be an overstatement."

"You say that every year," he teases. "You're gonna kill it, though. You always do."

The compliment makes me feel weightless, but my feet remain firmly planted on the ground. "Thanks," I reply, holding up my crossed fingers. "Fingers crossed."

"Good luck." Dread washes over him. "Wait, shit, that's the one thing you're not supposed to say, right?"

"You're fi—"

"Did I just curse the whole show? Should I throw salt over my shoulder? Knock on wood?"

Before I can reply, he takes it upon himself to knock on the faux wood lunch table.

"I think we'll be fine," I say between laughs as he rips open one of the abandoned salt packets on the table and tosses it haphazardly over his left shoulder, salting a disgruntled cheerleader walking past him. "It'll take a lot more than a curse to mess with us."

My reassurance soothes him. "That's the Ive I know." As he beams at me, it feels like everything might be okay. Like we can be who we used to be. And, for once, it doesn't feel like wishful thinking. "I'll see you?"

He starts to back away slowly, and I wish I could hold on to this moment, to *him,* for a little longer. But his words feel like a promise. The kind I'd hoped for but never would've dared to ask for. A chance to start again. "I'll see you," I reply.

He turns on his heel and disappears into the throng of seniors swapping signatures and snapping selfies with their yearbooks held proudly. Calm washes over me, a type of peace I haven't felt in months. There's still so much up in the air—about him, about us, about who we'll be when we're hundreds of miles apart in a few months. But even if everything falls apart, if he decides staying friends isn't what he wants, I'm glad I was honest.

Because he deserves to know that my happiest memories all end with him too.

CHAPTER TWENTY-TWO

IF WE CAN GET through opening night without this balcony falling on someone's head, it'll be a miracle sent by Shakespeare himself.

"How many minutes to curtain?" I shout into my headset.

One of the screws holding the balcony upright disappeared at some point, and I can't in good conscience have people running around next to a structure that's missing a vital screw.

I can barely make out Anna's voice over the steady hum of Lucentio muttering, "I burn, I pine, I perish!" behind me.

"How many what?" she asks.

"Minutes to curtain!"

One of the ensemble members glares at me as my shout interrupts her vocal warm-up. I give her one right back that screams, "Shove it and let me work unless you want to break an arm tonight." With a startled squeak, she scuttles off to the opposite end of the stage where her castmates have started a round of hamstring stretches.

Anna's voice crackles through the decade-old headset. "You get that?"

"Sorry, say that again."

"You have fifteen minutes."

Shit, less time than I thought. If I can't finish screwing down this base, we'll have to hold curtain, and nothing pisses off an overcaffeinated theater kid like telling them you need to delay the show twenty minutes. Anna speaks up again when I don't reply. "You need me to come down there?"

I shake my head even though she can't see me from up in the light booth. "No, no, I have it handled. You woman the fort."

"Aye aye, Captain."

Anna's end of the line goes quiet, and beyond the curtain her "Showtunes except they're cool" playlist—a collection of jazz covers of Broadway classics—kicks on through the speakers. The rumble of the waiting audience quiets down, their conversations reduced to whispers as they settle in for the last stretch before the show officially begins.

That's if I can find that goddamn screw.

I call over Emily Z, the only Emily who isn't carrying an armful of props, and have her help me scour the floor. If I could go back in time and strangle past Ivelisse for not thinking to have a backup set of these annoyingly specific screws, I would. Because holy shit is this a high-pressure situation.

"Ivelisse?" Anna says, the worried tone of her voice sending my panic into overdrive.

I stop scouring the flowerpot beneath the balcony to give her my full attention. "What happened? Did a spotlight go out?"

"No."

"Did a set piece fall apart?"

"No, but—"

"Is something wrong?"

"Well, no, but—"

"Then it can wait."

I'll apologize for being snippy and shower her with praise and her favorite candy at the wrap party, but right now I do *not* have time for anything that isn't finding this goddamned motherfucking screw.

Across the stage, the rest of the Emilys are gathered around the edge of the curtain, giggling and whispering among themselves as they sneak peeks at the audience. Whatever's going on past the curtain has them worked up—each one flushing an even deeper pink than the strawberry stage blush lathered onto the cast's cheeks.

"Hey!" I snap. "Either help me find this screw or go backstage."

The Emilys frown, casting longing glances out at the audience before ultimately getting onto their hands and knees.

"Ive," Anna says again, her voice more insistent this time.

"What?!" I shout, regretting it instantly. Anna doesn't deserve the brunt of my rage—especially considering she's the only person who understands what kind of stress we're under. But, as I go to apologize, a silver glimmer catches my eye. The screw, stuck in a crack in the floor.

I dive for it before it can disappear or roll away or God knows what, cradling it in the palm of my hand like a piece of solid gold and letting out a victory yelp.

"You should look at the audience," Anna says, her voice unusually apprehensive.

My brow furrows. So much for celebrating my miraculous find. "Why?" I ask, already bolting back to the tower to finish screwing things back into place.

"You'll see."

Well, that's totally not ominous or anything.

Dread creeping up the back of my neck, I dismiss the Emilys and carefully reinsert the screw (and therefore saving the play, thank you, Shakespeare). Once I'm done, I head toward the edge of the stage. With less than ten minutes to curtain, everyone has made their way to the backstage pen. All that's left behind the curtain is me and our no-longer-wobbling balcony. Sucking in a deep breath, I crack open the curtain prepared to see pandemonium, gore, or a UFO abducting our audience.

But all I see is Joaquin. Sitting in the front row, in the seat I'd always save him, except this year because I didn't think I'd need to. A bouquet of peonies in his hands.

"What is he doing here?" I don't remember pressing the speak button on my headset, and I don't even know if that was meant to be said out loud or privately obsessed over in the recesses of my mind, but Anna's response grounds me.

"He's here for you."

He's here for me, like he always has been. And, maybe, he always will be.

"Thought you might want to know now. Instead of hearing it from one of the Emilys gagging over him."

While I know I should thank her, I can only focus on him.

The curve of his lips and the way he taps his foot along to the music. His glossy brown curls. The peonies, blush pink and ten times more beautiful than the dried petals that used to sit on my living room mantel.

I have to talk to him. Hug him. Tell him I never want to let him go again.

"I'll be right back," I say into the headset before whipping it off and rushing to the stage exit.

The clock is ticking until curtain, but I've wasted enough time running away from what I feel. For once, I want to face it head-on, and I can't risk letting that feeling fade when the lights go down, and I lose him to the darkness.

The backstage area is a maze. Props and costume pieces litter the ground, and at one point I stub my toe so hard my life flashes before my eyes. Once visions of my third birthday party have faded, I take a careful step forward, only to trip over my backpack.

"Dammit," I mutter under my breath as the contents of my bag go spilling all over the stage. Professions of love get pushed onto the back burner as I scramble to scoop up my things and shove them back into my bag. Unless I want Tampax to be scattered across Padua, I need to act fast. My attempt to cram everything into my bag at lightning speed falters when I get to the last item—my yearbook.

The book is facedown on the ground, a dog-eared page catching my attention. I definitely didn't do that. I only had my yearbook for a matter of minutes before tucking it into my bag, and the only other person who had it was Joaquin . . .

Lunging for the book, I open to the flagged page so quickly I cut the tip of my finger on the stiff paper. I let out a hiss and suck my thumb, catching any blood before it can drip onto the page.

The page is a familiar one—Joaquin's memorial-esque spread. In the lower left corner, there's a message written beneath an image I didn't notice earlier. Joaquin and I in the Dino World photobooth, him licking my cheek, sandwiched between a photo of him running through the outfield, and a selfie of him and Doña Carmen before junior prom. A photo he must've asked them to include.

Ive—I'll always want to be next to you.

Every part of me swells with a type of exhilaration I've never felt before. Better than every roller-coaster drop combined, and more dizzying than any corkscrew turn or inversion loop. The words ring in my ears like a song on repeat. The boy I never want to let go of doesn't want to let go either.

An idea pops into my mind—a chance to give Joaquin the promposal moment he deserves.

An idea that *could* majorly backfire but is worth the risk.

Eileen, the stage manager, appears out of the darkness like a ghost—her face and arms the only thing left visible thanks to her all-black ensemble. "Are we good to get started or—"

"One second."

Without giving myself time to overthink or doubt, I dash toward the stage as fast as my jelly legs will carry me. I grab the AUX cord for the onstage speaker, plugging in my phone and pulling up the playlist Joaquin sent me weeks ago with only a single song on it—a song I've played enough times to know all the lyrics by heart. Whose lyrics have never felt more relevant than when I stared out into a crowd of hundreds and only saw one person.

Whipping the curtain aside, I burst onto the stage and directly into the blinding spotlight like an overeager ingenue as the opening notes of "Can't Take My Eyes Off You" ring throughout the auditorium.

At first, I wince against the harsh glare and heat of the light. Anyone who can dance, sing, and act at the same time under this kind of pressure deserves a gold medal. Anna, God bless her, must notice the way the light catches me off guard, the brightness dimming until I can slightly make out the audience.

Joaquin comes into view just in the nick of time, our eyes locking as I lunge for the microphone seconds before the first lyric of the song.

"You're just too good to be true," I mouth along, careful not to actually sing so as not to destroy everyone's eardrums. Instead, I commit to the bit, doing my best to match Frankie Valli's energy as the crowd giggles and hides smiles behind their hands. Who knows how long I have before Eileen tries to pull me off the stage with a cane like a vaudeville gag, so I've got to sell it while I can.

Anna, a true angel, gives me a hand. She quickly reprograms the lights, allowing the spotlight to follow me as I attempt to sway my way off the stage and into the audience. As I near the edge of the curtain, I narrowly dodge Eileen's outstretched hand.

"What're you doing?!" she mutters to me from backstage, still attempting to grab the back of my shirt.

During the instrumental interlude, I take advantage of the brief break from having to mouth along to dart across the stage and away from Eileen. The crowd breaks out into scattered laughter as I two-step my way to the other end of the stage, and it takes all of my willpower not to get too into my head about how mortifyingly embarrassing this could be. Eileen slowly edges out onto the stage, cloaked in darkness as the spotlight continues to follow me. Being generous, I probably have about thirty seconds until she tackles me and drags me backstage.

With what little time I have left, I give everything I have to the performance. I throw my head back and lip sync along to the chorus, faux-belting like I'm gunning for a Tony. I'm not much of a dancer, so I throw my free arm into the air and let the spirit of Frankie Valli take over. It's easy to give myself over to the music when the lyrics feel so relevant—true in every sense about the boy I'm singing them to.

Eileen is tight on my tail, her hand just barely missing me as I kick ball change and jazz hands away from her, using every musical theater dance move I've picked up to put distance between us. I hazard a peek over my shoulder, my performance faltering when I realize how close she is to catching up to me. She rears back, as if she's going to football tackle me to the ground. With one last literal leap of faith, I jump into the audience and slide on my knees until I'm directly in front of Joaquin.

"Let me love you . . . ," I say just for him.

My heart pounds as I wrench my eyes shut and lip-sync belt the last lyrics of the chorus, Anna fading out the song for me.

The crowd doesn't even wait for the music to fade before giving me a rousing round of applause and a standing ovation, while Eileen stews onstage.

Finally, I meet Joaquin's eyes, prepared to see him shielding his face from view, or attempting to gracefully sneak out of the room. Instead, he's beaming, his shoulders shaking with laughter as he gives me the most adoring look I've ever seen in my life.

In that moment, I wish I had more. A sign, or a banner, or something that asks the question for me. Instead, all I have is my voice.

"Joaquin Romero, I haven't been able to take my eyes off you since you came over to my house fourteen years ago and asked me if I wanted to play with your Legos. Will you go to prom with me?"

He deserves something bigger, more spectacular. Fireworks spelling his name in the sky. A full choir belting his favorite song. A lifetime supply of Marco's slushies. But this is what I can offer—putting myself and my heart on the line and praying that's enough for him.

An excited buzz spreads through the audience as they crane their necks for a peek at the guest of honor. While I wait for his response, my heart hammers so loud I'm sure the mic is picking it up and broadcasting it to the world. A blush creeps along the apples of his cheeks as he laughs quietly.

"Only if we can get slushies first."

The audience giggles like kids on the playground and my cheeks ache as I hold the mic back up to my mouth.

"Deal."

Cheers and hollers spread through the entire auditorium,

but everything fades to a hum. All that matters is him, and the way he looks at me like I'm made of stars.

Eileen appears out of nowhere, yanking the mic out of my hand. "Very nice, thank you for that, Ivelisse," she says, discreetly shoving me toward the exit.

I scurry backstage as quickly as I can, trying to return to the light booth before she can tear me limb from limb for disrupting her show. From stage right, with a wave and a mouthed *"I'll see you soon"* to Joaquin, I rush off the stage and let the real show begin.

I'm totally not biased, but this was the best damn spring play yet.

The cast gets a generous standing ovation that continues on through them thanking the band and pointing to me and Anna up in the light booth for our own moment of glory at our last ever Cordero show. Anna does a deep, dramatic bow even though no one can see us through the tinted glass, but I make up for it by giving her the hype she rightly deserves. After we've turned on the house lights and powered down the light board, Anna pulls open the door with a grand flourish.

"Go get your man."

Fear takes over as I come down from my promposal high and reality starts to sink in. I just asked my best friend to prom in front of hundreds of people. Via lip sync and passable dance. And now I have to walk right into the thick of it and try not have a semi-public meltdown because *Joaquin said yes.*

"I should probably clean up in here before we—"

"Nope," Anna interjects, making it clear that this is a demand, not a suggestion. "Go get your man."

Swallowing my nerves, I nod, accept her encouraging hug, and head out to "get my man."

Most of the audience lingers in the auditorium, waiting with bouquets and balloons for the cast to emerge fresh-faced and out of their period costumes. I scan the clusters of supportive parents, siblings, and friends for any sign of Joaquin, but his entire row is vacant. There's no curly mop of hair peeking out over the tops of the crowd like usual, and I will myself not to panic. He wouldn't leave now when he came to see me.

Unless he doesn't actually want to go to prom with me and ran away instead of telling me to my face.

Once I'm sure he's not in the auditorium, or in the hallway, I burst into the parking lot with the last shreds of my chill. The air is warm, almost humid, and the skyline beyond the lot is a shade of purple so vibrant it would stop me in my tracks if I wasn't already so enamored by what's right in front of me.

Joaquin, leaning against Herbert, with the bouquet and a smile that makes my knees weak.

"Sorry to make you come all the way out here," he says as he pushes off the door. "Emily W asked for a bunch of selfies, then told her friend to come get in them, and it was turning into a whole thing, so I snuck out here."

I snort at the thought. "You're so popular these days."

He shrugs, sheepishly scratching at the back of his neck. "I guess . . ."

Before I can rib him for his newfound superstardom, he brushes off his shyness and launches into a new train of thought.

"The show was great. Especially the part where this cute girl asked me to prom."

"She sounds pretty cool."

He grins, handing over the bouquet of flowers. "The coolest."

As I bury my nose in the flowers, my heart swells so wide it could burst right out of my chest.

"But don't tell my friend Ive," he continues. "I've kinda had a crush on her for forever—can't let her think I'm straying."

"Your secret's safe with me." I take a chance and another step toward him, the flowers pressed between our chests. I lower my voice even though there's no one around to eavesdrop and lean in until I'm close enough to watch his cheeks bloom pink as the peonies. "And I may have heard through the grapevine that she has a crush on you too."

His hands come to rest against my waist, my skin igniting under his touch. "You think?"

"I know."

I step even closer, resting my hand over his heart, the rapid pounding beneath my fingers making me blush down to my toes. But before I can move to close the distance, he grabs my wrist.

"Are you sure you want this?" he asks, his voice so soft and somber it makes my stomach clench. "Next year, you're gonna be in the city, and I'll just . . . be here."

It's the most vulnerable I've seen him since Mrs. Romero and Isabella left, his brown eyes glossy and his cheeks tinged pink. He avoids my gaze, as if he's ashamed of opening himself up to me.

I'm not sure what the future will hold for us. Whether the distance will tear us apart, or if it'll just make coming home that much sweeter. Two months ago, I wouldn't have thought it would be worth it. That we'd be doomed to end up like every cliché high school love story—like Mami and Papi. Like me and Danny. But I don't care, so long as it means I'll have him. Even if it's just for a moment.

I rest my hand on his cheek and tilt his face toward mine.

"All I want is you."

We move in sync, him leaning down and me going onto the tips of my toes until our lips meet halfway in a kiss that makes me lose my balance. His grip around me tightens, crushing the flowers between us as he pulls me against his chest, my body stretching to its limits just to meet him, but I don't mind so long as I'm kissing him until we're breathless.

When we break, his palm cups my cheek, a tender moment before he flips us around, gently hoisting me onto Herbert's hood before pulling my face back to his and kissing me harder, faster. It'd be so easy to lose myself to this feeling. The taste of peppermint ChapStick and honey, the scent of Irish Spring and coconut hand lotion, and the pad of his thumb digging into the bare skin where my shirt has ridden up.

Kissing Joaquin Romero is better than slushies, better than Marco's, better than roller coasters, because he is all of my favorite things at once.

The third time we pull apart, we're heaving for breath, our lips so close it takes the fear of passing out not to lean in and kiss him again. The boy in front of me is so familiar, and yet so startlingly different. His lips red and kiss swollen, his curls mussed in a way I've never seen before. I didn't think it was possible, but I fall even more in love with him.

Instead of leaning in for a fourth time, Joaquin's head falls against my shoulder, a soft laugh making his shoulders quiver. "I've wanted to do that for a really long time," he says, the words muffled by the fabric of my sweater.

"Did it meet your expectations?" I ask, a hint of nervousness behind it. What felt mind-blowing to me might not have felt that way for him, considering I haven't kissed someone since freshman year.

He leans back and tucks a strand of hair behind my ear, his fingers lingering on the edge of my jaw. "Surpassed them."

Unable to wait another second, I grab hold of his collar, pull him in, and give myself over to the purest joy I've ever known. Because I can kiss him again. Today, tomorrow, every day.

CHAPTER TWENTY-THREE

"STOP, STOP, I'M GOING to cry!" Mami squeals as I step out of my bedroom for the grand reveal, fanning away the tears threatening to ruin her mascara.

Nurse Oatmeal gives her seal of approval by nuzzling her head against my shoes.

"Ven pa'ca," Doña Carmen calls out, urging me to come back to the room I'd just made my dramatic exit from.

I teeter back to her, struggling to balance in my just-bought-last-night heels, and praying I don't break my neck before Joaquin gets here. She's waiting at the edge of my bed with a safety pin and a determined expression on her face. She fusses with the back of my left sleeve, pinching and tucking until it's pulled more tightly across my shoulder.

"So you can dance," she explains once the last pin has been slipped into place.

I give her a twirl in the mirror. As promised, I can move

freely now without the fear of my left shoulder strap sliding down and exposing my goods to the world.

The fact that I'm even in this dress right now is miraculous. Anna wasn't kidding, the pickings for prom dresses this late in the game were dreadfully slim. With less than a week to find something, I either had to buy a dress in store ASAP or cough up another three figures for express shipping. With my in-person options being various types of unflattering animal print, I was ready to show up to prom in jeans.

Thankfully, Mami is a sentimental clothing hoarder, and we just happen to be the same size.

"It looks better now than it did when I bought it!" Mami exclaims as she joins me in front of the mirror.

The dress did go through a Cinderella-esque makeover. Doña Carmen, former seamstress extraordinaire, was able to fix the imperfections in the timeless pink dress Mami wore to her sophomore homecoming. She adjusted the too-wide straps to a more modern Bardot top, added a layer of tulle, and patched the holes left behind from our brief but very terrifying moth infestation with embroidered flowers. The moths also ate up the bottom of the skirt, but thankfully it still works as a tea-length dress, too. Plus, Doña Carmen cinched the waist to make up for the fact that I didn't inherit Mami's hourglass curves. My clavicle looks great, though.

It's not at all what I expected—it's better.

"La más hermosa nenita en todo el mundo," Doña Carmen proclaims as she admires her handiwork before giving me a kiss on the cheek. In this dress, with my hair tumbling down my shoulders in soft waves pinned to one side, my eyes smoldering thanks to a smoky glitter eyeshadow and lined with wings sharp enough to kill, and my tanned skin shimmering like a mythical goddess—thank you, Rihanna—it's impossible not to feel like she's right. I am the most beautiful girl in the world.

A knock startles the three of us. We turn to find Joaquin in the doorway, hands covering his eyes. "Am I allowed to look? Or is that bad luck?"

"It's not a wedding dress," I tease, crossing the room and pulling his hands down to his sides. The thrill of his fingers sliding into mine still doesn't feel any less surreal, and I hope it never does.

Doña Carmen whispers something to Mami that makes her nod vigorously. The two of them shuffle out of the room as quickly as they can, mumbling about needing to go grab the corsage and boutonniere.

"Door open!" Mami calls out from the hallway, leaving the door to my room cracked just enough that we have some privacy without her needing to worry about any funny business. Not that I have any interest in getting out of this dress when it took twenty minutes to put it on.

When their voices have faded, we finally take each other in. I already knew Joaquin cleaned up well from previous dances we've been to over the years, but his newly rented black suit is especially on point. Impeccably cut to every slope of his body, with a soft pink silk tie that matches my dress so perfectly it's as if they were designed to be worn together.

"You look gorgeous," he whispers, an awed expression on his

face as he cradles my cheek in his palm. His thumb runs along the curve of my lower lip, careful not to disrupt the gloss. "You always do, but a little extra today."

"Only a little?"

He chuckles, letting his chin fall to his chest. "Fine. A lot."

His hand shifts to the back of my neck, pulling me in for a kiss that makes me even more unsteady than I already was in these heels. His movements are careful, minding my hair and the pins holding my dress together as he rests a hand on my waist. There are a thousand things to love about kissing him, but this is one of my favorites. The way he takes so much care in every touch, letting us set the pace together. Never too much, or too fast. And, somehow, never enough.

While I'd be very happy with kissing the most handsome boy I know until my lip gloss is smeared and my body is too numb to stand, we're not dressed up for nothing.

Our attentive audience makes sure to gasp and ooh and aah when we come out to the living room as if they didn't see us five minutes ago. The loudest cheer comes from Joaquin's phone, Mami holding it up and around so we can see Mrs. Romero. Meanwhile, from my laptop, Isabella gives us a vigorous round of applause.

"Daaaaaaaaamn, bro!" Isabella shouts as Joaquin steps toward the cameras and does a proper spin for her. "You actually look halfway decent."

"Please, you wish you could look this good in a suit," he says with a wink.

Isabella rolls her eyes. "See, now why did you have to go and ruin the moment?"

Mrs. Romero hushes her daughter before leaning in so close to her camera, we can see up her nose. "You look beautiful, Ivelisse."

My already rosy cheeks go red as apples when Joaquin's hand slides around my waist and gives me a squeeze, as if to back up his mom's compliment.

"Thank you, Mrs. Romero," I reply, praying, based on how grainy the image of her nostril is, that she can't see how hard I'm blushing.

"All right, picture time!" Mami announces, handing Mrs. Romero to Doña Carmen before rushing to grab her own phone off the dining table.

Since we have about a dozen dances under our belts, Joaquin and I assume our usual positions. We start at the base of the stairs, as always. Joaquin's hand shifts to my low back as we make our way over. The camera shutter goes off before we're even settled, Mami making sure to document every moment of us walking to the stairs, then stopping at the stairs, then getting into position.

While the pose is as cliché as all the dances before, there's something easier about it this year. And in the way I lean back against Joaquin's chest and rest my hands on top of his where they're clasped at the base of my stomach. For once, I don't dread the thought of Mami sending these to every tía and tío in the family WhatsApp thread or having to scroll through the hundreds of photos to find one where I don't look like I'm in pain.

When Mami's satisfied with her two-hundred-plus options, we head over to our next and final pose spot in front of the decorative fireplace in the living room.

"Ten cuidado," Doña Carmen warns as she hands me the boutonniere and Joaquin the corsage. Both made of light pink peonies.

I get the honors of going first, doing my best to avoid jabbing it into his chest.

"Ow!" he shouts as I adjust the pin to straighten it out.

"Shit. Are you okay?! Where does it hurt?" I scramble to pull the boutonniere off and check for blood, but his shaking shoulders give him away. "You dick!" Once I whack him on the shoulder, he gives up on trying to hold in his laugh.

"Sorry, had to." He backs away with his hands raised in surrender. "Your reaction was adorable, though."

I pout, mumbling under my breath as I finish pinning his boutonniere without any fanfare. "Yeah, well, giving me a premature heart attack isn't very adorable."

Joaquin takes my hand before I can pull away, delicately sliding the corsage onto my wrist. "A humble price to pay for a really good joke."

I could pinch him or come up with a witty comeback, but I don't do either. Instead, I revel in the way our hands slot together like we've been doing this for years and close my eyes when he leans in to press a kiss to my cheek.

"That's the one!" Mami waves her phone in triumph, rushing over to me so quickly she nearly trips on the carpet.

Her phone is open to the last photo she took, capturing the serenity on my face as Joaquin kisses my cheek. It's startling at first, seeing something so intimate. Mami's usually a crappy photographer, but I have to give her props for this one. Somehow she's managed to immortalize the way I feel about him in a single photo.

That, when I'm with him, I feel at home.

"Text me that one?" I ask, struggling to drag my eyes away from the photo.

"Me too," Joaquin adds, pulling me closer.

Moments after she sends it, he lets me go and taps at something on his phone before tucking it back into his pocket, the photo of us now set as his lock screen.

Twenty minutes later, and I've realized that leaving the house is more difficult than either of us thought. Mami insists on showing us every photo she took and FaceTiming my abuela. While being showered with compliments is very flattering, these shoes are starting to pinch my toes, and I want to get at least one dance in before giving up on them entirely.

"Take pictures! Drive safe!" Mami calls out to us from the doorway as we finally head out.

"She does *not* need more pictures," I mutter to Joaquin as he takes my hand in an iron grip, helping me stumble down the driveway.

"You sure you don't want to wear chanclas?" Joaquin asks as I move at a snail's pace of two steps a minute. "Because at this rate, we're gonna get to prom in time to watch everybody leave for the after-party."

I stick my tongue out at him and quicken my stride, nearly

breaking my neck in the process. To avoid getting myself killed before I can even get to the car, I readjust my grip and cling to him like a lifeline, relying on his sturdiness to move more quickly. "I did not spend the last of my savings on these just to show up wearing flip-flops."

Once we've made it over to Herbert, Joaquin carefully lets go of me long enough to open the passenger side door. "Your chariot awaits."

Thanks to our last-minute reunion, we won't be showing up to prom in style. All of the pre-prom limos were booked, and while Tío Tony insisted that he could hook us up with a Lamborghini for the night, going in good ol' Herbert feels more fitting.

Though, Joaquin did clean him for the occasion.

"Really pulling out all the stops here," I say as I take my seat, running my finger along the freshly wiped down dashboard. No abandoned protein bar wrappers, or clumps of dust in sight. With the back seat free of dirty sneakers, cleats, and spare T-shirts, Herbert might as well have just rolled fresh off the lot. Well, a used lot.

"Special occasion." Joaquin leans down with a mischievous smirk. "Forgot something. Be right back," he says before pressing a kiss to my cheek and racing back to his house.

So much for hustling.

My date returns soon enough, hiding something behind his back. I roll down my window as he stands beside the passenger seat, gasping when he reveals two Marco's slushies.

"For you," he says with a grin as he hands me the piña colada slushie, taking the cherry one for himself.

"You're a genius," I tell him before closing my eyes and taking my first sip. It's been way too long since we've had these. The first sip is as glorious as I remembered, my entire body shivering from the cold. That ultimate slushie champion title was well-deserved.

Joaquin gets in on the driver's side, not replying until he's taken his own first mind-blowing sip. "I *did* say I'd only go to prom with you if we got slushies first."

"And you are a man of your word."

I follow his lead, savoring the rush of artificial coconut on my tongue, the taste of lazy summers and long drives with my favorite person. "Best Uber Eats driver ever. Five stars."

"I'm honored."

After a few sips, and a synchronized shoulder-shimmy celebration dance, we pop open the lids of our cups and combine our slushies together—creating our favorite cherry colada masterpiece. We sit in silence, basking in the sugar high and brain freeze until we realize it's almost seven. No one shows up to prom at five like they're supposed to, but two hours seems excessive. We kick Herbert into gear, and while stopped at a red light down the block, Joaquin goes to turn on the radio. I stop him.

"Can I play something?"

His brow furrows, but he switches the radio off without protest. I reach into the back seat for the hiding spot I'd stashed *my* surprise in last night, pulling out the "Driving with Joaquin" CD I burned on Mami's ancient desktop computer. A playlist of *his* favorite songs—the ones we don't often get to listen to because he's so willing to let my music taste come first. Starting with "I Want You to Want Me."

It feels strange at first, hearing the opening chords of a song he'd meant to dedicate to Tessa. But the smile that blossoms on his face is well worth it.

The stoplight switches from red to green, but his gaze stays locked on me instead of the road for what seems like hours.

"You okay?" I ask, my voice barely audible over the song.

"Yeah," he replies, taking his hand off the gear shift to brush a loose lock of hair over my shoulder. "You're just really beautiful."

His touch against the bare skin of my shoulder is enough to make me melt, but the press of his lips on mine, quick and sweet and tasting of cherry and coconut, makes stars burst behind my closed eyes. Even in Herbert's cramped front seat, kissing Joaquin makes me feel like we're in the clouds.

The blare of a car horn ruins the moment.

"Let's go already!" the man in the car behind us yells between honks.

"My bad!" Joaquin shouts out the open window before slamming on the gas. "Sorry," he says to me once we've put a decent amount of distance between us and the intersection. "You're very distracting." He takes my hand and lifts it to his lips, pressing a kiss to my knuckles, his lips sticky from the gloss on mine.

I smile and settle back into my seat, heart pounding and feeling so, so alive.

By the time we make it to the Elmwood Hilton, prom is in full swing. The prom committee has transformed the standard hotel ballroom into an underwater oasis complete with red and gold coral, ocean-blue streamers, and a tasteful variety of fish-themed décor. I guess all that stucco money *does* go to good use.

The dance floor is packed, our classmates gyrating to a remix of a song from the '90s. Dated as the music is, it doesn't seem like anyone cares. So long as they can grind on each other with minimal supervision, they're happy.

We skip the massive line for the photo booth in favor of parting ways for a bit. Joaquin heads over to the makeshift stage at the front of the room to check in with the prom committee and assure them that their last court member has arrived in one piece, while I search for Anna. Her dress, a mermaid-style strapless gown bedazzled with sequins in a gradient pattern matching the colors of the lesbian flag, makes her easy to spot in the sea of one-tone ensembles.

"You're here!" she squeals when I come up behind her, her breath smelling like Smirnoff Peach.

"*You're* here!" I squeal back. Even without the booze, it's impossible not to match her energy.

We pull each other in for a hug that almost sends both of us toppling over.

"How was the A-list limo?" I ask with a raised brow.

With Tessa as her date, Anna got a hand-delivered invitation from Casey Zosnowski, co-captain of the cheerleading squad, to join their pre-prom limo—dubbed (by Casey) to be *the* most exclusive ride to prom this year. Joaquin was bestowed the same honor, only to commit the high crime of turning down the offer once he realized he wouldn't be going with Tessa like he'd originally thought.

Anna's eyes gleam with delight. "I really wanted it to be overrated, but I can't lie, it was sick as hell." She grabs her hot-pink sequined clutch off the table, popping it open and whipping out a pig in a blanket. "Want one?" she asks before grabbing one for herself.

While I know I probably shouldn't accept food that just came out of a purse, I'm powerless to the lure of free appetizers.

"Damn," I mumble after downing the pig in a blanket in one bite. Even after sitting in Anna's clutch for who knows how long, it still hits. Maybe Casey wasn't overhyping their limo.

Anna nods in approval, offering me a second one while showing off some of their pre-prom photos, one of which includes Mr. Hernandez smiling brightly in between Anna and Tessa, pressing a kiss to his daughter's head. She's about to swipe to another when Principal Contreras steps onto the stage at the front of the ballroom. The DJ fades out the music, the lights turn up slightly, and conversations fall to a quiet hum as Contreras clears his throat directly into the mic.

"I hate to pause the party." He holds as if he's waiting to be booed off the stage and continues when he isn't. "But I'm sure we're all eager to hear who this year's Prom King and Queen are." He waves a gold envelope that sends the crowd into a frenzy, applause and cheers drowning out whatever he says next.

Anna and I both let out a loud whoop, clapping along with the crowd until Contreras signals for us to quiet down.

"And your Prom King is . . ." He pauses for dramatic effect, the DJ starting up a drum-roll sound effect. "Joaquin Romero!"

It's not a surprise in the slightest, but I scream as loud as my lungs let me anyway. Our classmates also erupt into cries of excitement, and I bounce on my toes as best I can without tipping over, cheering until my voice cracks.

Joaquin steps onto the stage and gives his attentive audience a humble wave. When he bends down to accept the crown from Contreras, his eyes find mine in the crowd, and it feels like we're the only two people here.

"And your Queen . . ." Contreras has to shout over the roar of the crowd. The interruption does the trick, getting everyone to simmer down for their next monarch.

"Is . . . Tessa Hernandez!"

Not a surprise either. They're the perfect couple on paper.

The room gives Tessa the same treatment, proclamations of love and cheers ring through the hall as she accepts her tiara and a bouquet of roses with grace. She's a textbook image of a prom queen, her hair done up in a series of intricate braids and adorned with small crystals, her purple lace gown clinging perfectly to her curves. She even has the queen wave nailed, looking as regal as the royal family as she thanks the crowd for their support. Beside me, Anna claps with enough force to make her whole body shake.

Following tradition, Joaquin offers Tessa his hand and guides her to the dance floor for the first official slow dance of the night. There are a few wolf whistles that the two of them brush off with good-natured smiles, and the jealous rage that used to consume me at the thought of them together is gone.

It's funny, seeing the two of them illuminated by the dim light of the disco ball as they approach the center of the dance floor. They wound up together in the end, just not quite how they'd expected. Instead, they've defied an ages-old high school cliché—the two most popular kids in school falling for the tech crew nerds.

I head toward the closest available seat at Anna's table, planning to give my feet a rest from these cursed heels while I can, when a low murmur spreads among the crowd. I lift my head, expecting to see someone trying to steal the crown, or something equally shocking, but instead Cordero's newly crowned Prom King is walking directly toward me.

"What're you doing?" I hiss once Joaquin is in earshot.

He ignores the question and offers up his hand. "Can I have this dance?"

As sweet as the gesture is, I can't just leave Tessa standing on the dance floor confused and abandoned by her king. We're not exactly best friends now, but leaving someone hanging so you can get your rom-com-worthy prom moment is a dick move. "But you're supposed to—"

As if on cue, Tessa appears beside him. The two share a knowing look before she moves past us, eyes set on her own target.

"Wanna dance?" she asks, holding her hand out to Anna.

Anna grins, tossing aside the half-eaten mini quiche she just pulled out of her clutch, and takes Tessa's hand. "I thought you'd never ask."

"Did you—"

Joaquin shushes me before I can finish the question. "Yes, I knew. And yes, we planned this together," he responds with a smirk.

Before I can throw another line of questioning at him, Tessa halts beside us, hand in hand with Anna. "You coming?" she asks, the question aimed at me.

Normally, the pressure of this many eyes on me would make

me crumble, but tonight it makes me stand a little taller. Feel a little bolder.

"Yeah," I reply, taking Joaquin's hand. "We are."

The four of us make our way to the dance floor to the tune of a hundred whispers. Tomorrow morning we'll be front page news, but for now we're just us—four kids who fell in love with their best friends.

Principal Contreras seems flustered, but ultimately doesn't stop our small act of rebellion. With a disgruntled nod, he signals to the DJ to turn up the music and let us have our moment. It seems his dance partner isn't the only thing Joaquin managed to coordinate, as the opening notes of an all-too-familiar song begin playing over the speakers.

"You're never going to let me live that down, are you?" I ask, resting my forehead against his shoulder as we sway to the opening notes of a smooth, slowed-down cover of "Can't Take My Eyes Off You."

"Why would I?" he teases. "Top ten moment of my life."

Sure enough, my off-the-cuff promposal made the rounds through the Cordero gossip mill. More people knew Joaquin and I were dating before I did, considering they managed to circulate the video during the two hours I was occupied in the light booth. It's strange, being catapulted back into the social spotlight for a second time in my high school career because of a boy. But there's no shock this time. No confusion as to how someone like me landed someone like Joaquin. If anything, the bigger question is why we waited so long to make it official.

"How long did it take you to plan this?" I ask after he insists on lowering me into a dramatic dip. Despite my uneasiness on my feet, he doesn't drop me. And, I've gotta admit, it's as swoony as the movies make it seem.

"About four minutes," he replies with a shrug. "I'm in love with you, Tessa's in love with Anna, just made sense."

"Oh, so you're in love with me now?"

He chuckles softly, letting his forehead come to rest against mine. "Always have been."

"And what if I told you I loved you too?"

"Then I'd say I'm a pretty lucky guy."

Before doubt can flood my mind, I close the distance between us and kiss him, because I want the world to know that he saw me. For me. A girl who hides in the background and builds happy endings for others, who found her own with the boy who was beside her the whole time.

Everything about our future is still unclear—whether the distance will tear us apart, whether we crash and burn before ultimately going our separate ways. But, for once, I don't see all of those haunting what-ifs. I see something beautiful, something that takes my breath away. A life full of memories with my best friend.

When we separate and he gazes at me with the type of love I never thought I could have with him, it's easy to see how he can believe in all of those cheesy love songs.

1 THING I LOVE ABOUT PROM

I get to spend the night dancing with you.

ACKNOWLEDGMENTS

Well, would you look at that, we're doing this again! It's an honor beyond my wildest dreams to be able to publish not one but *two (!!!!!!)* books with the Joy Revolution team. Thank you, Bria, David, and Nicola, for continuing to believe in me and my stories. This year has been the best kind of whirlwind, and I owe it all to you. Thank you, thank you, thank you.

This book wouldn't exist without the wonderful team at Assemble Media! One thousand thank-yous to Steven Salpeter for trusting me with this story, and to Jack Heller, Caitlin de Lisser-Ellen, Madison Wolk, and Jiayun Yang for helping me create Ive, Joaquin, and their love story.

Thank you to my marvelous agent, Uwe Stender, for captaining the Elle Gonzalez Rose ship. I'd be lost at sea without you.

I'm beyond lucky to be able to work with the phenomenal Casey Moses on yet another cover straight out of my dreams, which was brought to life by the incredible Rebeca Alvarez. Thank you to interior designer Cathy Bobak for bringing these pages to life.

It takes a village to put out a book! Endless thank-yous to the most amazing publicists, Kris Kam and Kim Small, for all the work they did to share my debut with the world. Thank you to Colleen Fellingham, Alison Kolani, Carrie Andrews, Caroline

Kirk, and Maggie Hart-Sandor for combing through these pages and making them shine.

I wouldn't have had the courage to pursue this strange and beautiful life if it weren't for the endless support of my family. It means the world that I have all of you in my corner. Mami, you always knew this was the path I was meant to go down. Thank you for leading me to it. Daddy, I carry you with me in every word I write. Thank you to all of my tías, tíos, and cousins for the love and encouragement throughout this wild year.

GILWCTI, I'm so lucky to have a safe space in the three of you. Special thank you to Leila for your incredible commentary while reading this book!

Writing is a lonely process, but I have never been alone on this journey, thanks to the friends I've made along the way! Thank you to my beloved nemesis, Zach Humphrey, for the dinners and sleepovers and afternoons with my gremlin dog. Thank you to my Joy Revolution sibling, Angela Montoya, for being such a wonderful friend and an endless source of light in the writing community. And thank you to Gabriel Torres for being such an amazing early supporter of my work.

Ye Olde Penthouse LLC—I'm so lucky to call all of you my friends. Flag flag!

Thank you to my therapist for helping me brave this roller coaster of a year.

Many thanks to the Myrick Magidson family for their love and support—especially to my music consultant, Dustin, for teaching me what a short chorus and interlude are, and David, for accidentally calling our dog Nurse Oatmeal. Sorry I stole a nickname from you again!

To all the readers who picked up my debut, *Caught in a Bad Fauxmance,* and are now picking up this book, I'll never have enough words to thank you properly. I get to live my dreams all because you decided to take a chance on me and my stories. Thank you for all the kind words, for the time you took to read or listen to my work, and for embracing these stories. It means the absolute world to me.

And last, but never least, Duncan. Life is easy with you.

ABOUT THE AUTHOR

ELLE GONZALEZ ROSE is a television producer from New York who's better at writing love stories than she is at writing bios. Her dog thinks she's okay. She is also the author of *Caught in a Bad Fauxmance*. Elle, not the dog.

ellegonzalezrose.com

Turn the page for a sneak peek at . . .

★ "A sweet hopeful LGBTQIA+ love story—this is a must-have."
—*School Library Journal*

"This energetic and hilarious tale boasts fun-in-the-sun shenanigans
and a Shakespearean aura." —*Publishers Weekly*

CHAPTER ONE

Thirty minutes in the backseat together and my sister wants to kill me—a new record.

"Devin." Maya snaps her manicured fingers in my face when I ignore her. "Move over."

It's the third time she's made that demand since we piled into the car. Any other day I would pack up my drawing tablet and laptop and give her free rein over the backseat, but I'm holding my ground this time.

I push her hand away. "No, I'm working."

"No, you're not," she scoffs. "You've been looking at your phone this whole time. Your tablet isn't even on."

Up in the peaceful driver's seat, Dad sighs while Andy tries and fails to hold back a snort. We should've seen this coming when we let Andy call shotgun. It made sense at the time—shoving our six-foot-three stepbrother into the cramped backseat of our Honda Civic wouldn't have been fair—but Maya hates long drives, and my tablet takes up all the extra leg space. It was a recipe for disaster.

"I'm doing research," I reply indignantly.

I turn my attention back to the profile I was scouring, only for Maya to snatch the phone out of my hand. She tucks it right into the one place she knows I'm not willing to go: her bra. "Social media stalking your classmates doesn't count as research."

Scoping out the competition absolutely counts as research. "Yes, it does."

She gives me a deadpan look.

Okay fine, it doesn't.

Not that I'd ever admit it to her, but Maya's right. If I want any chance of not shooting my barely existent art career in the foot, I *should* be working on my application for the Cardarelli mentorship. Every spring semester, one CalArts freshman is whisked away to undergrad stardom by Professor Lila Cardarelli, an animator with so many accolades under her belt she needs a separate Wikipedia page to list them all.

Professor Cardarelli's protégés are basically gods, according to my roommate, my advisor, and just about everyone else at CalArts. You give up any semblance of free time in exchange for shadowing one of the most iconic names in animation. Internships at Pixar and Disney are essentially guaranteed once you've got a recommendation letter from Lila Cardarelli, who has the Disney family on speed dial. No one has any clue how Cardarelli picks her mentees, but it's the same application every year. Standard background information, and one enormously daunting assignment: attach *one* piece that you feel best expresses who you are as an artist.

Which sounds easy enough, except I barely have any idea who I am as a person, let alone an artist.

My first semester of almost-adulthood was less than stellar. Being surrounded by people who have been creating since they could hold a pencil and can produce gallery-worthy art in their sleep isn't exactly encouraging when you can barely grasp the basics of color theory. Especially when you're like me, someone who didn't consider animation as a profession until their junior year of high school. Six months ago, I thought I'd be in my element—living the cool, aloof LA art school kid life I'd seen in movies. Instead, I spent the past four months hardly ever leaving my dorm room just so I could keep up with all the homework. I've been in the land of eternal sunshine for three months and I'm even paler than when I arrived, and I've spent more time with the vending machine on my floor than my roommate.

So, yeah, I could really use a win right now.

The application isn't actually due until the first day of spring semester, and while procrastination has never done me any favors, I can't focus on productivity when my innocent phone is being held captive in my sister's gross, sweaty clutches.

"C'mon, give it back," I whine, nudging my knee against Maya's.

"Nope." She smacks her bubblegum and waves a finger at my tablet. "Pack it up or get drawing."

I can explain to her for the hundredth time that that's not how my artistic process works, or I can play dirty.

"Dad, Maya stole my phone."

"Give your brother his phone back," Dad mumbles, squinting at a sign about road closures.

Maya's glare would turn me to stone if I wasn't so used to being on the receiving end of her rage. Whoever said twins have a special psychic bond lied. The last time Maya and I were on the same page was when we sent Mami into labor ten weeks before our due date. We've been menaces since the day we were born.

We stare each other down, unblinking and unrelenting, until she lunges at me. On instinct, I curl around my tablet, protecting it from her wrath. She goes for the cord connecting it to my laptop instead, ready to yank it free, when Dad springs into action.

"Hey!" he shouts, startling all of us, even Andy, into total silence. "Watch it around the tablet," he warns, focusing back on the road once Maya retreats to her side of the car.

She begrudgingly hands me back my phone, sticking her tongue out at Dad when he's distracted by a Prius that gets too close to us. "Sometimes I think you love that thing more than you love either of us."

"With how much I paid for it, yes, I do," Dad replies.

Guilt settles too comfortably in the pit of my stomach. It's no secret that my tablet's price tag was more than we should've spent, but Dad had insisted we splurge on the CalArts recommended model instead of the used three-generations-old one I'd found on eBay. It was for a special occasion—an eighteenth birthday and "congrats on getting into art school" gift rolled into one—but bills like ours don't leave room for five-hundred-dollar special occasions, as Maya, the golden child who abandoned her grand plan to move to New York and study cosmetology for the more affordable option of staying home and commuting to Florida State, loves to remind me.

Case in point: this entire trip. We haven't been to our cabin in Lake Andreas for four years, but Dad begrudgingly kept up with the payments for the sake of nostalgia. Swinging the extra couple hundred bucks a month felt worthwhile when there was still a slim chance we'd spend another summer or winter break at the lake. Especially after we gave up our childhood home to find a place big enough for Andy and his mom, Isabel, to move in last year.

With two college tuitions, a new mortgage, and unpaid medical bills that have been sitting on the kitchen counter for what feels like eons to keep up with, nostalgia doesn't make the cut anymore. As much as it might suck, avoiding lifelong debt outweighs sentimentality.

That's the part none of the therapists warned us about— grief is hell on your bank account.

Not that I'm not grateful for our "special occasions." The tablet makes me feel more like a serious artist than the now-infected nose ring I let my roommate Marcus talk me into because "all artists have cool piercings." And at least we're getting a chance to say goodbye to the cabin. Christmases since our last trip to Lake Andreas have been . . . weird. We rarely even acknowledge holidays anymore. Christmas is just a day. Sometimes we sit around an undecorated pine tree in the living room and exchange gifts, but the first year we didn't even do that. It must be odd for Andy and Isabel, walking into a family that acts like one of the biggest holidays in the world doesn't exist.

Which is why I pinched myself when Dad suggested this

trip in the first place. He always made vague promises that next year we'd do something different, and now he's finally delivering. One last nostalgic, and very strictly budgeted, Christmas in Lake Andreas before our cabin heads onto the market.

With my phone back in my pocket and Maya in full-on sulking mode, I finally return to my tablet. Instead of doing work like I promised myself, I let my gaze wander over to her when I'm sure she's not looking.

She's been on edge since I came home two days ago. Not that she's usually a happy-go-lucky person—snark has always been her brand—but she's especially huffy lately. Every time I deign to mention any of the three Cs—California, CalArts, or Cardarelli—she either scoffs, rolls her eyes, or leaves the room when we don't switch to a new topic. Yesterday she snapped at me for taking too long to get a glass of water. Maya's had problems with controlling her anger since we were old enough to talk, and I'm still not able to tell whether she's mad at me, our family, or the world at large. But I do know that the Devin Báez Reunion Tour is going terribly so far.

A four-hour road trip no longer feels like the right place to work on finding who I am as an artist. The application isn't due for another month, and not pissing off my sister is higher priority right now. Especially if I want to make it back to CalArts with all of my limbs, and electronics, intact.

Once my tablet is tucked away, Maya stretches herself out like a cat in the sun. She doesn't grace me with a smile or even the basic decency of eye contact, but her shoulders slacken, and her frown softens. That's Maya for "thank you."

Three hours and two bathroom breaks later, Dad takes the exit for Lake Andreas and lowers the volume on his trusty road trip mixtape. "Nearly there," he says, and rolls down our windows.

Andy leaps up, hanging his head out of his window like a golden retriever. I unbuckle my seat belt when Dad isn't looking, sliding in beside Maya to peek at the familiar welcome sign.

LAKE ANDREAS: THE HAPPIEST PLACE IN FLORIDA

The sign is frayed and has yellowed at the edges, but it warms my jaded little heart.

The car slows down as highways turn into one-way streets, giving us time to take in the scenery. Oak trees sprawl as far as the eye can see, shielding the rustic wooden cabins along the side of the street from view. Tire swings and Little Free Libraries on every corner. Bikes and paddleboards abandoned on front lawns and the smell of saltwater and sunscreen in the air.

Pure magic.

I lean out my window as we pull onto the main strip, ready to *ooh* and *aah* over all the places Maya and I would terrorize as kids, except . . .

They're gone.

Well, not all of them. The deli that gave me and Dad food poisoning is still around. The shops on Fulton Drive are still painted pastel pinks, blues, and greens, but their windows are shuttered and doors barred, lining the street like rotten gumdrops. The entire block, like the welcome sign, feels frayed and yellowed at the edges. The abandoned shops haven't even been replaced by a Starbucks or a Chipotle, or one of those business-casual places that charge $16 for salad. They're just empty. Sad, forgotten shells of a town that once meant so much to us.

"Huh," Maya murmurs as Dad parks in front of what was once a pretty decent Thai restaurant. "Was the lake always this depressing?"

Dad takes off his Florida State cap, his hair in sweaty disarray. "I don't think so."

"Me neither," I reply. I know kids see the world through rose-tinted glasses and all that jazz, but this is *definitely* not our Lake Andreas. At least not the one we remember. Even if my memories are kinder than reality, there's no way Mami would've let us spend our Christmases in a ghost town every year when we could've skipped the four-hour drive from Tallahassee and stayed home.

"Probably just an off year." Dad slips his cap back on and turns off the car, gesturing for us to follow him as he steps out.

Most of our favorite places have bit the dust. The Winter Wonderland miniature village—complete with fake snow and a Ferris wheel made of chocolate—in the front window of the candy store has been replaced with a foreclosure notice and cobwebs. Our favorite bakery, Loafin' Around, looks like it's been boarded up for months. A hunger pang rips through my empty stomach at the thought of never having their sundried tomato and rosemary focaccia again.

Sam's Superior Souvenirs is hanging in, though. And so are their signature I GOT CRABS IN LAKE ANDREAS shirts. Wonderful.

The streets somehow feel emptier than they look, with only the distant sound of seagulls and the echo of our footsteps for company. The kind of empty that feels ominous even in broad daylight. I stick close to Maya as Dad leads us toward the grocery store at the end of the block.

"Watch it," she hisses when I accidentally step on the back of her chancla. Forget playing nice—if an ax murderer decides to come after us, I'm using her as a shield.

I fall back, lingering beside Andy instead. He's a foot taller and lifts weights heavier than me during football practice. No way I can force him into being my unwilling shield. So, I guess this is the end of me. Can't say this is how I thought I'd go.

We make it to the grocery store without coming across any other signs of life. Not even the usual swarm of bloodhungry mosquitoes. I'm half expecting the store to be abandoned, but when the bell over the door announces our arrival, we're greeted by a familiar face.

"Well, I'll be damned," Old Bob says with a slap to his knee.

Well, *I'll* be damned. The candy shop didn't survive, but Old Bob did.

It's a relief, really. Old Bob is a Lake Andreas staple, welcoming families with open arms and hard candy year after year. Once upon a time, he'd been the mayor of this place, winning two consecutive landslide elections before passing the mayoral torch to his wife, Janine, and opening up the General Store. He's the kind of person who always remembered our birthdays and what sports we were into and whether we preferred soft serve or Popsicles. And one of the few locals who actually looked forward to visitors like us coming around to wreak havoc on their usually quiet community, never minding the extra noise and bigger crowds. He always said folks like us kept life at the lake exciting.

"Tony Báez, come 'ere you bastard." It's not until he's pulling Dad in for a hug that I remember we don't actually know Old Bob's real name. It had been a joke at the time, but it suits him. He looks like a Bob, and he *is* old. Five-year-old Devin and Maya were on to something.

"It's been a while . . ." Dad hesitates, slapping his hand down on Old Bob's shoulder. "My friend." Nice save.

Old Bob settles back down on his stool behind the front counter. "What brings the Báezes to our neck of the woods?" He stiffens suddenly, eyes narrowing. "You passing through on the way to that new water park across the lake?"

Andy's eyes light up. "There's a water park?!"

Old Bob bristles, nodding sternly. "Allegheny Park. Thing's been taking up most of our usual business. Everyone wants to stay over in Hillsdale these days. Something about a state-of-the-art waterslide."

That explains the tumbleweeds. The opposite end of the lake, better known as Hillsdale, was usually for the more up-scale "round of golf before lunch at the country club" types, but maybe some money-hungry developers decided to cash in on the Lake Andreas crowd and create more budget-friendly options.

Well, at least we won't have to wait in line at the kayak rental stand . . . if it's still around.

"How's the family been?" Old Bob continues, back in good spirits. "Think I can talk Ximena into letting me sneak a piece of that tres leches cake again this year?"

Without missing a beat, Dad pulls out the shopping list Isabel left on the kitchen counter that morning, handing it to Maya. "Think you guys can handle grabbing everything? We've got some catching up to do."

Maya and I nod, dragging Andy away as Dad turns back to Old Bob. This is the part we're not supposed to see. The smiles that turn into frowns. The *I'm so sorry*s and *I had no idea*s. A bitter reminder that this town isn't the only thing that's changed. I put as much distance as I can between us and the counter, heading toward the far corner of the store. Nothing says happy holidays like avoiding your dad's practiced spiel about how your mom died.

Once we're safely hidden between the produce and fish bait aisles, Maya carefully tears the shopping list down the middle, handing me the lengthier half. "Meet you up front in ten?"

Andy and I nod, grabbing a basket from a stack beside the apples before heading to the opposite end of the store. All we've managed to grab is ice cream and pasta sauce when we're brought to a complete halt in the cereal aisle.

"Just pick one already!" I shout after Andy puts back the box he was holding for the hundredth time.

"I'm trying!" He carefully picks up a family-size box of Count Chocula, looking at it longingly before shaking his head and setting it back down. "Do you think we can get two?"

"No." I hold up our half of the list, pointing to the bright red total Isabel marked at the bottom of the page, and the price tags on the shelves. "Not in the budget."

"Stupid budget," Andy grumbles under his breath as he picks the Count Chocula back up.

"I'm going to the next aisle. Meet me when you're done."

Andy doesn't respond, turning his full attention to a box of Honey Nut Cheerios. I should've known better than to get between him and sugar. For a seventeen-year-old linebacker, he has the diet of a picky toddler. Grabbing our basket, I head to the next aisle.

Miraculously, there's another sign of human life. A guy around my age, tall with taut shoulders and a jaw that could cut me in half. He doesn't strike me as the Lake Andreas type; he's decked out in designer sneakers and a name-brand hoodie. Not the usual Crocs and Hawaiian shirt crowd. I can't quite make out his face, but even with what little I can see, there's no denying that he's startlingly handsome.

Guys like him don't exist in places like this. Lake Andreas is for families who want a break from the oppressive Florida humidity but can only afford to go somewhere with a light breeze. Not for hot guys who wear designer sneakers to go grocery shopping. Though a cute new local in town does have a very Hallmark movie ring to it. The charming lumberjack to my jaded big-city businessman. Or maybe I'm the lumberjack in this situation? I *do* wear a lot of plaid. . . .

One second I'm admiring Hot Guy's forearm as he reaches for a gallon of milk, and the next I'm tripping over my shoelaces. Story of my life.

The jar in my basket shatters the second I hit the ground,

splattering pasta sauce and glass across the floor while the ice cream rolls down the aisle. What're the odds that Hot Guy didn't notice any of that?

"Oh my God, are you okay?"

Great.

I gingerly push up onto my elbows before I can embarrass myself any more. No broken bones, but my dignity has seen better days.

Hot Guy delicately navigates around the sea of broken glass, coming to stand beside me. "Are you all right?" he asks again.

His voice is as strangely familiar as the acoustic song blaring through the store's speakers. I hold a hand over my eyes, squinting to make out his face against the harsh fluorescent lighting. He leans down, his face slowly coming into view. My mouth goes dry as I reach two very important conclusions in a matter of seconds.

One: Hot Guy's face is as hot as the rest of him.

Two: I know him.

"Devin?" Julian Seo-Cooke chokes out, brows shooting up to his hairline.

Awesome, our awful next-door neighbors are still around.

"Julian," I reply through gritted teeth, wishing I'd stuck through Andy's indecisiveness in the cereal aisle.